HOUSE
DIVIDED

ALSO AVAILABLE

TurningPoints
SONS OF LIBERTY
MARSHALL POE
LELAND PURVIS

TurningPoints
LITTLE ROCK NINE
MARSHALL POE
ELLEN LINDNER
Vote against Integration!
SEPARATE BUT EQUAL

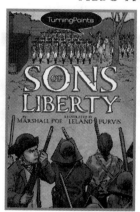

HOUSE
DIVIDED

BY MARSHALL POE

ILLUSTRATED BY LELAND PURVIS

ALADDIN PAPERBACKS
NEW YORK LONDON TORONTO SYDNEY

To Julianna and Isaiah —M. P.

To Elizabeth, and the blessings of houses undivided —L. P.

Each book is faithful in spirit to the values and experiences that influenced the person's development. History is fleshed out with fictionalized details, and conversations have been added to make the stories come alive to today's reader, but every reasonable effort has been made to make the stories consistent with the events, ethics, and character of their subjects.

☛ ALADDIN PAPERBACKS • An imprint of Simon & Schuster Children's Publishing Division 1230 Avenue of the Americas, New York, NY 10020 • Text copyright © 2009 by Marshall Poe • Illustrations copyright © 2009 by Leland Purvis • All rights reserved, including the right of reproduction in whole or in part in any form. • ALADDIN PAPERBACKS and related logo are registered trademarks of Simon & Schuster, Inc. • The text of the frontmatter of this book is set in Turning Points, created by Dalton Webb • Manufactured in the United States of America • First Aladdin Paperbacks edition January 2009 • 10 9 8 7 6 5 4 3 2 1
Library of Congress Control Number 2008929317
ISBN-13: 978-1-4169-5057-8 • ISBN-10: 1-4169-5057-5

ACKNOWLEDGMENTS:

MARSHALL POE

In writing A *House Divided*, I felt a little like a traveler in an unfamiliar country. I needed a lot of guidance. Happily, I got it. First from my agent, Bob Mecoy, who pointed the way. Next from Leland Purvis, who drew an excellent map. Then, when I was too thick to understand the said map, from the remarkable Carla Jablonski, who put me (and the book) firmly back on track. And finally from my editor at Simon & Schuster, Liesa Abrams, and from Matt Madden, who both greeted me when I arrived, at long last, safe and sound.

LELAND PURVIS

Special thanks to Liesa Abrams, Matt Madden, all at Deep Six Studio, and a deep bow and humble gratitude to Carla Jablonski, for her reliably extraordinary contributions.

Boston, Massachusetts
Early Spring, 1856

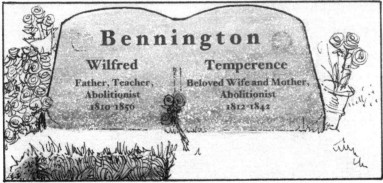

Bennington

Wilfred
Father, Teacher,
Abolitionist
1810-1856

Temperence
Beloved Wife and Mother,
Abolitionist
1812-1842

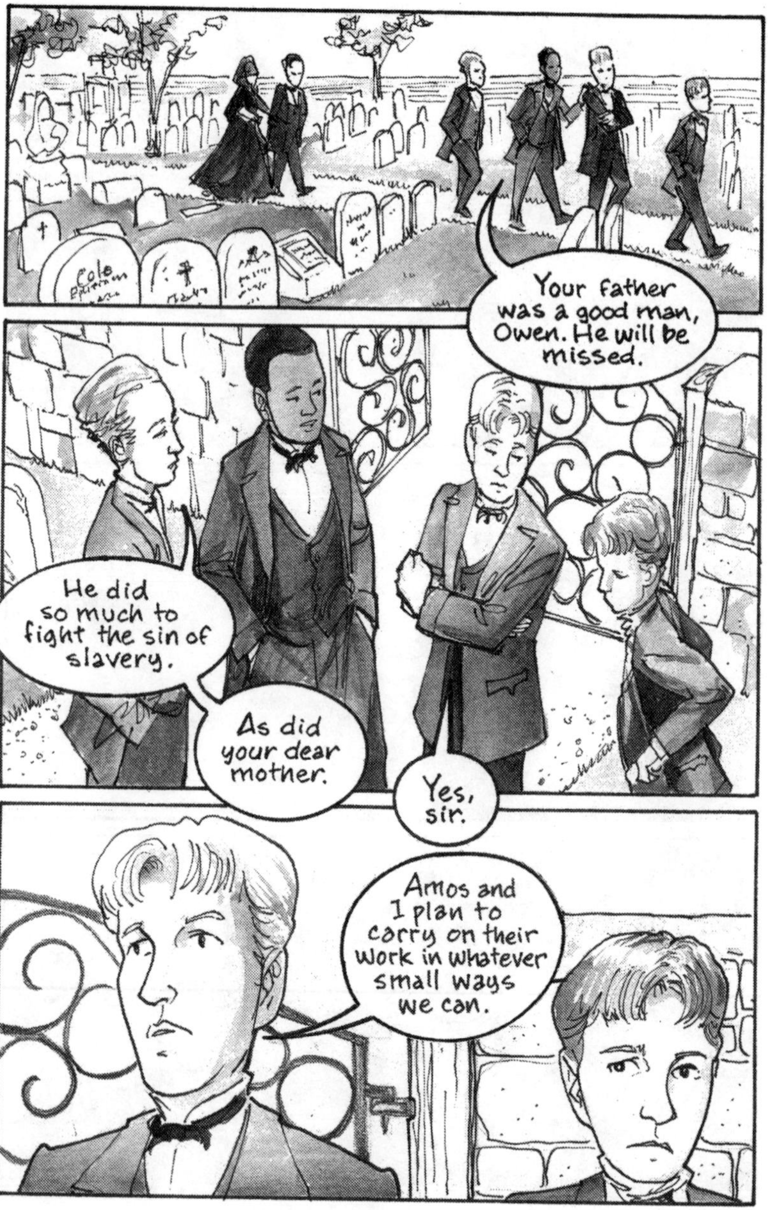
Your father was a good man, Owen. He will be missed.
He did so much to fight the sin of slavery.
As did your dear mother.
Yes, sir.
Amos and I plan to carry on their work in whatever small ways we can.

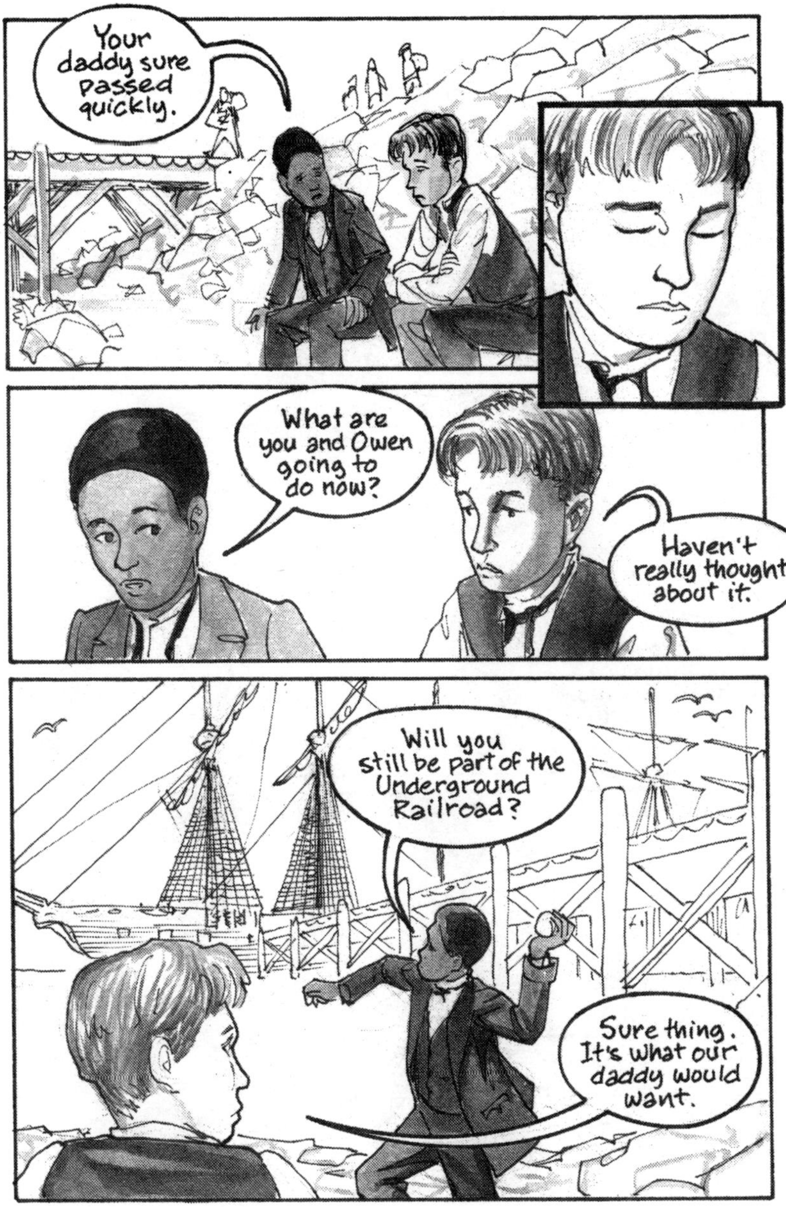
Your daddy sure passed quickly.
What are you and Owen going to do now?
Haven't really thought about it.
Will you still be part of the Underground Railroad?
Sure thing. It's what our daddy would want.

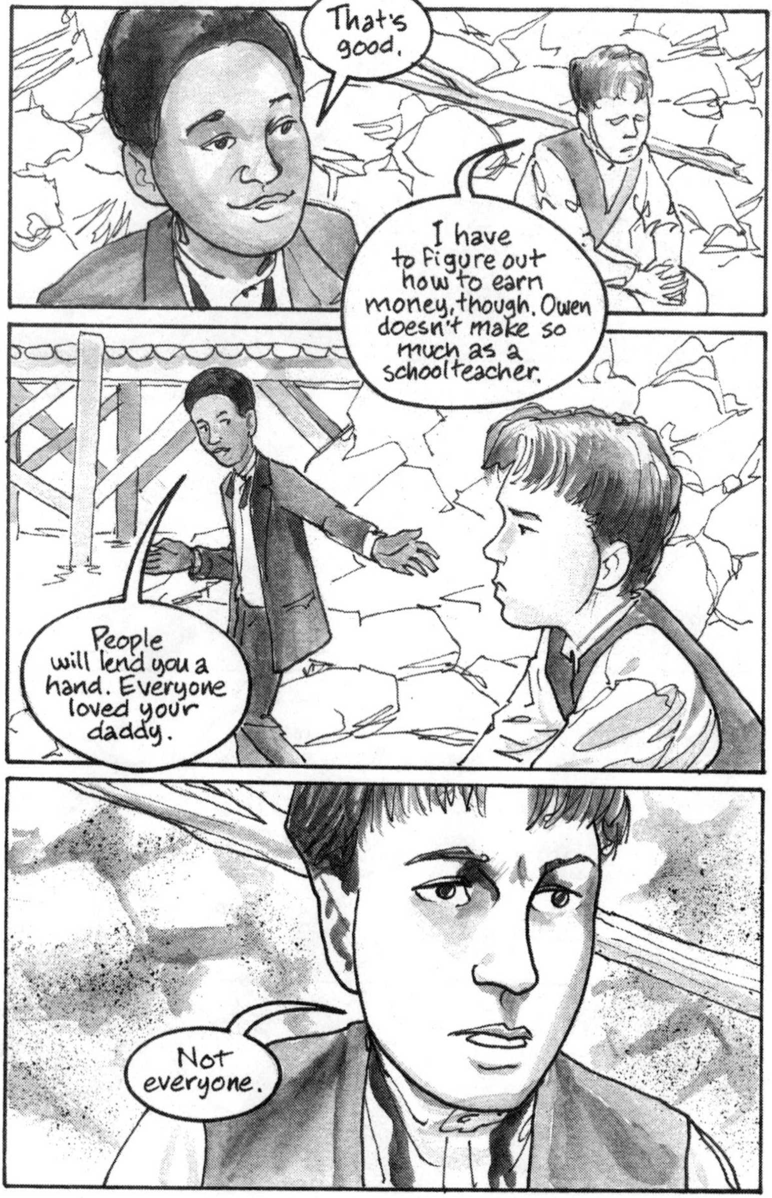
That's good.
I have to figure out how to earn money, though. Owen doesn't make so much as a schoolteacher.
People will lend you a hand. Everyone loved your daddy.
Not everyone.

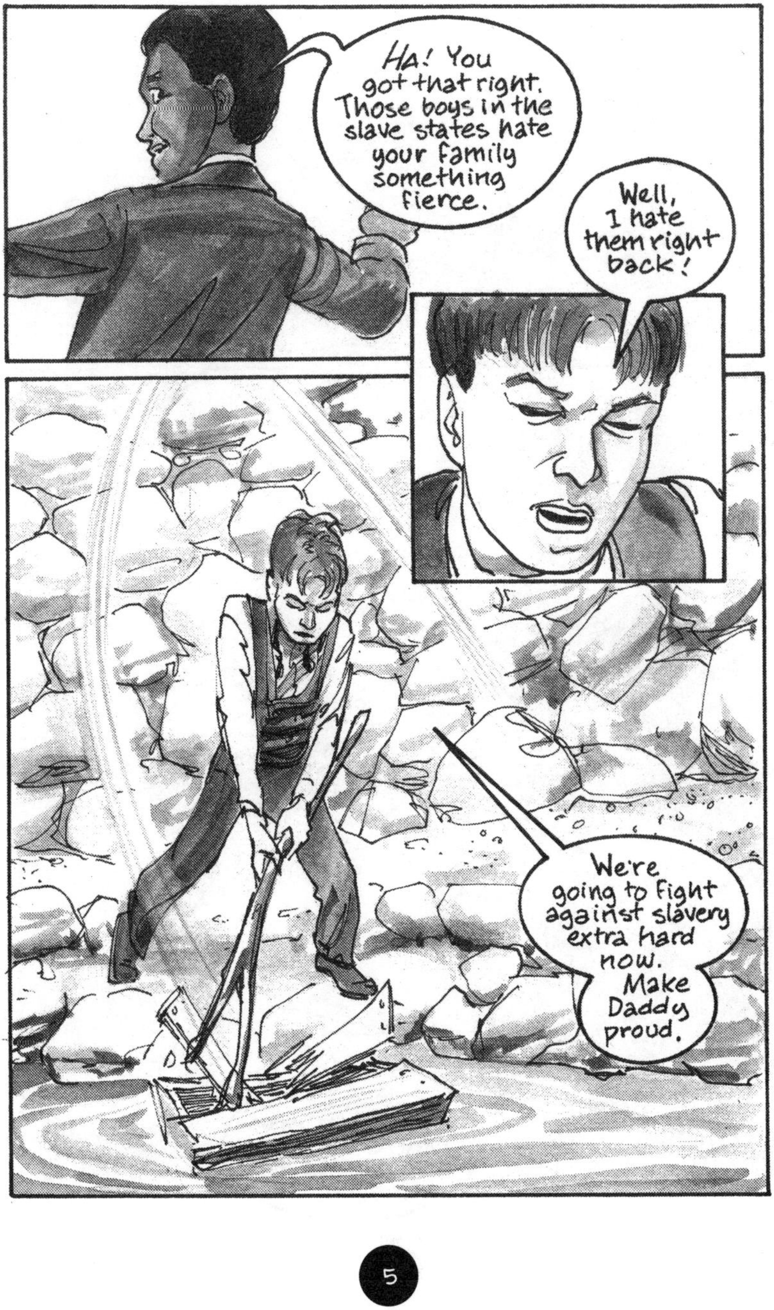
HA! You got that right. Those boys in the slave states hate your family something fierce.
Well, I hate them right back!
We're going to fight against slavery extra hard now.
Make Daddy proud.

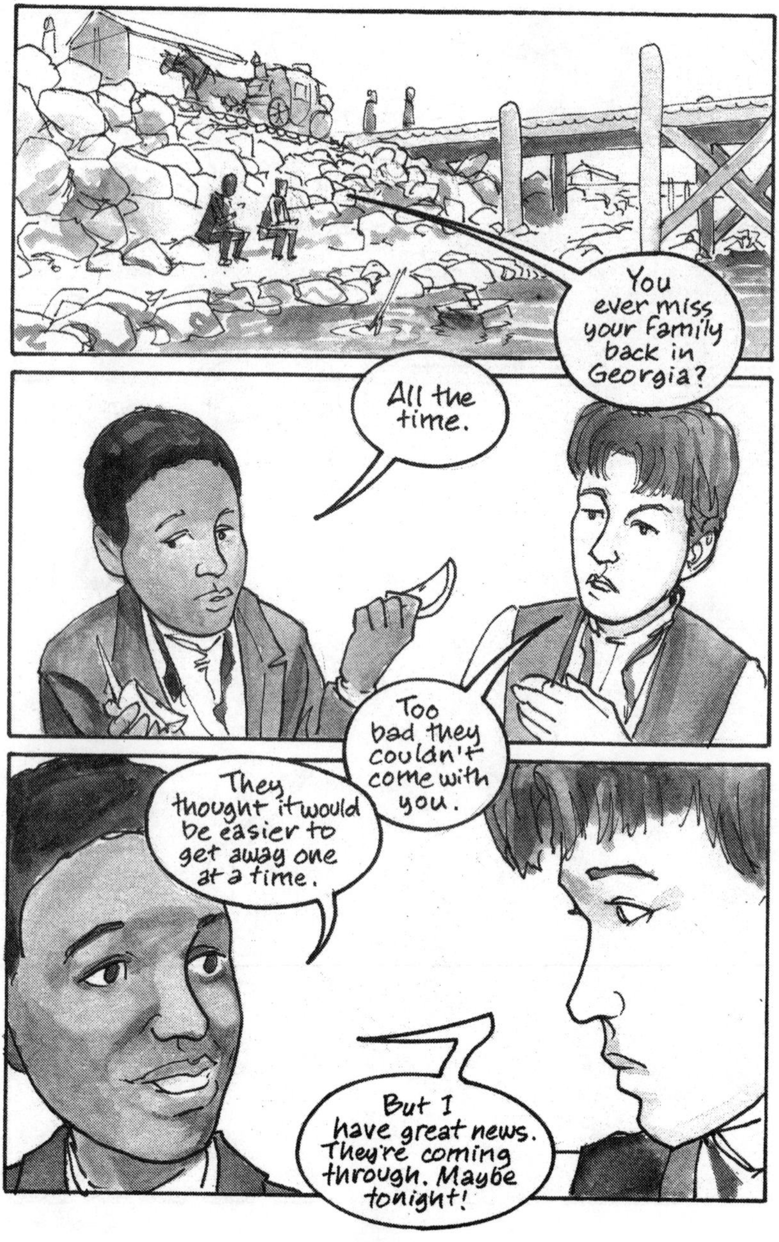
You ever miss your family back in Georgia?
All the time.
Too bad they couldn't come with you.
They thought it would be easier to get away one at a time.
But I have great news. They're coming through. Maybe tonight!

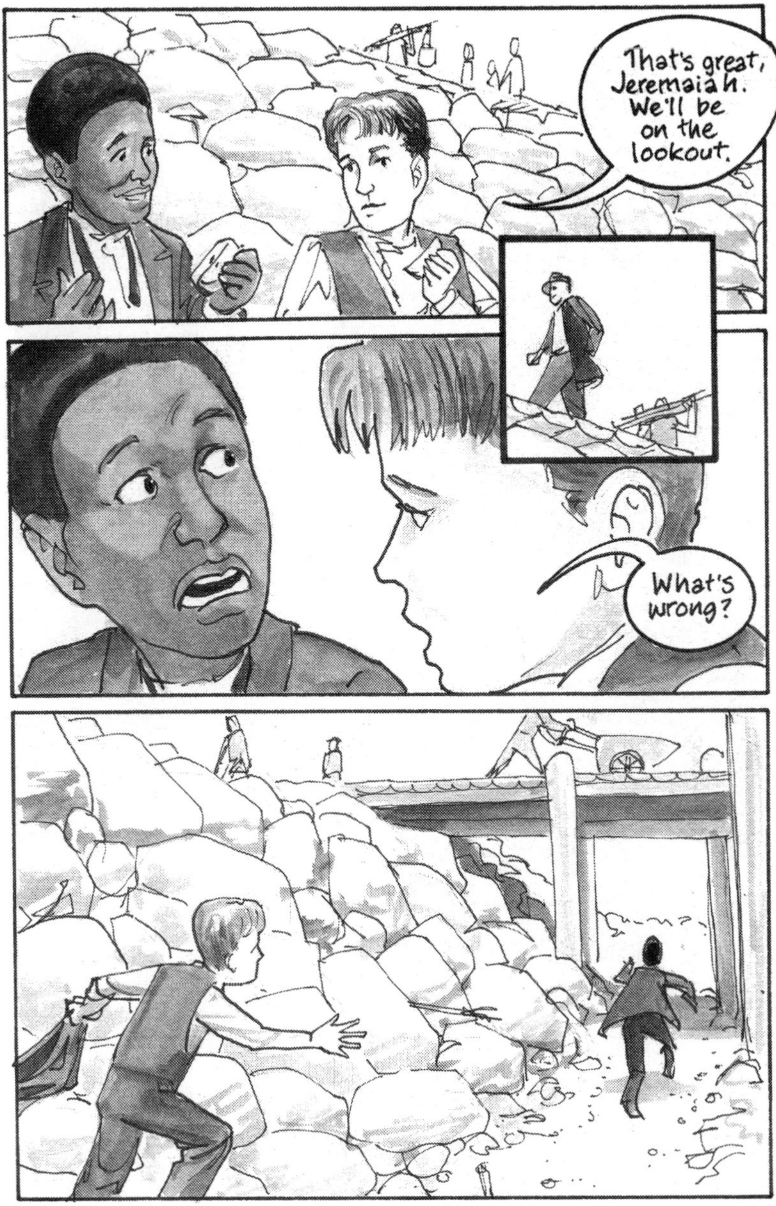
That's great, Jeremaiah. We'll be on the lookout.
What's wrong?

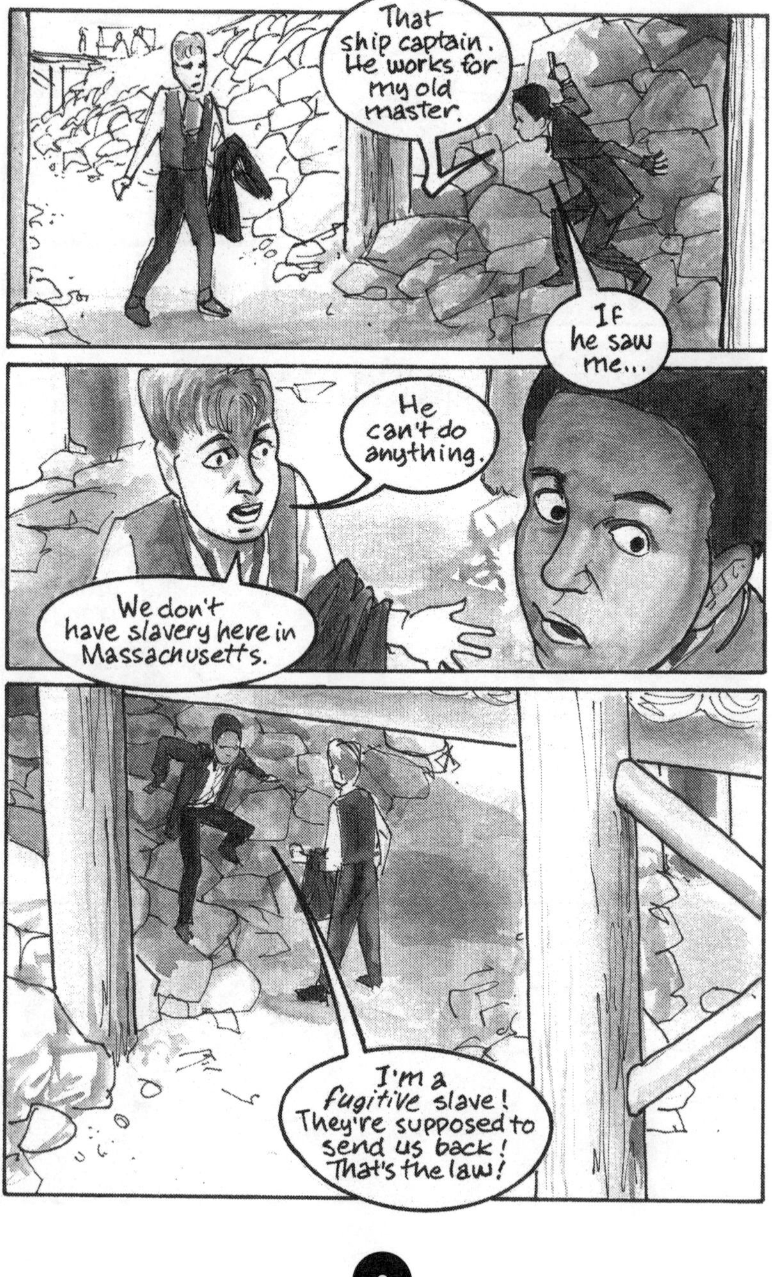
That ship captain. He works for my old master.
If he saw me...
He can't do anything.
We don't have slavery here in Massachusetts.
I'm a *fugitive* slave! They're supposed to send us back! That's the law!

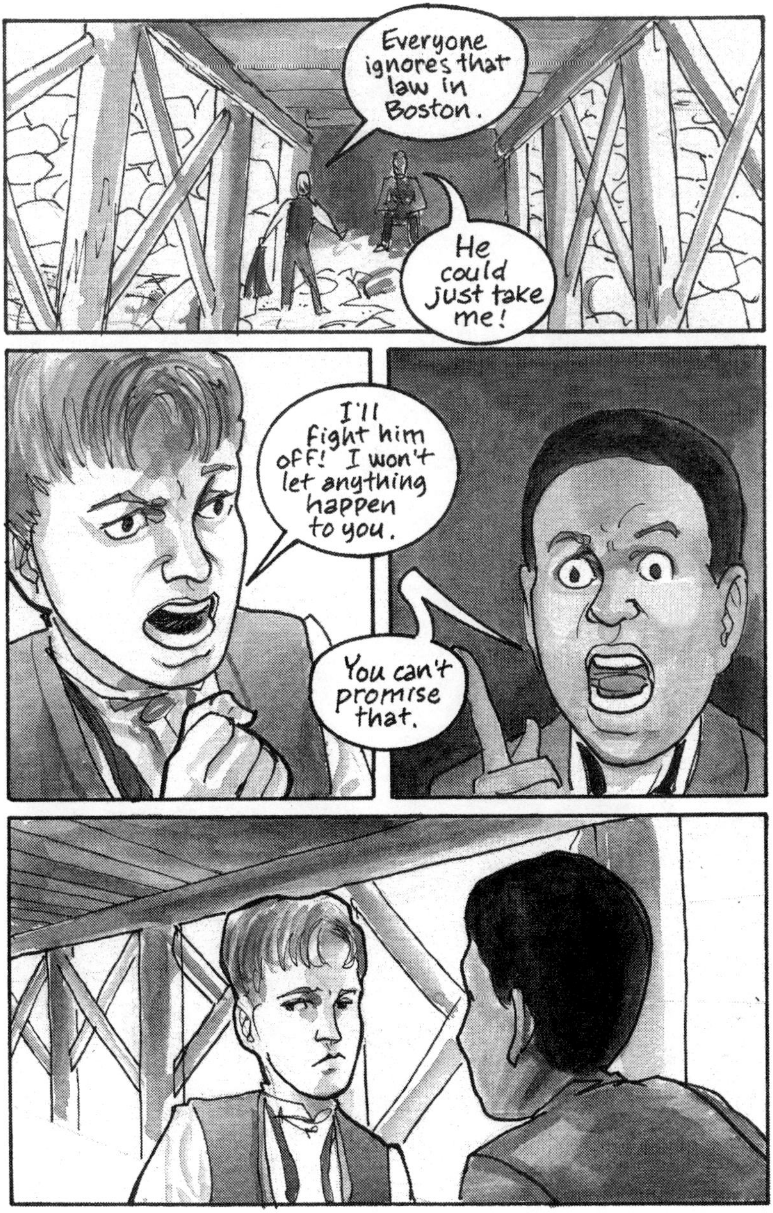
Everyone ignores that law in Boston.
He could just take me!
I'll fight him off! I won't let anything happen to you.
You can't promise that.

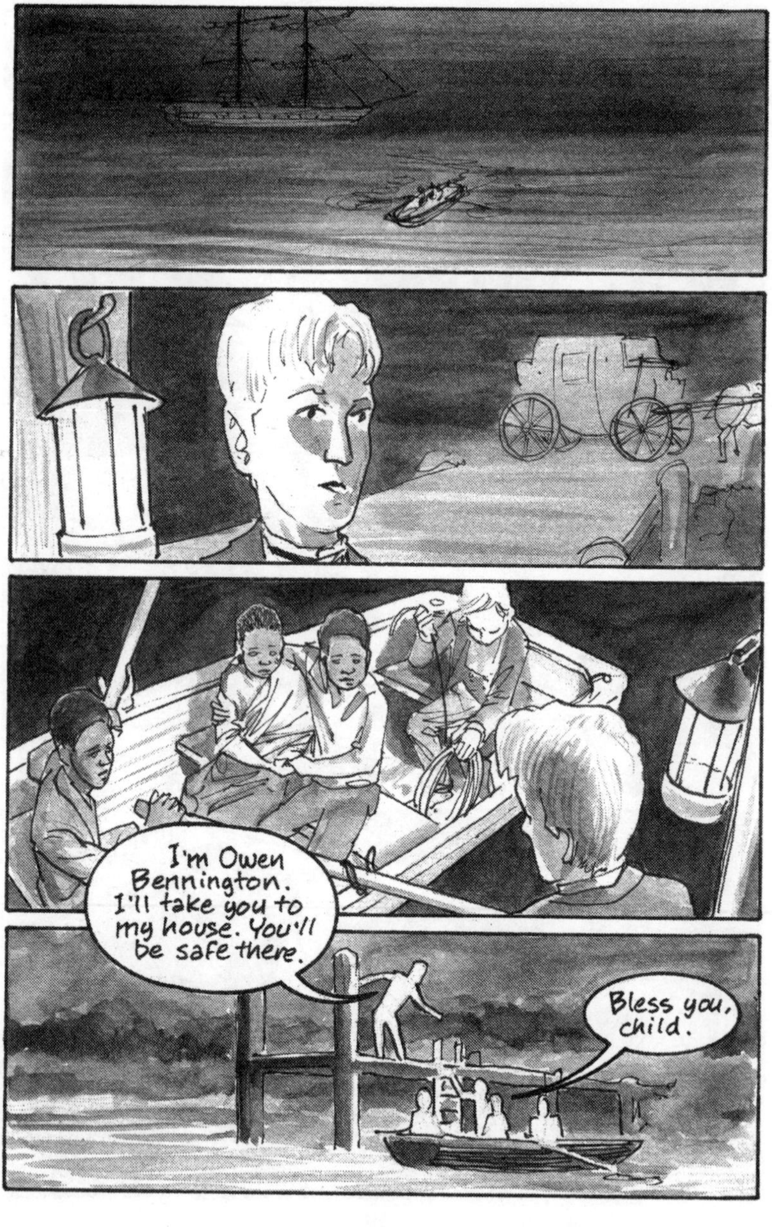
I'm Owen Bennington. I'll take you to my house. You'll be safe there.
Bless you, child.

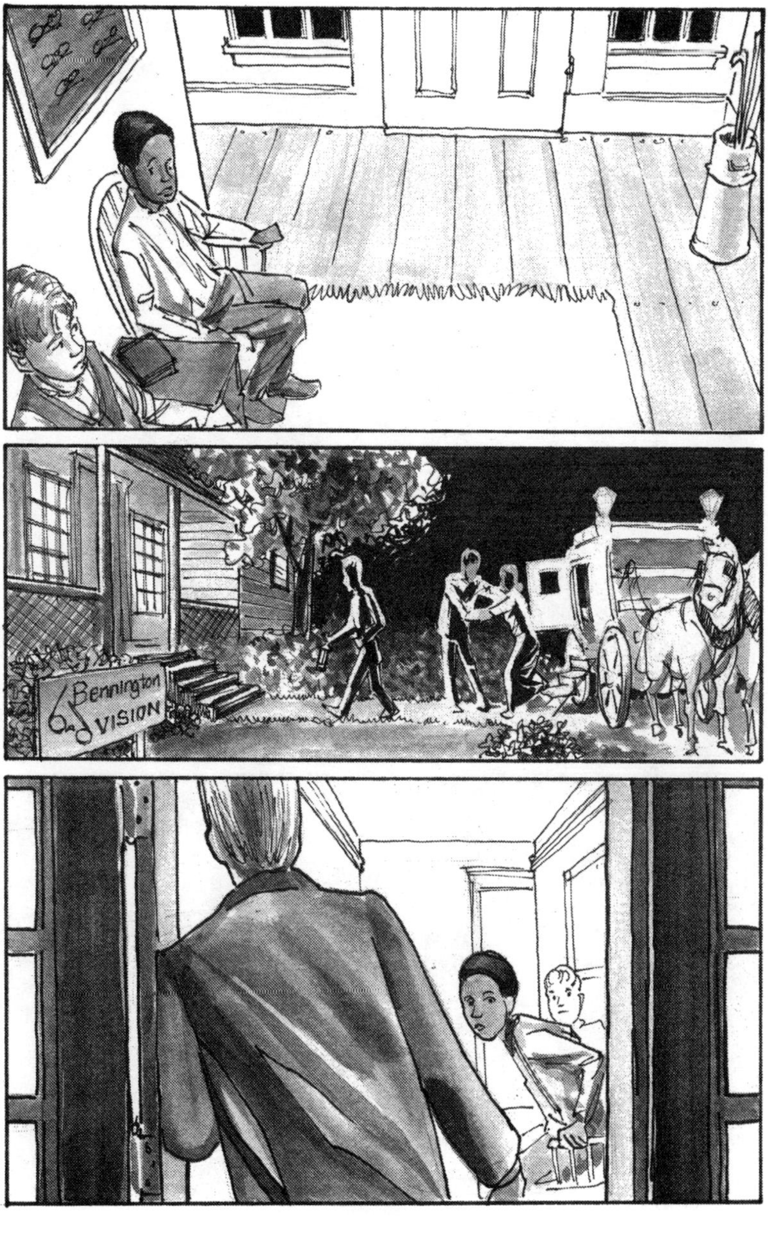
Bennington
VISION

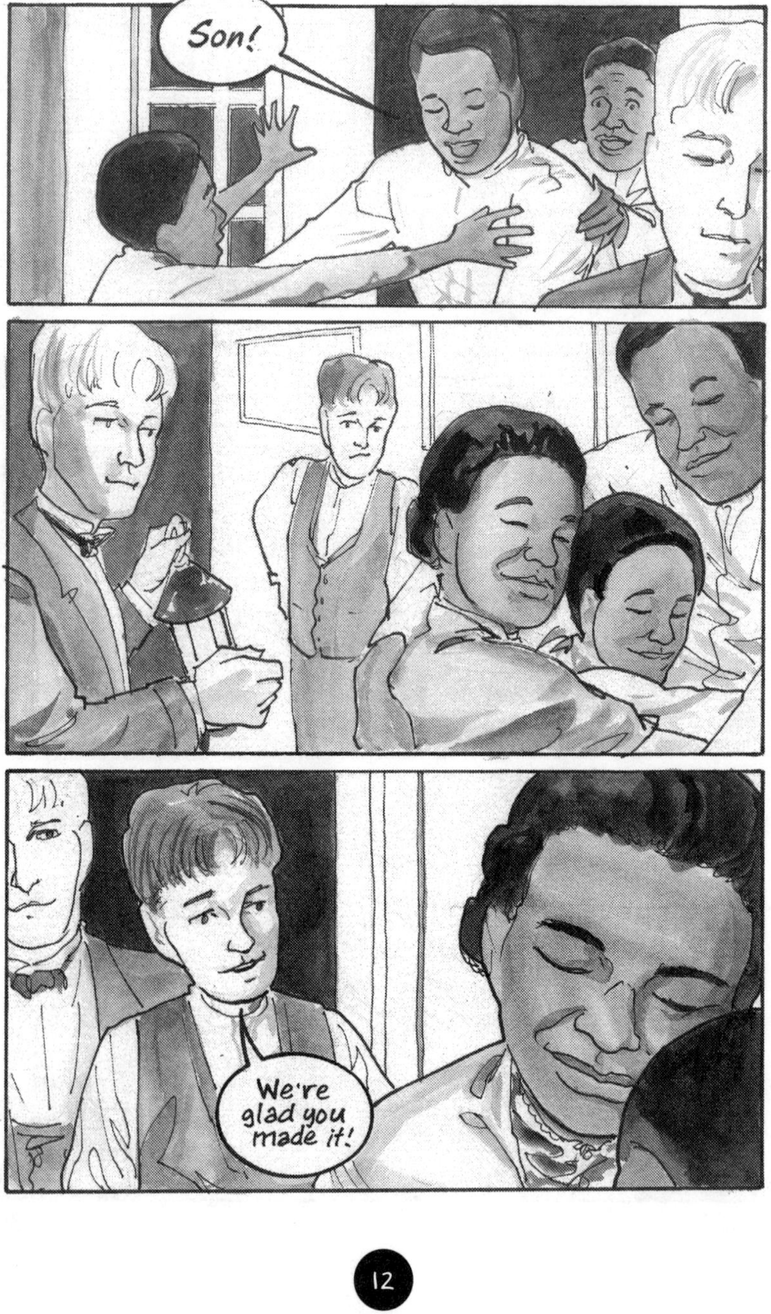
Son!
We're glad you made it!

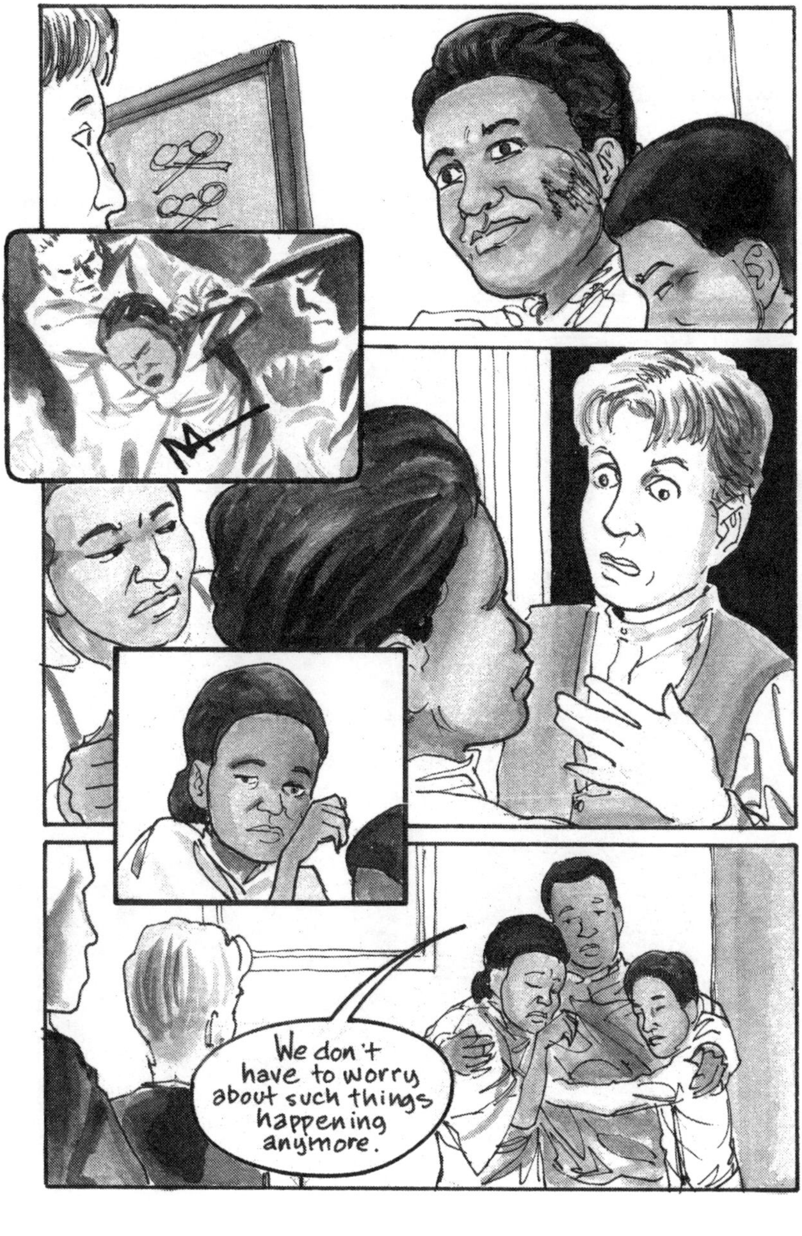
We don't have to worry about such things happening anymore.

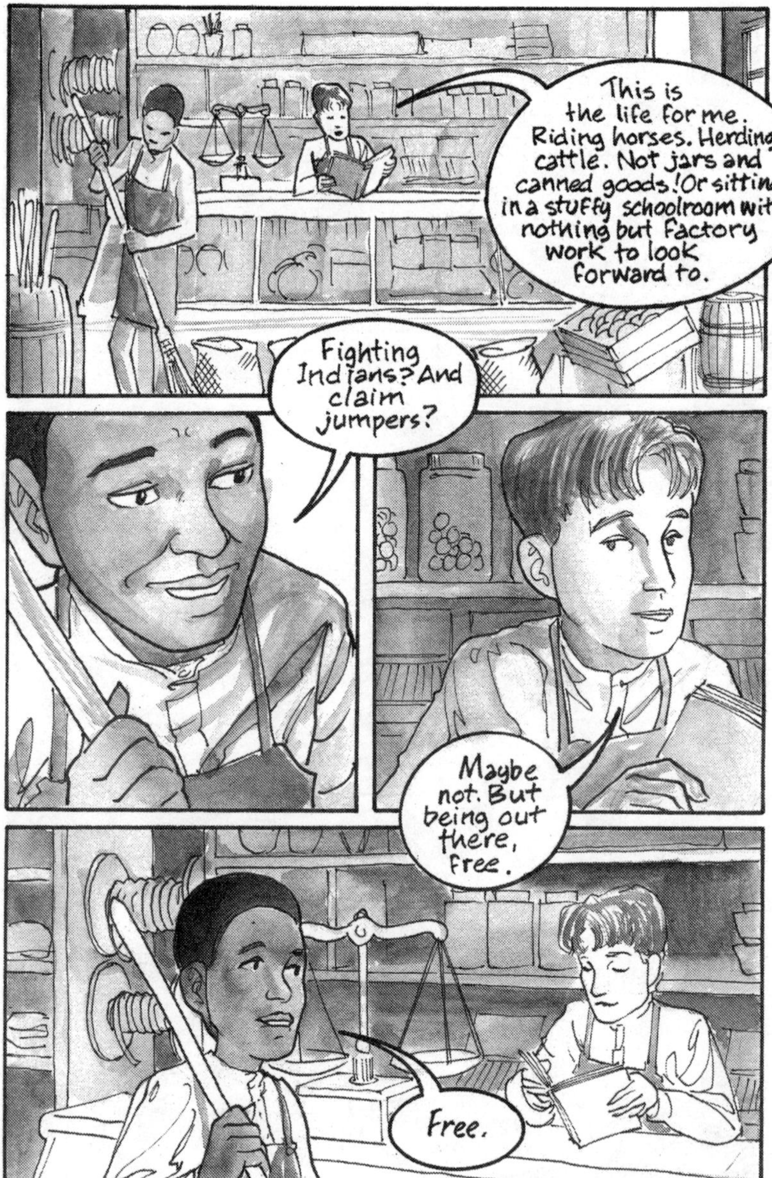
This is the life for me. Riding horses. Herding cattle. Not jars and canned goods! Or sitting in a stuffy schoolroom with nothing but factory work to look forward to.
Fighting Indians? And claim jumpers?
Maybe not. But being out there, free.
Free.

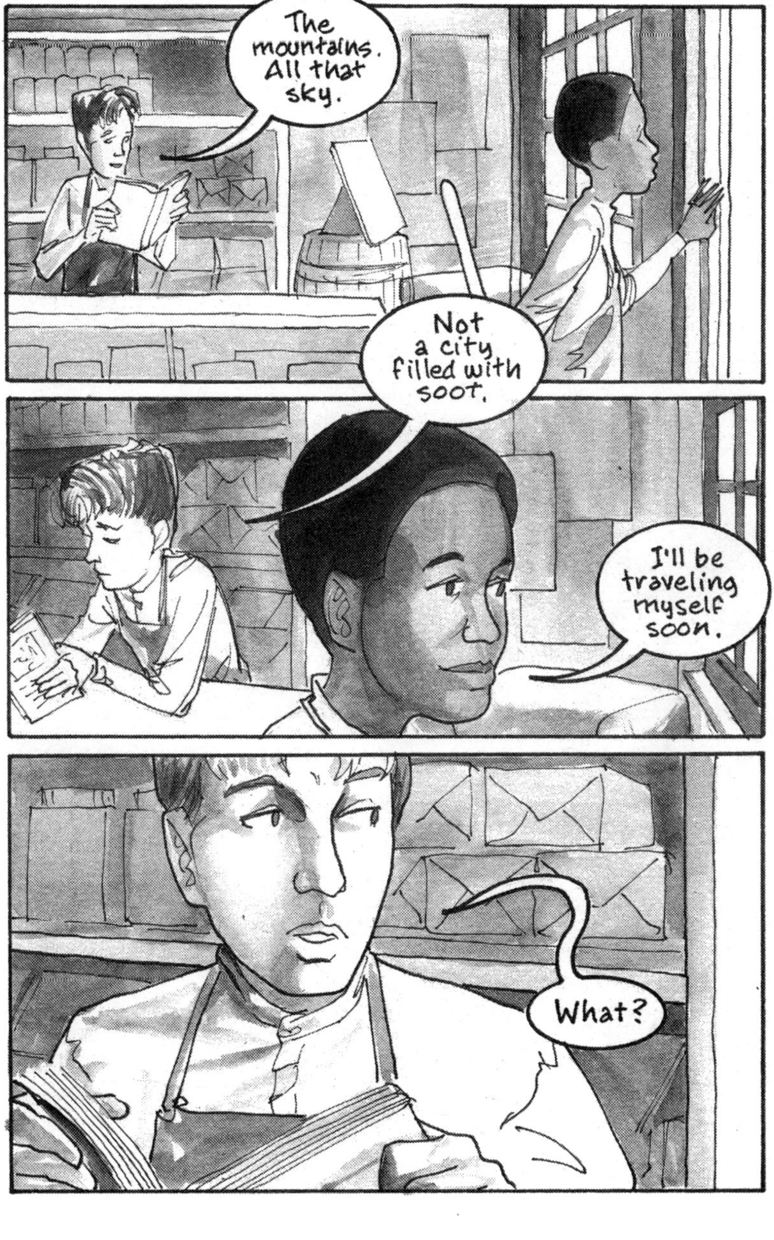
The mountains. All that sky.
Not a city filled with soot.
I'll be traveling myself soon.
What?

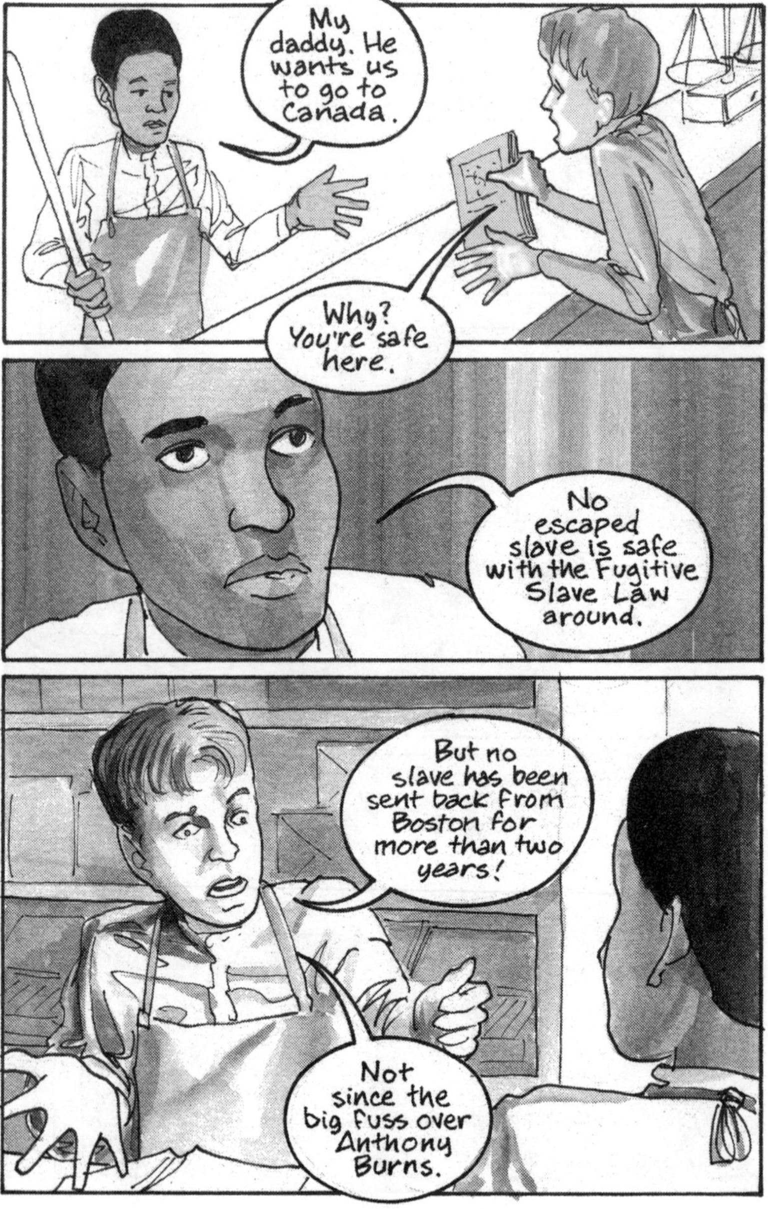
My daddy. He wants us to go to Canada.
Why? You're safe here.
No escaped slave is safe with the Fugitive Slave Law around.
But no slave has been sent back from Boston for more than two years!
Not since the big fuss over Anthony Burns.

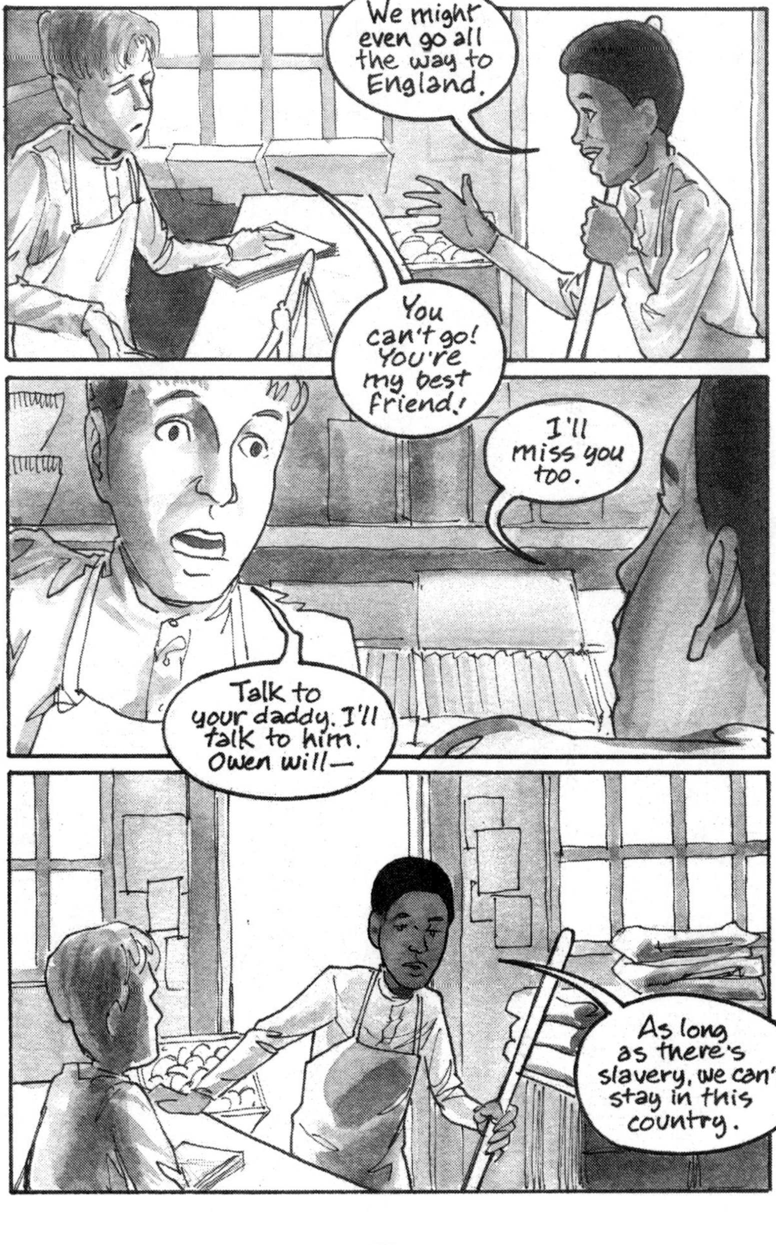
We might even go all the way to England.
You can't go! You're my best friend!
I'll miss you too.
Talk to your daddy. I'll talk to him. Owen will—
As long as there's slavery, we can't stay in this country.

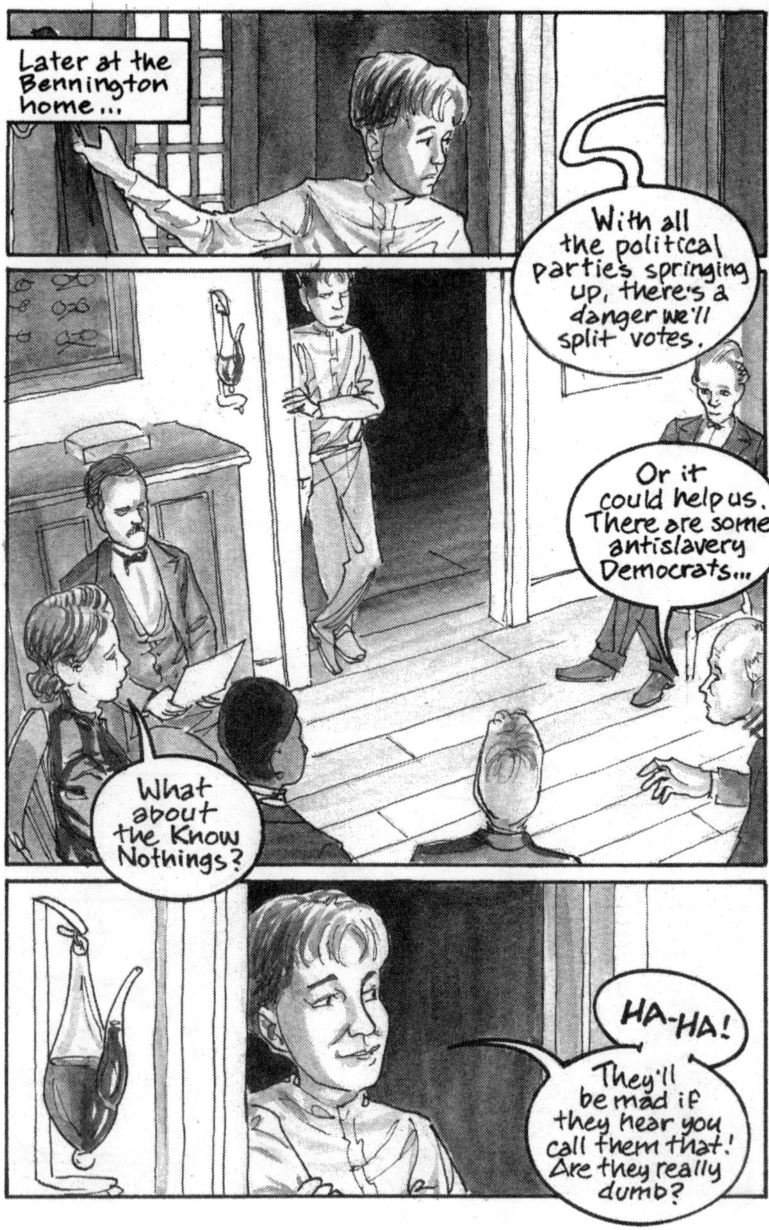
Later at the Bennington home...
With all the political parties springing up, there's a danger we'll split votes.
Or it could help us. There are some antislavery Democrats...
What about the Know Nothings?
HA-HA!
They'll be mad if they hear you call them that! Are they really dumb?

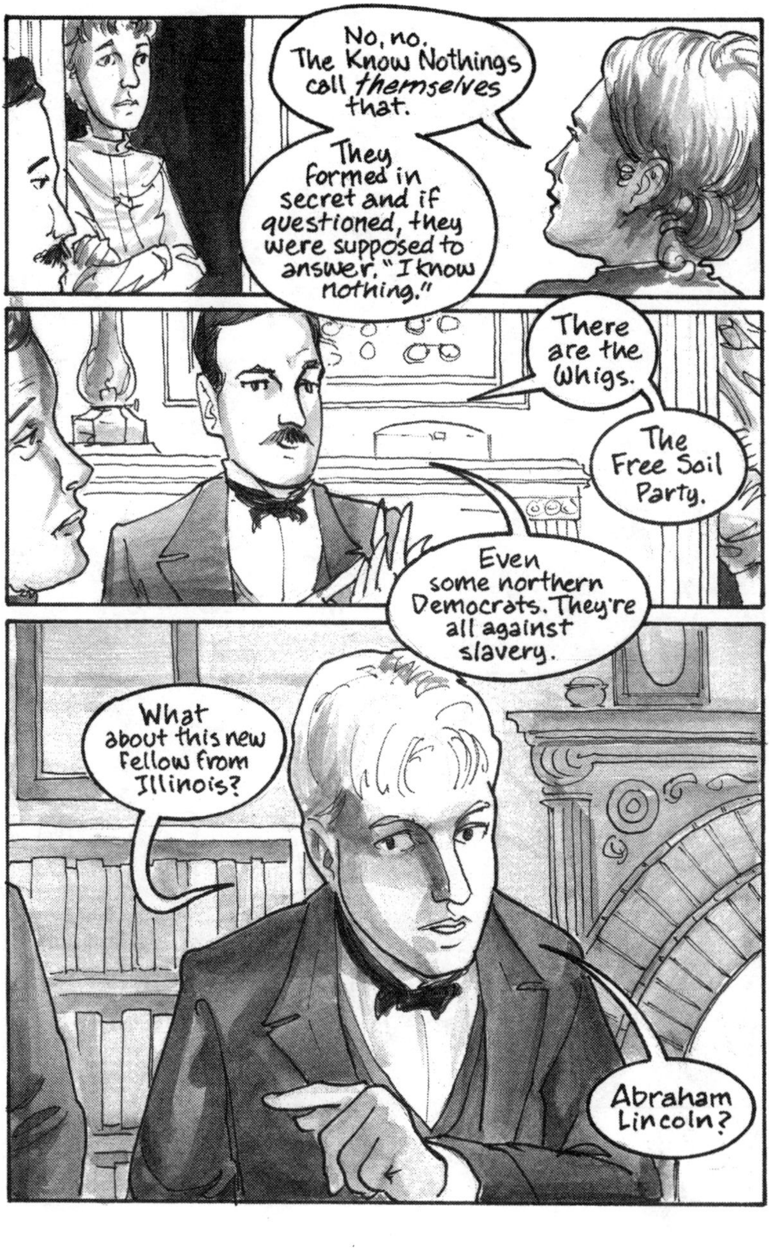
No, no. The Know Nothings call *themselves* that.
They formed in secret and if questioned, they were supposed to answer, "I know nothing."
There are the Whigs.
The Free Soil Party.
Even some northern Democrats. They're all against slavery.
What about this new fellow from Illinois?
Abraham Lincoln?

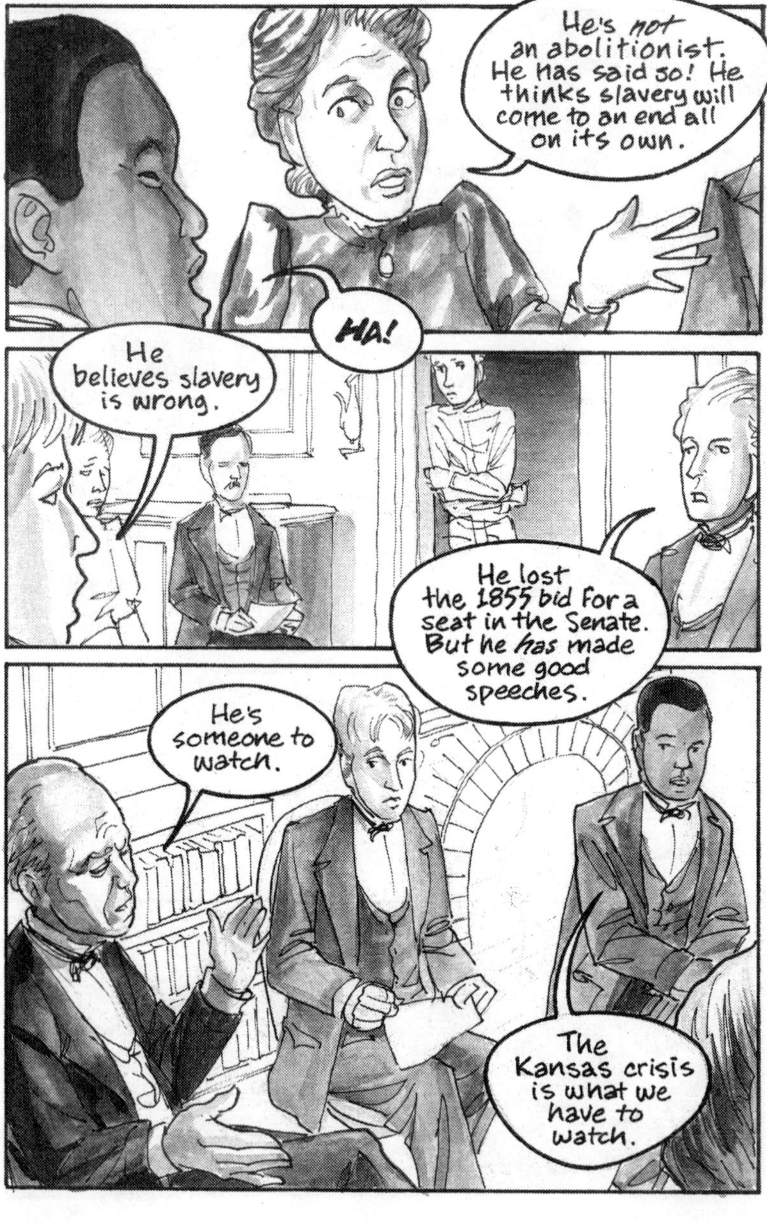
He's *not* an abolitionist. He has said so! He thinks slavery will come to an end all on its own.
HA!
He believes slavery is wrong.
He lost the 1855 bid for a seat in the Senate. But he *has* made some good speeches.
He's someone to watch.
The Kansas crisis is what we have to watch.

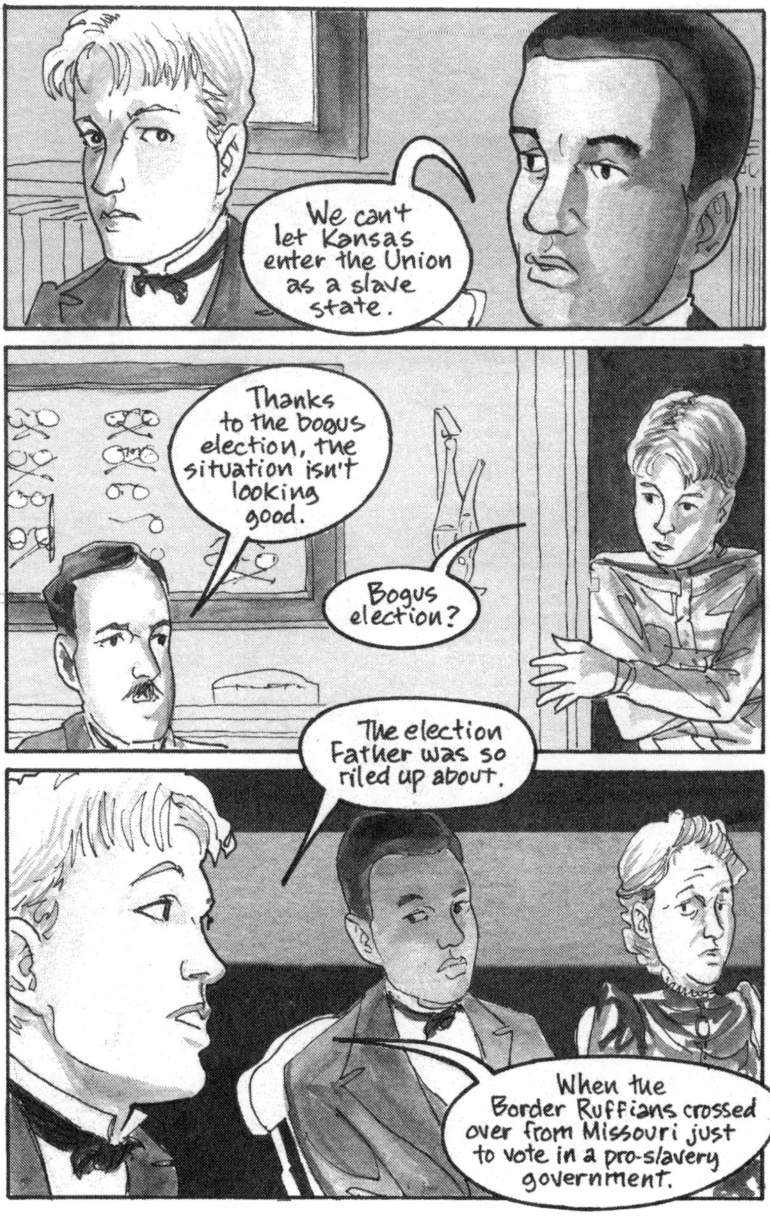
We can't let Kansas enter the Union as a slave state.
Thanks to the bogus election, the situation isn't looking good.
Bogus election?
The election Father was so riled up about.
When the Border Ruffians crossed over from Missouri just to vote in a pro-slavery government.

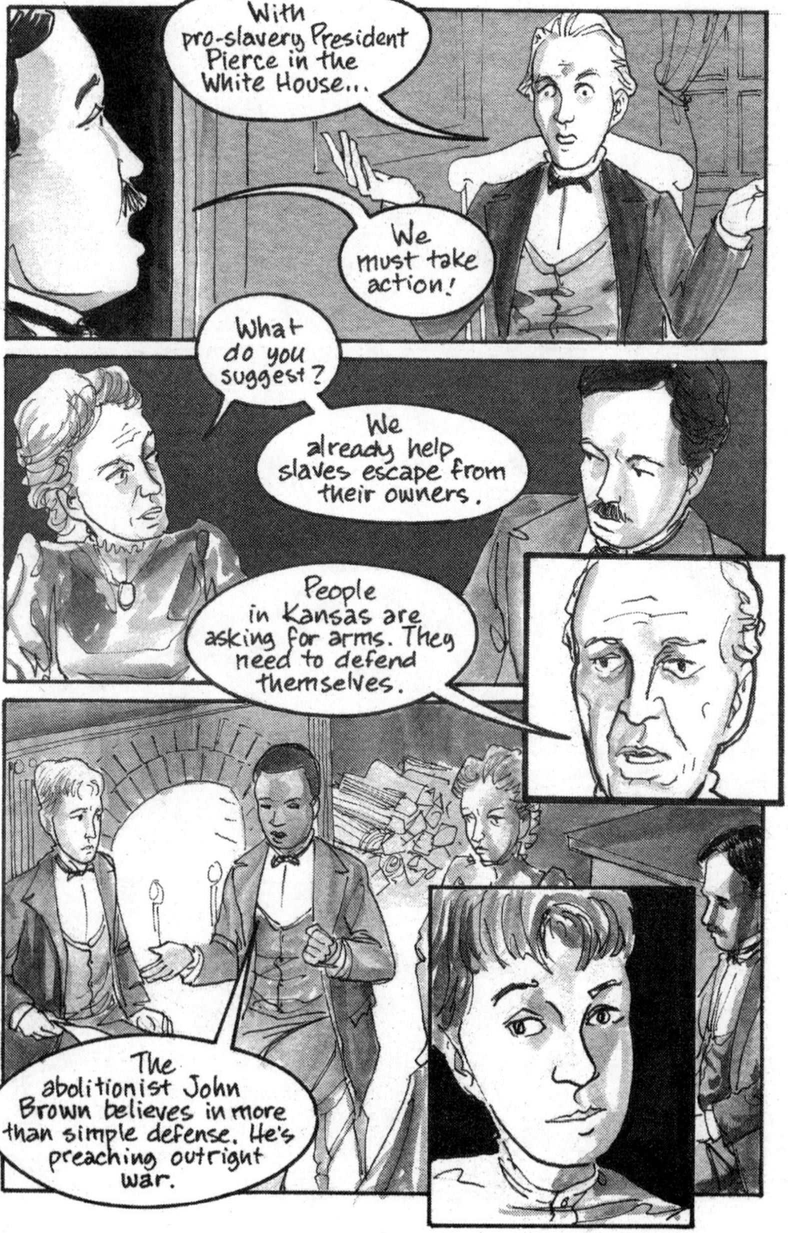
With pro-slavery President Pierce in the White House...
We must take action!
What do you suggest?
We already help slaves escape from their owners.
People in Kansas are asking for arms. They need to defend themselves.
The abolitionist John Brown believes in more than simple defense. He's preaching outright war.

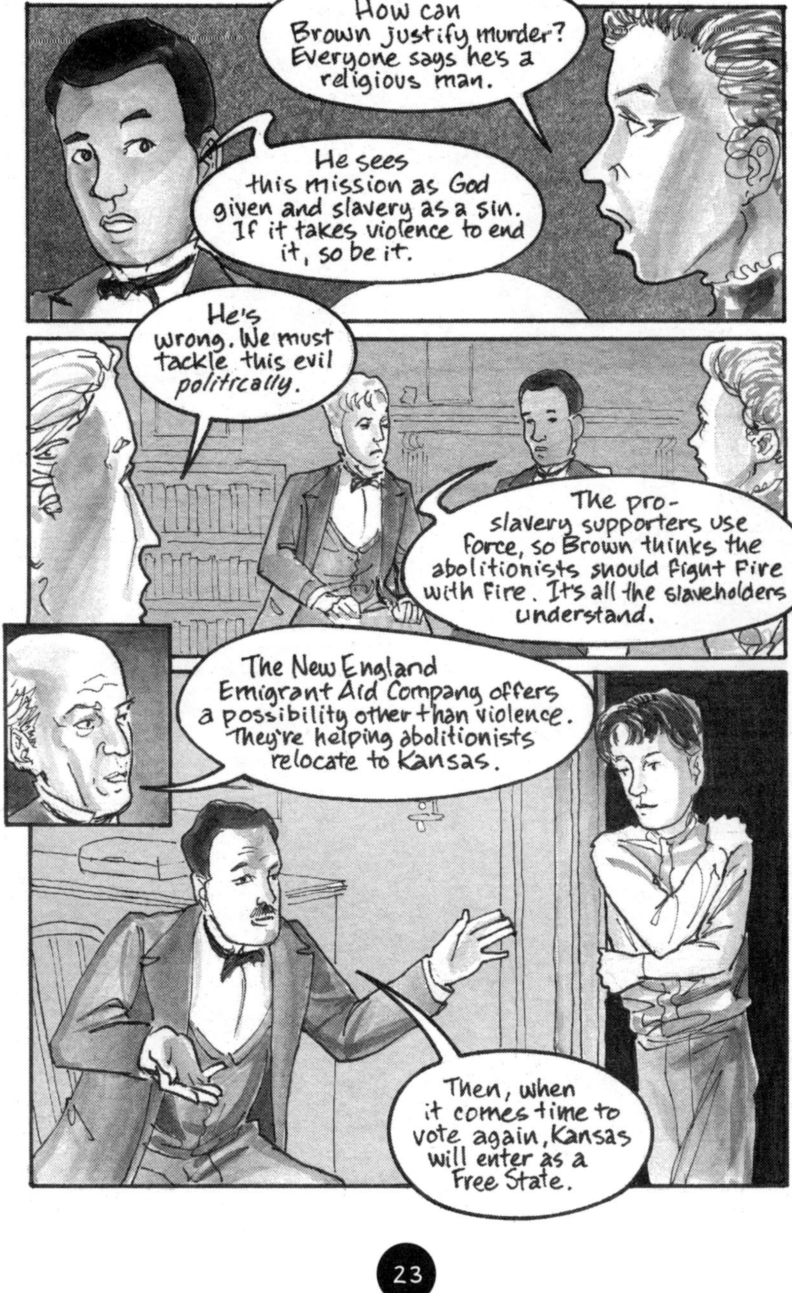
How can Brown justify murder? Everyone says he's a religious man.
He sees this mission as God given and slavery as a sin. If it takes violence to end it, so be it.
He's wrong. We must tackle this evil *politically*.
The pro-slavery supporters use force, so Brown thinks the abolitionists should fight fire with fire. It's all the slaveholders understand.
The New England Emigrant Aid Company offers a possibility other than violence. They're helping abolitionists relocate to Kansas.
Then, when it comes time to vote again, Kansas will enter as a Free State.

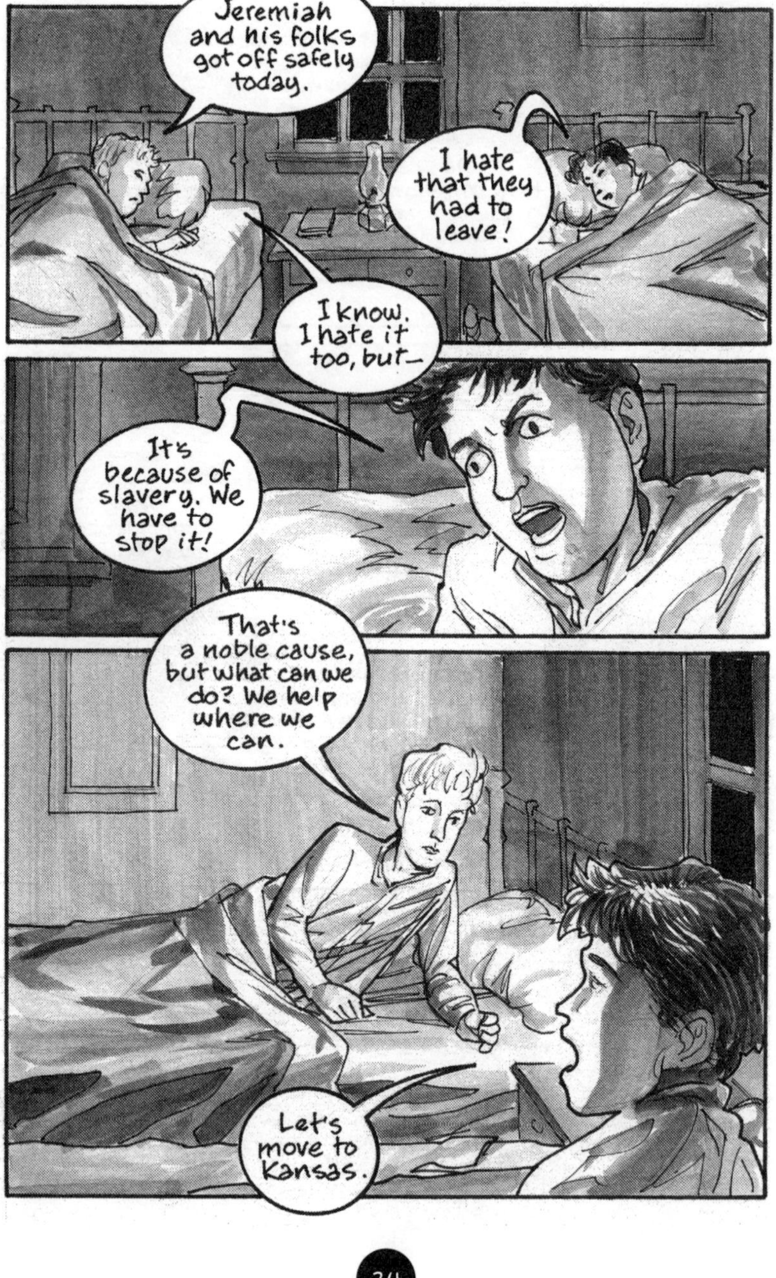
Jeremiah and his folks got off safely today.
I hate that they had to leave!
I know. I hate it too, but—
It's because of slavery. We have to stop it!
That's a noble cause, but what can we do? We help where we can.
Let's move to Kansas.

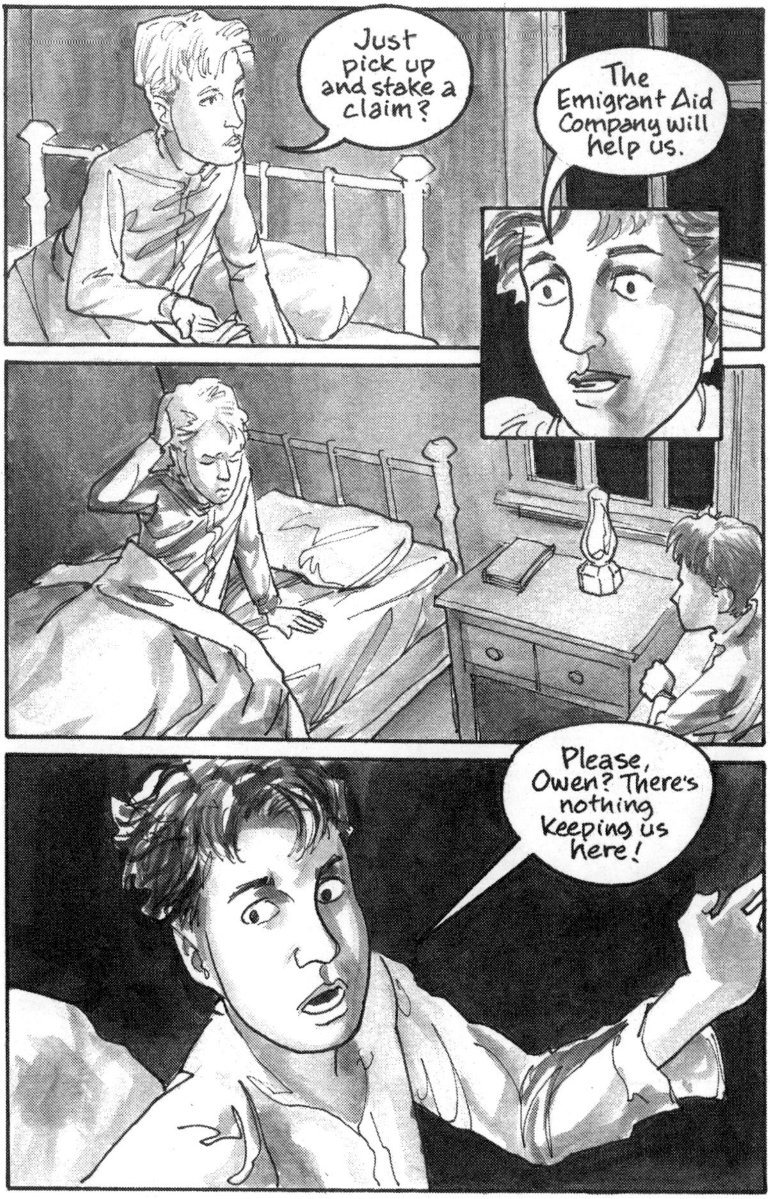
Just pick up and stake a claim?
The Emigrant Aid Company will help us.
Please, Owen? There's nothing keeping us here!

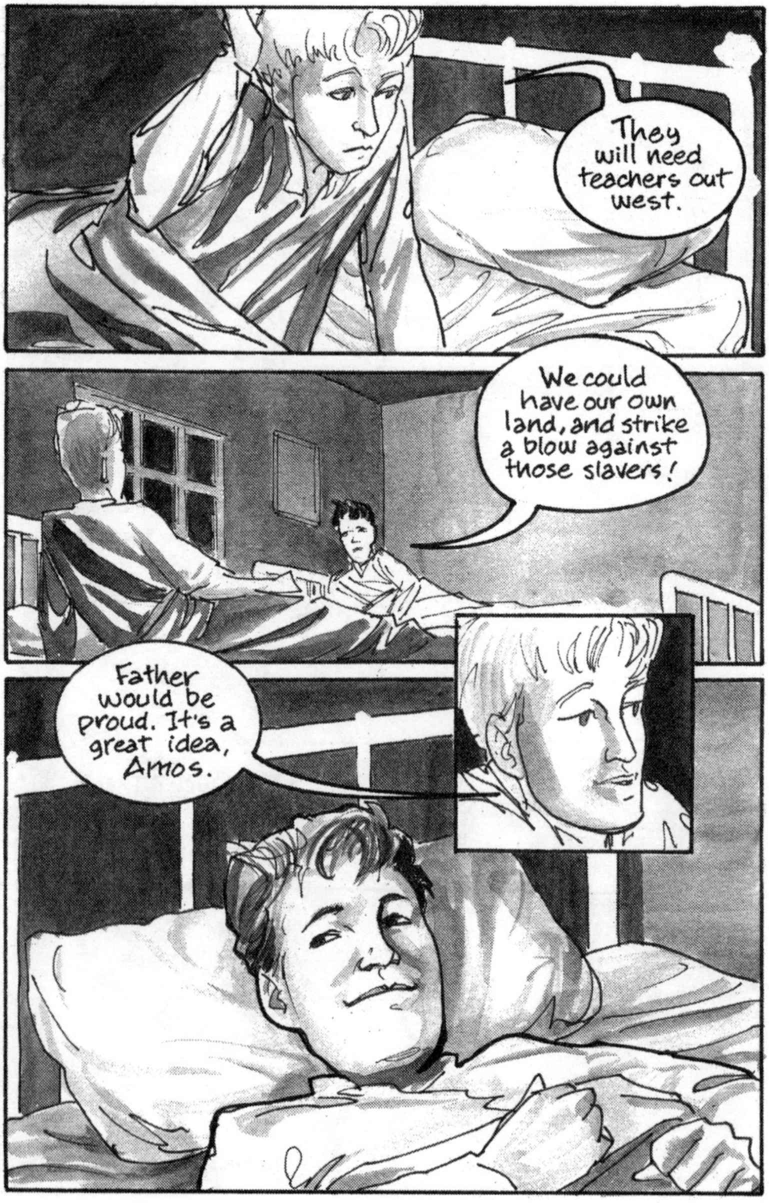
They will need teachers out west.
We could have our own land, and strike a blow against those slavers!
Father would be proud. It's a great idea, Amos.

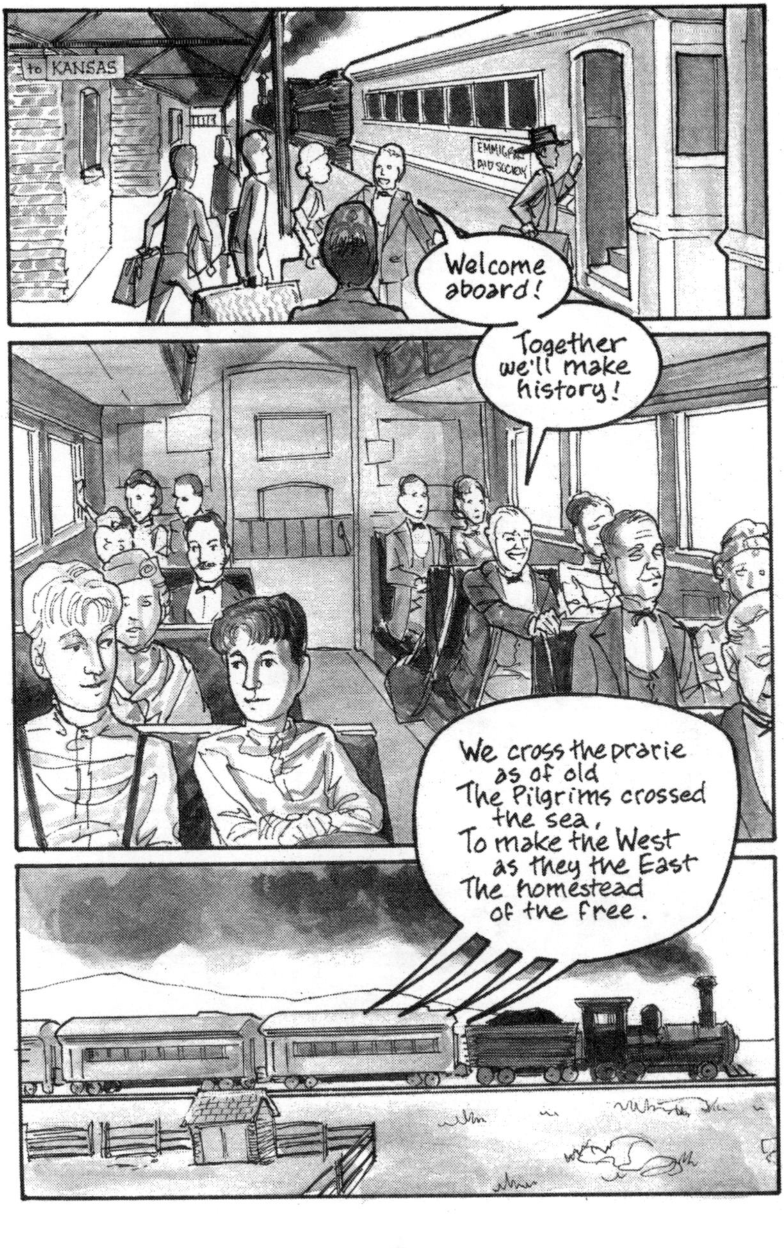
to KANSAS
Welcome aboard!
Together we'll make history!
We cross the prarie as of old The Pilgrims crossed the sea, To make the West as they the East The homestead of the free.

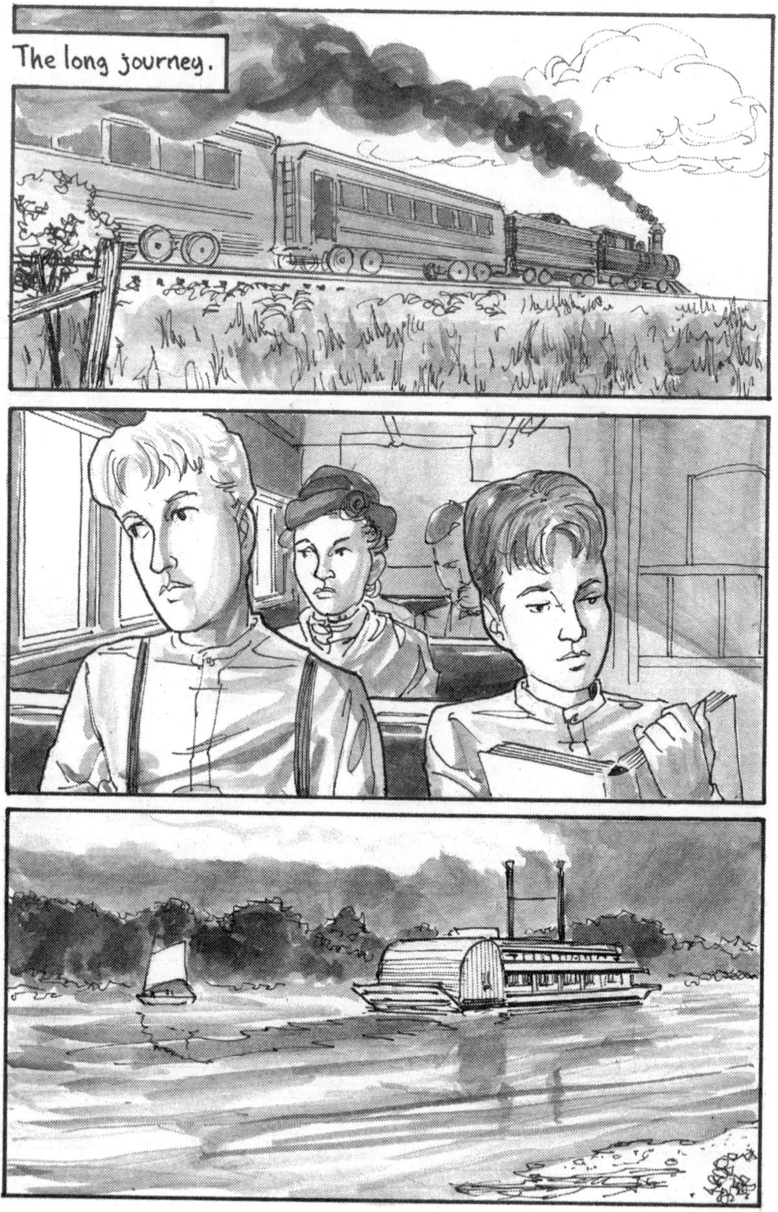
The long journey.

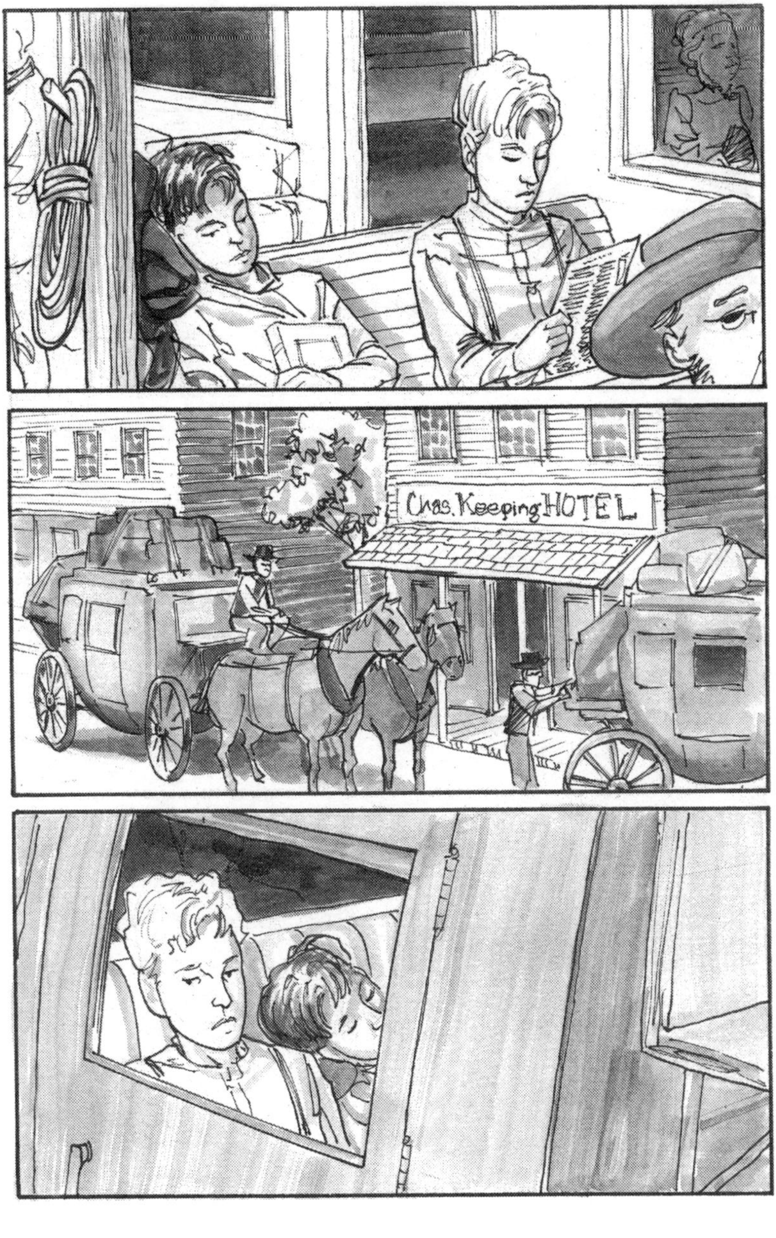
Chas. Keeping HOTEL

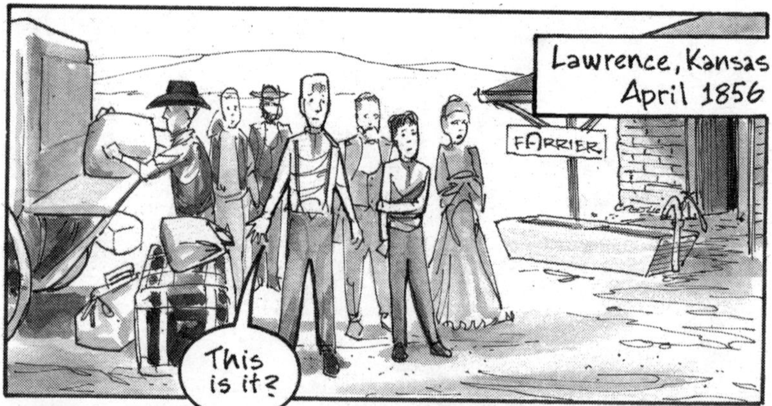
Lawrence, Kansas
April 1856
FARRIER
This is it?

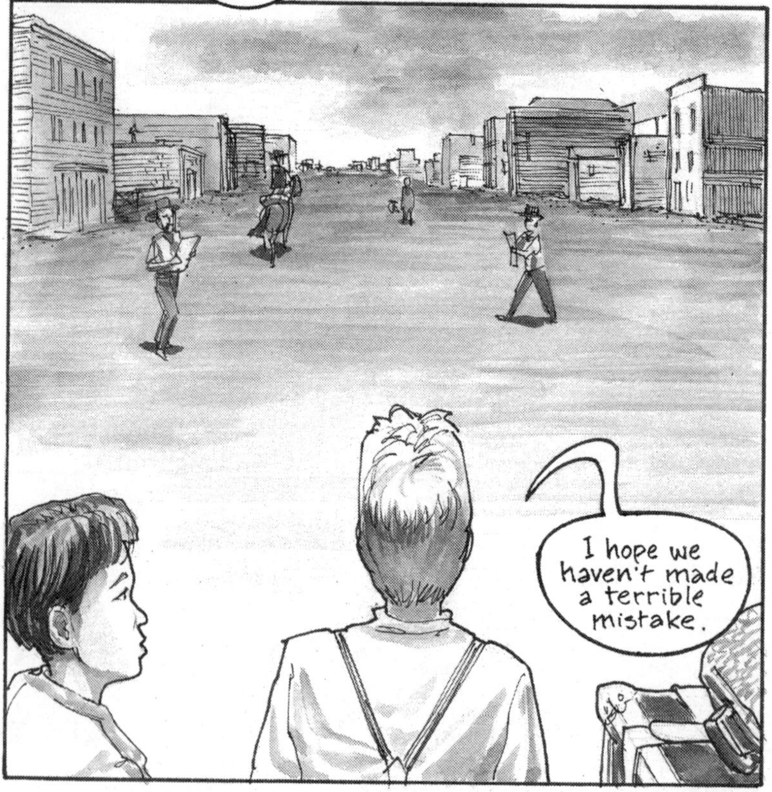
I hope we haven't made a terrible mistake.

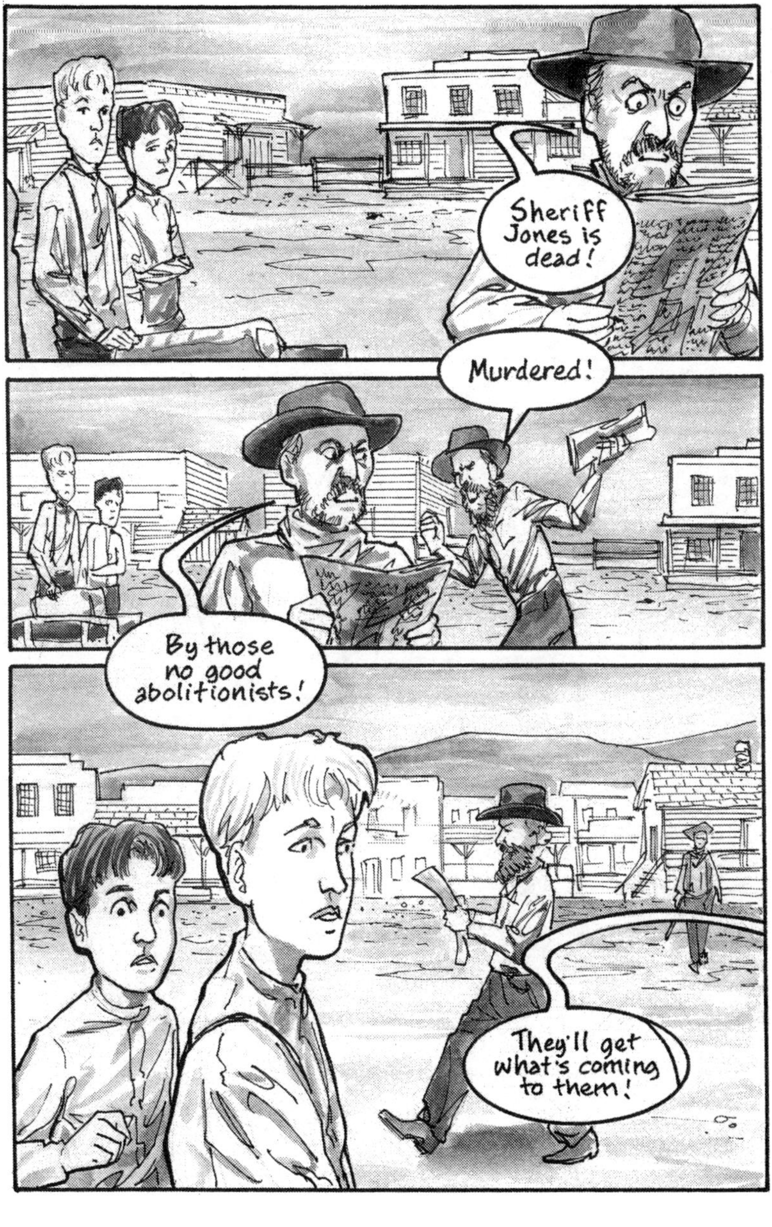
Sheriff Jones is dead!
Murdered!
By those no good abolitionists!
They'll get what's coming to them!

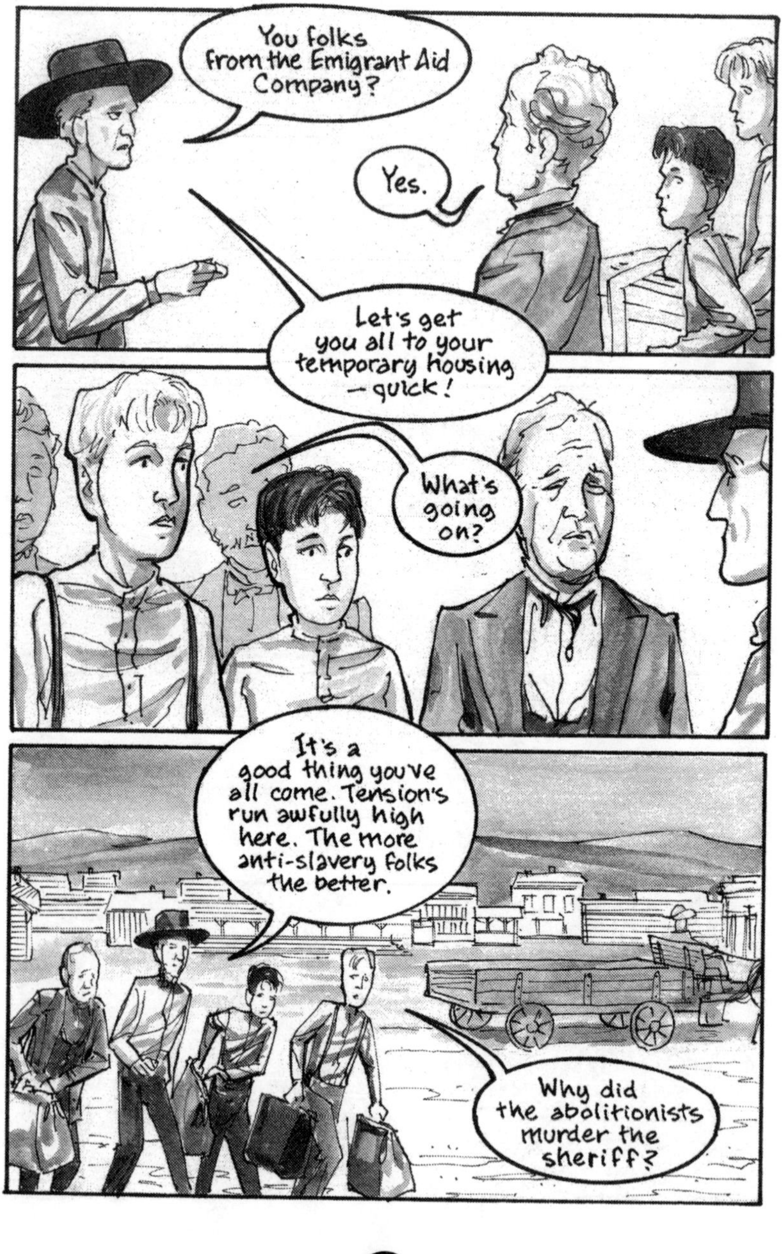
You folks from the Emigrant Aid Company?
Yes.
Let's get you all to your temporary housing — quick!
What's going on?
It's a good thing you've all come. Tension's run awfully high here. The more anti-slavery folks the better.
Why did the abolitionists murder the sheriff?

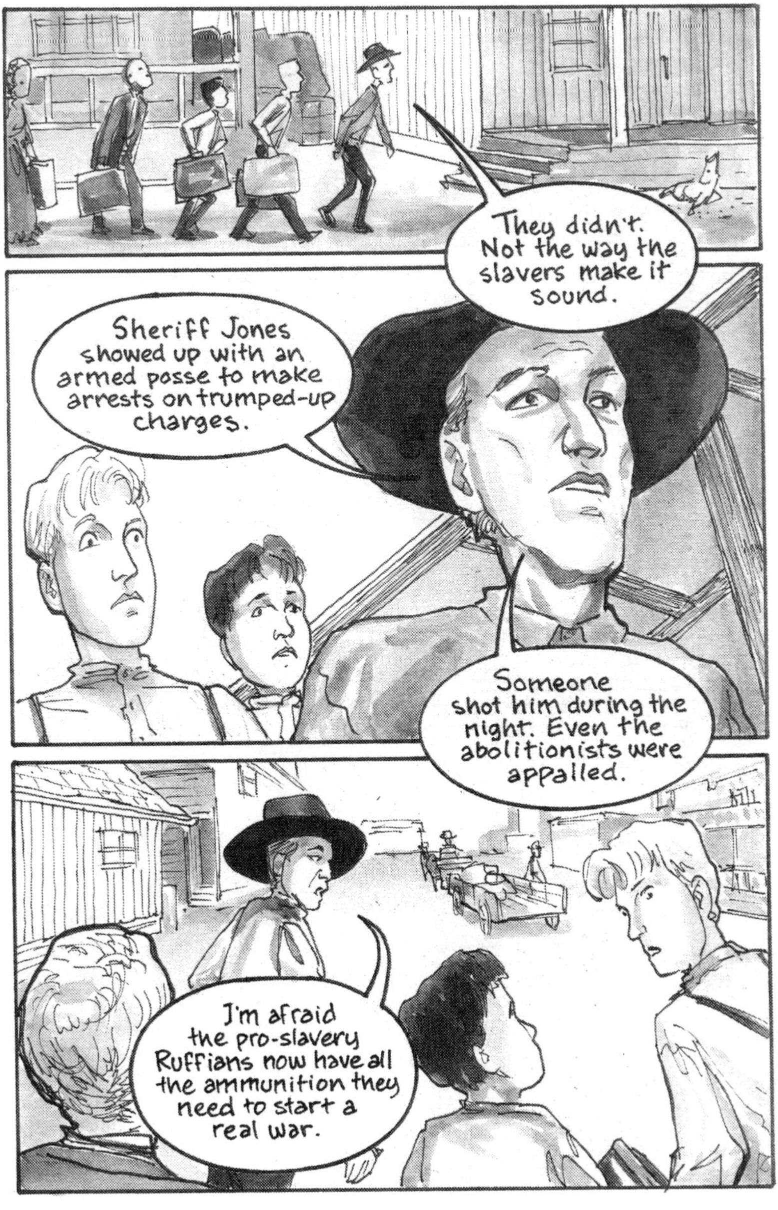
They didn't. Not the way the slavers make it sound.
Sheriff Jones showed up with an armed posse to make arrests on trumped-up charges.
Someone shot him during the night. Even the abolitionists were appalled.
I'm afraid the pro-slavery Ruffians now have all the ammunition they need to start a real war.

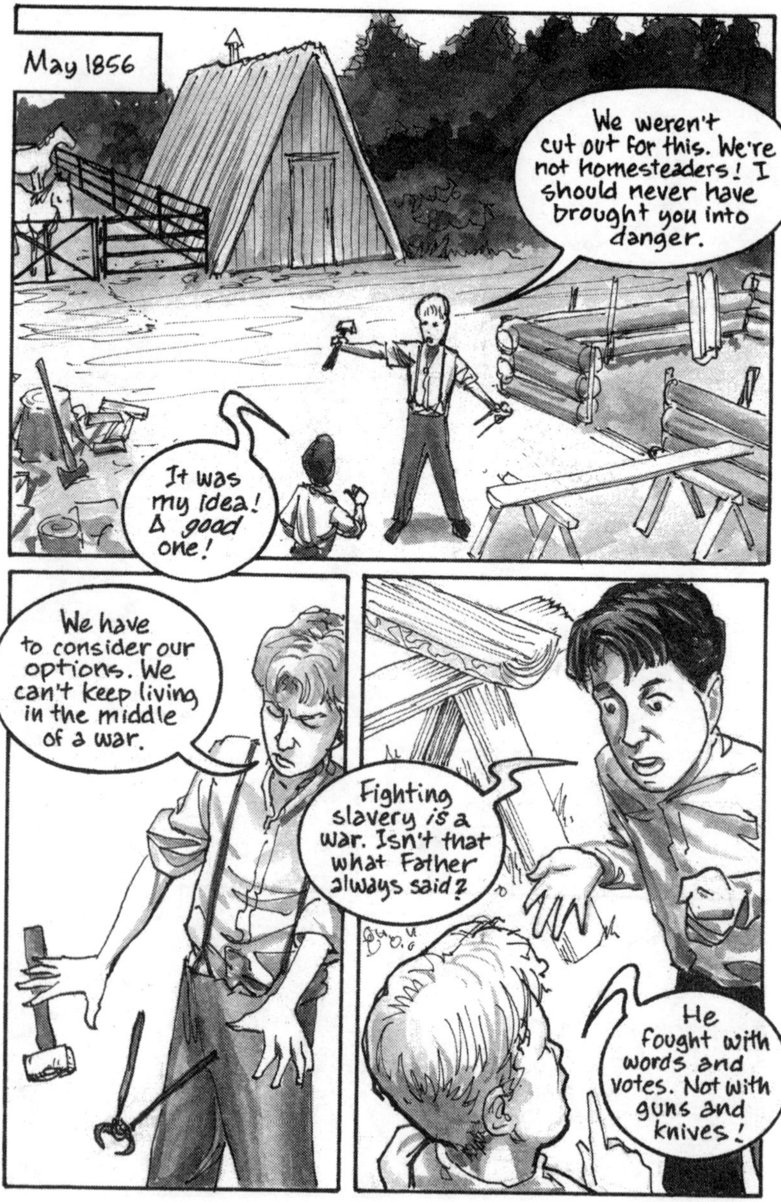
May 1856
We weren't cut out for this. We're not homesteaders! I should never have brought you into danger.
It was my idea! A good one!
We have to consider our options. We can't keep living in the middle of a war.
Fighting slavery is a war. Isn't that what Father always said?
He fought with words and votes. Not with guns and knives!

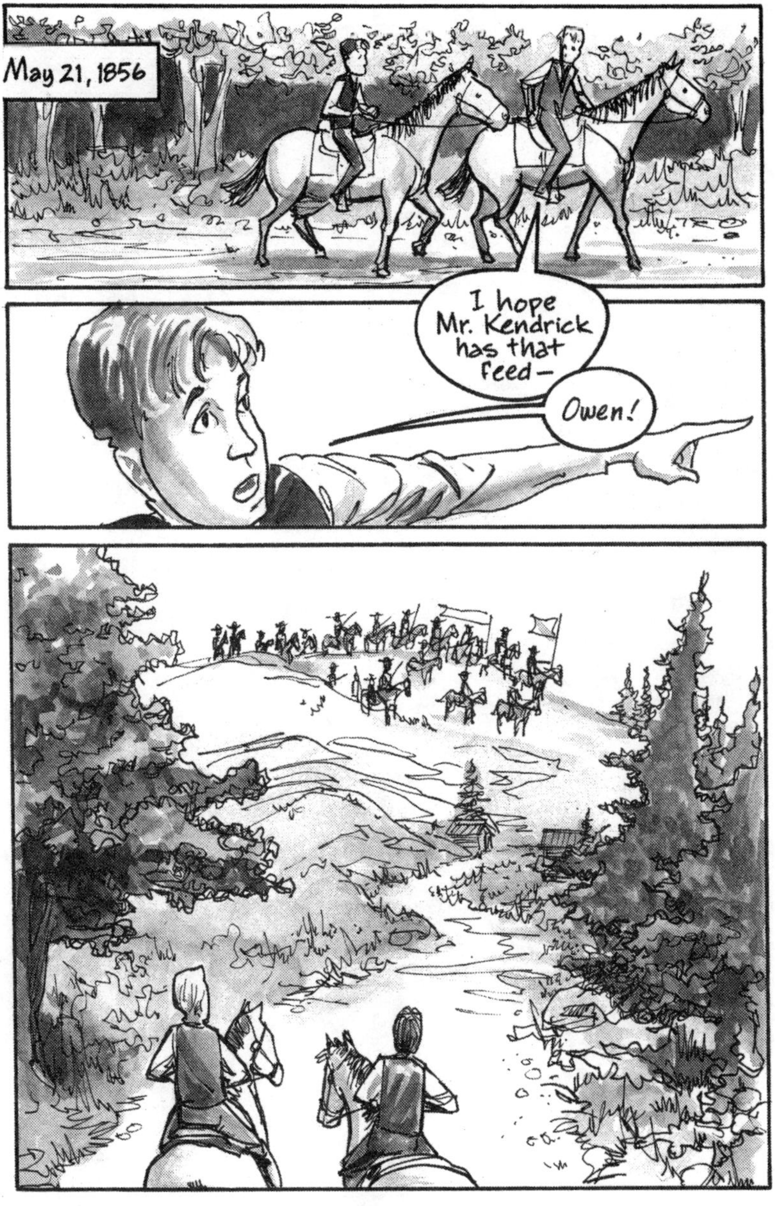

May 21, 1856
I hope Mr. Kendrick has that feed—
Owen!

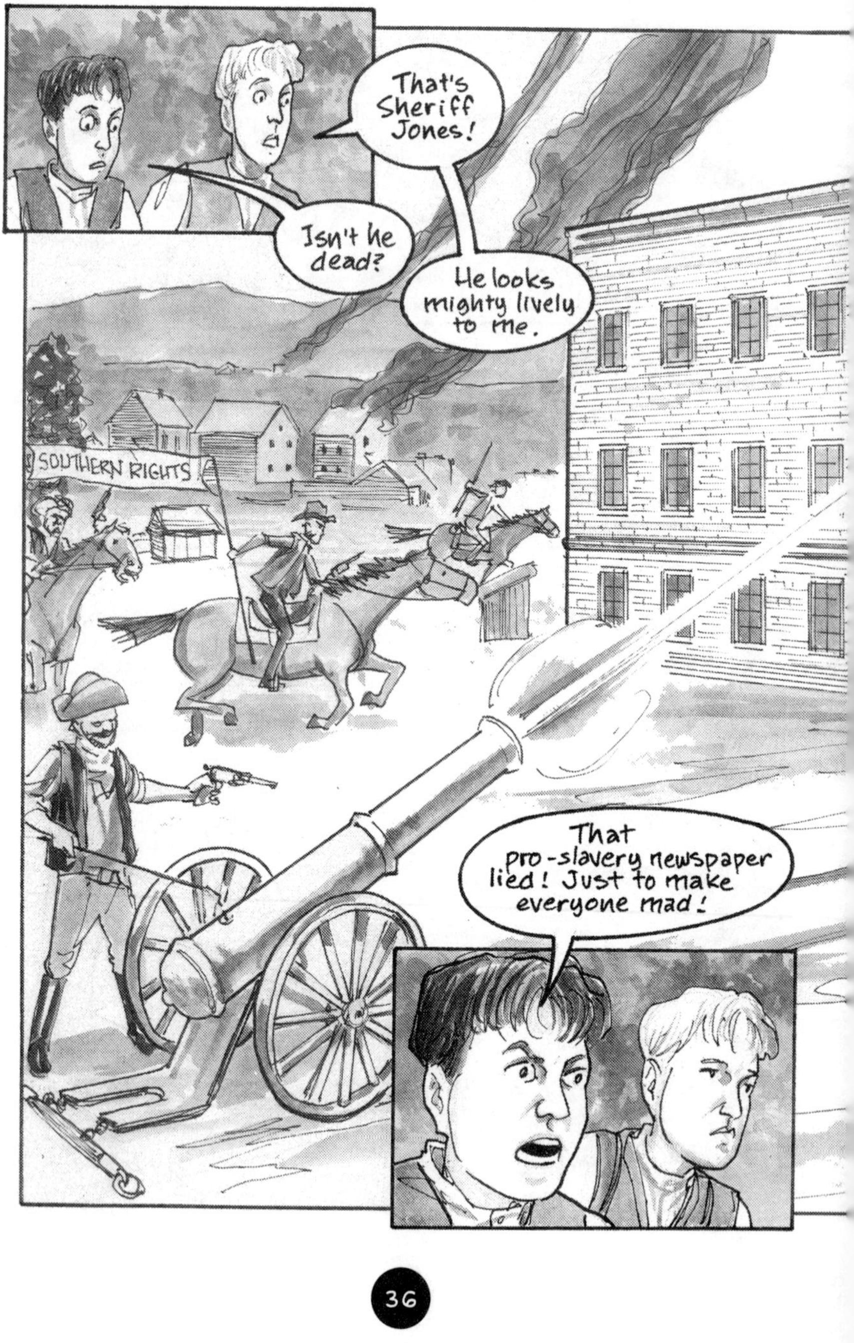
That's Sheriff Jones!
Isn't he dead?
He looks mighty lively to me.
SOUTHERN RIGHTS
That pro-slavery newspaper lied! Just to make everyone mad!

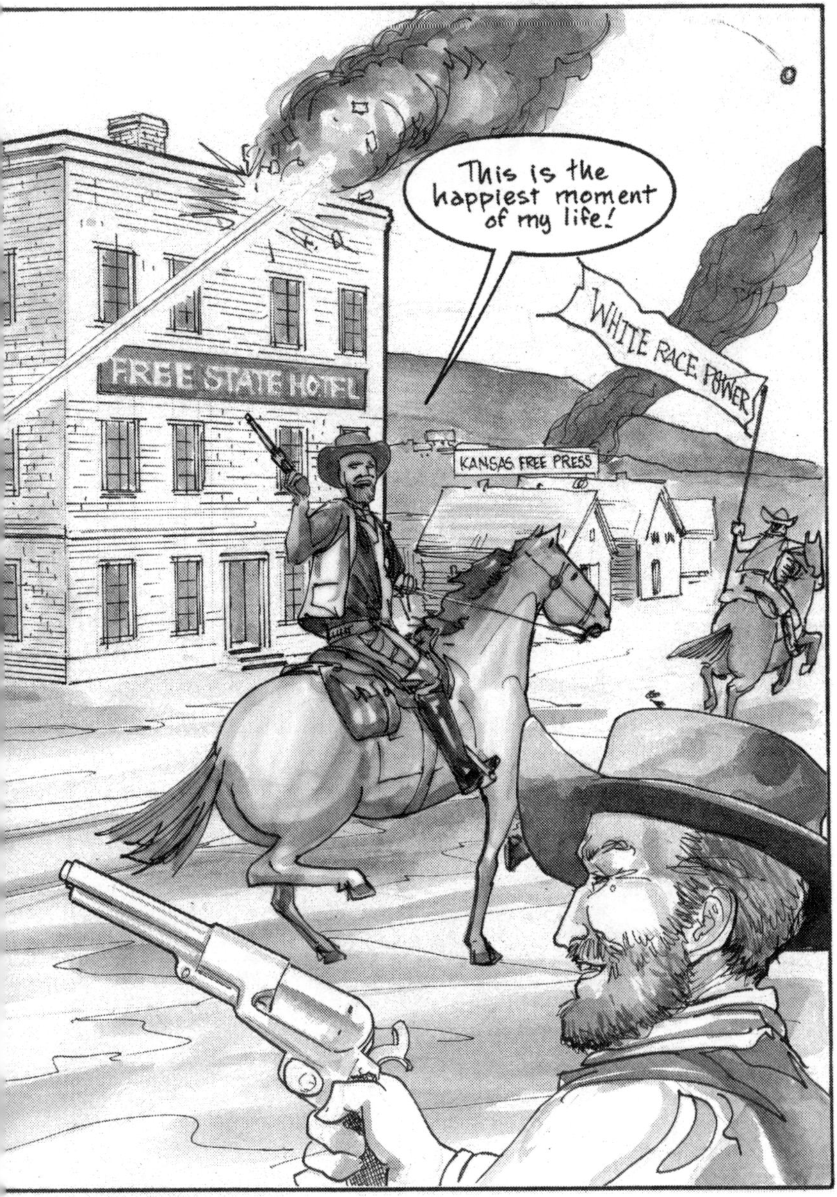
This is the happiest moment of my life!
FREE STATE HOTEL
KANSAS FREE PRESS
WHITE RACE POWER

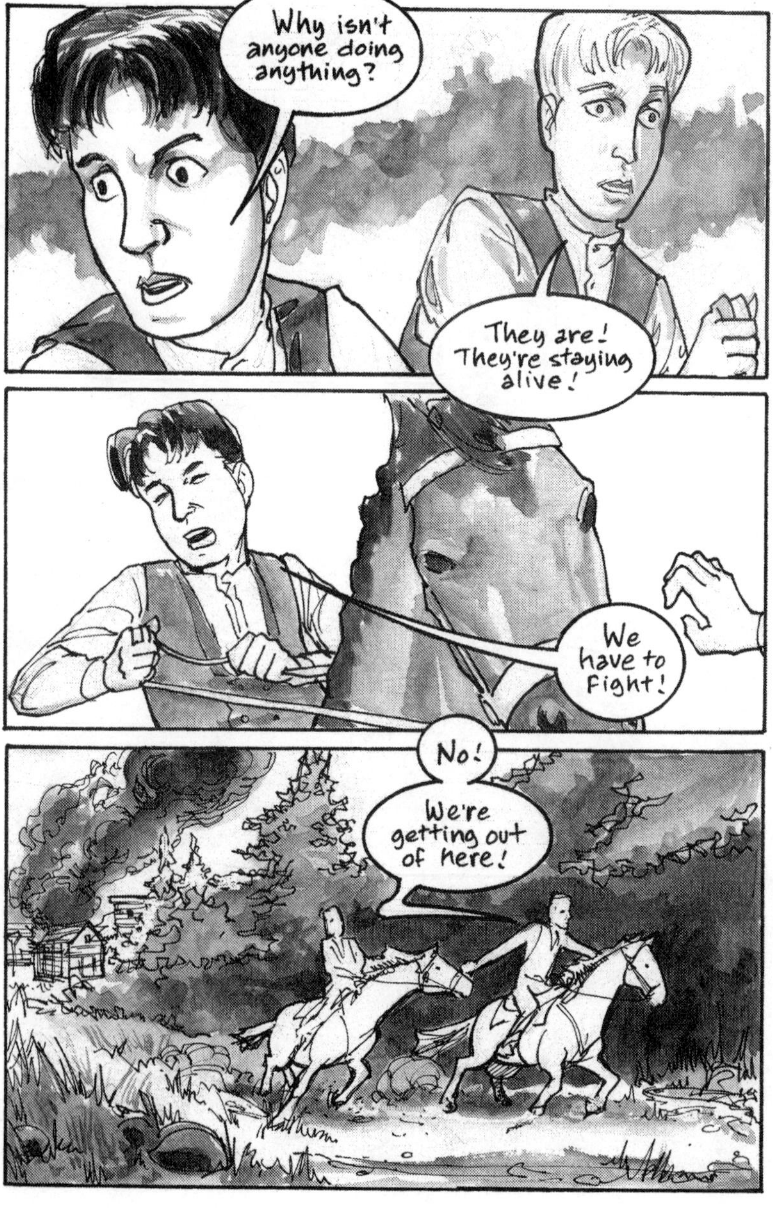
Why isn't anyone doing anything?
They are! They're staying alive!
We have to fight!
No!
We're getting out of here!

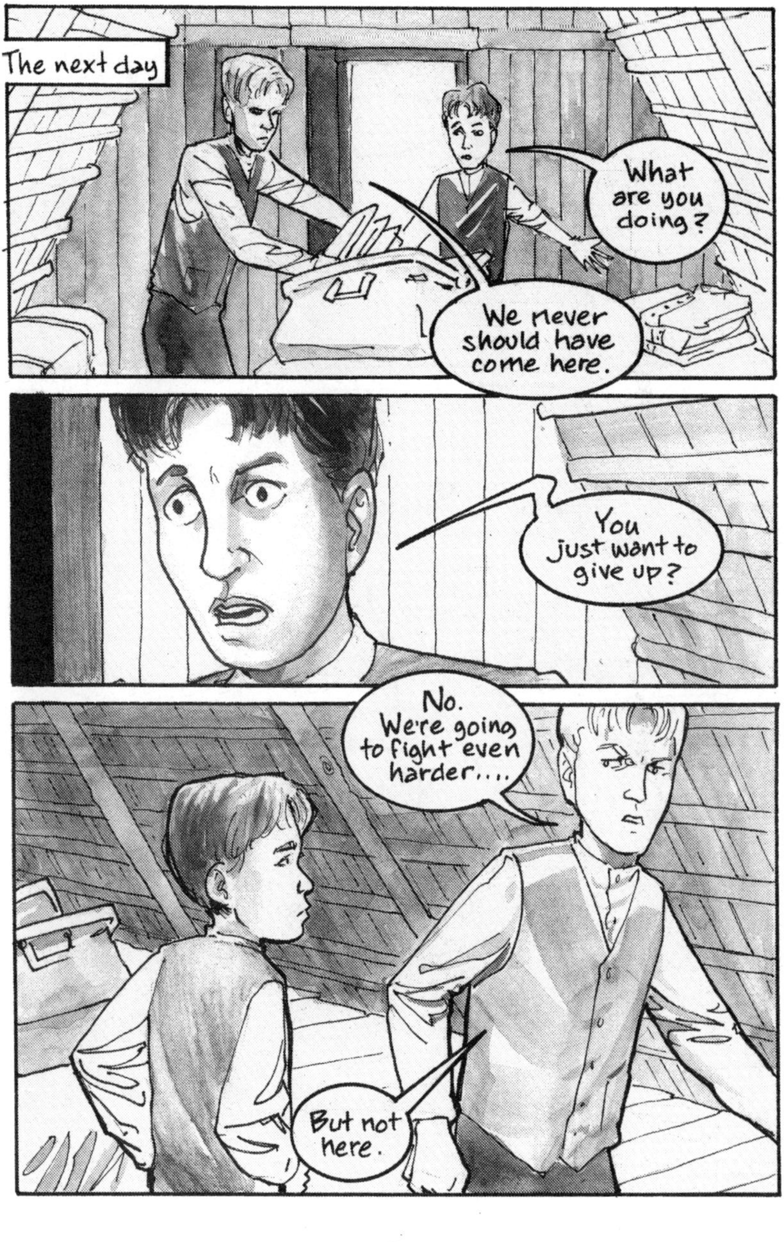
The next day
What are you doing?
We never should have come here.
You just want to give up?
No. We're going to fight even harder....
But not here.

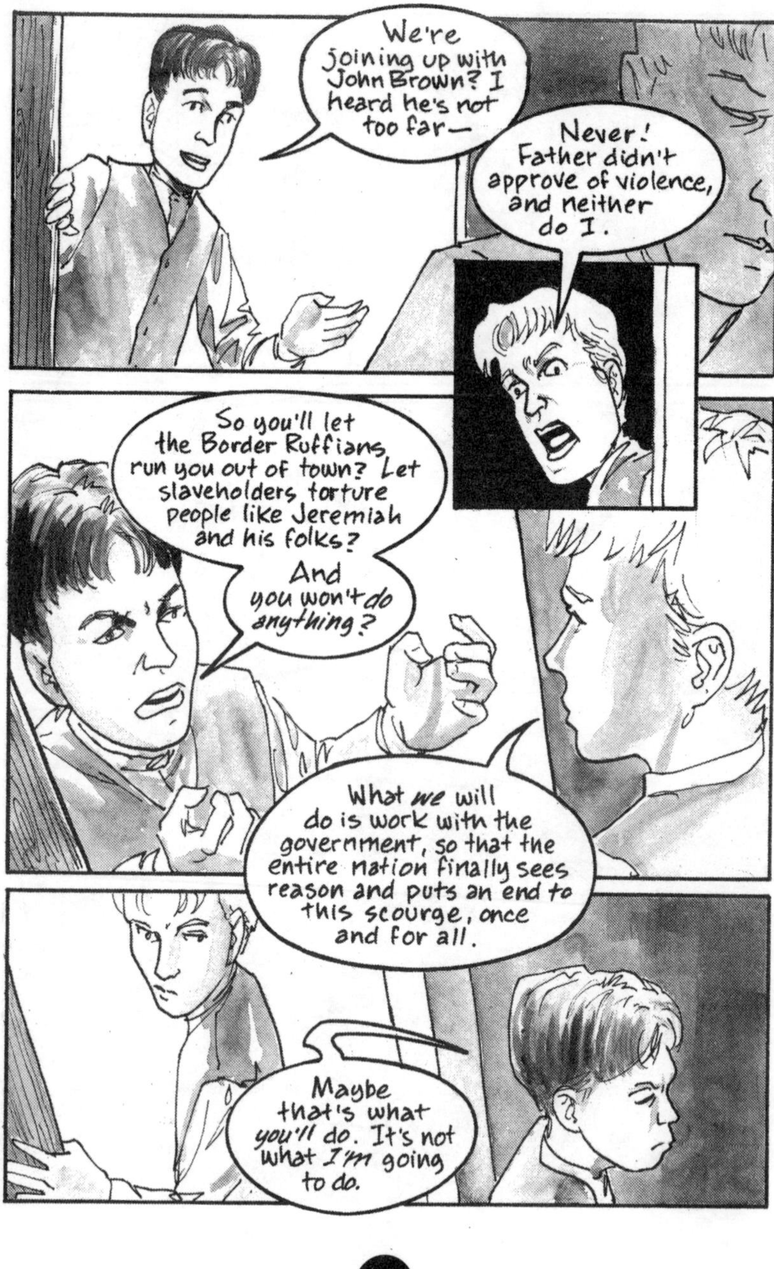
We're joining up with John Brown? I heard he's not too far—
Never! Father didn't approve of violence, and neither do I.
So you'll let the Border Ruffians run you out of town? Let slaveholders torture people like Jeremiah and his folks?
And you won't *do anything*?
What *we* will do is work with the government, so that the entire nation finally sees reason and puts an end to this scourge, once and for all.
Maybe that's what *you'll* do. It's not what *I'm* going to do.

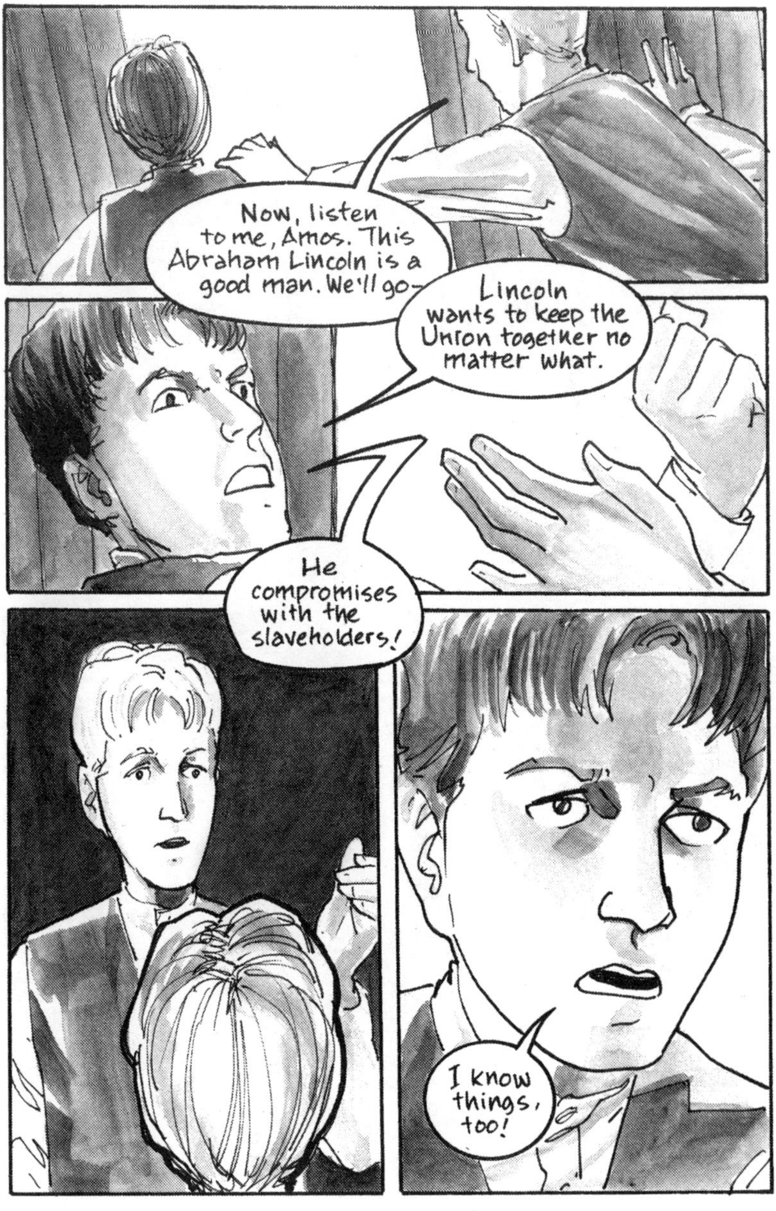
Now, listen to me, Amos. This Abraham Lincoln is a good man. We'll go–
Lincoln wants to keep the Union together no matter what.
He compromises with the slaveholders!
I know things, too!

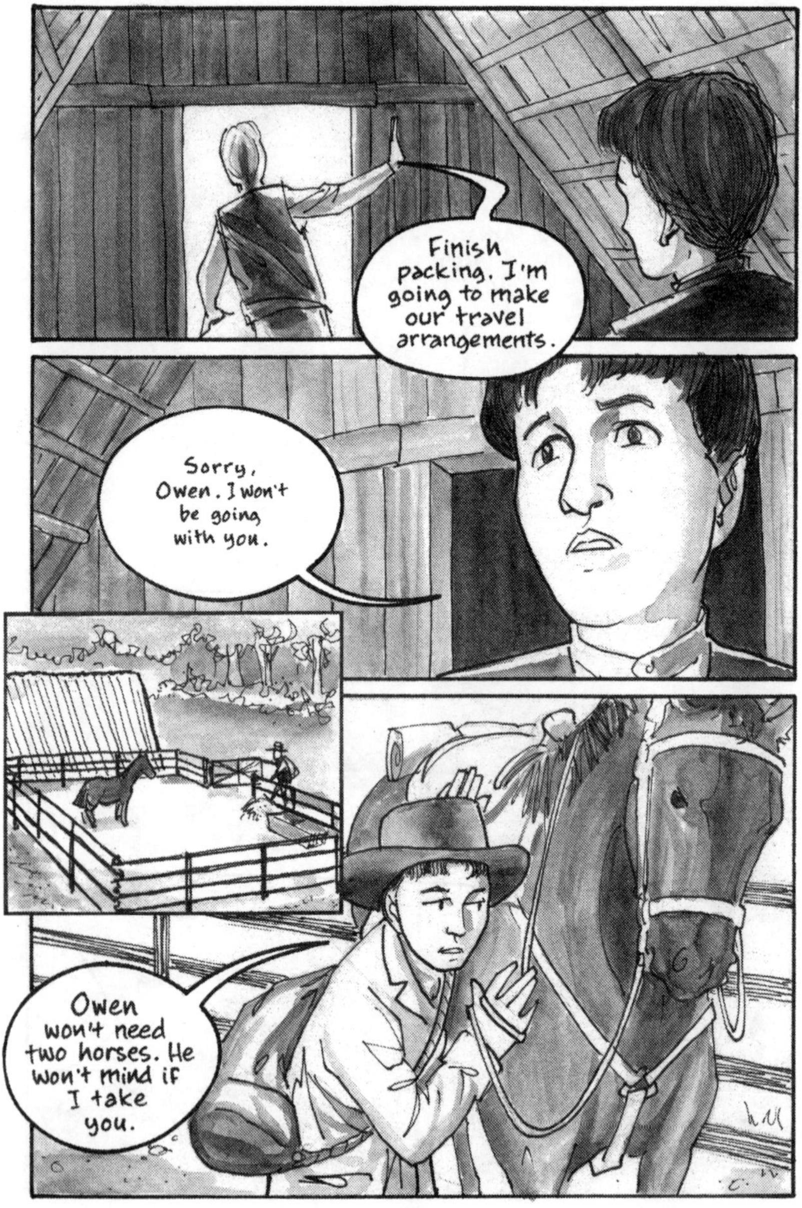
Finish packing. I'm going to make our travel arrangements.
Sorry, Owen. I won't be going with you.
Owen won't need two horses. He won't mind if I take you.

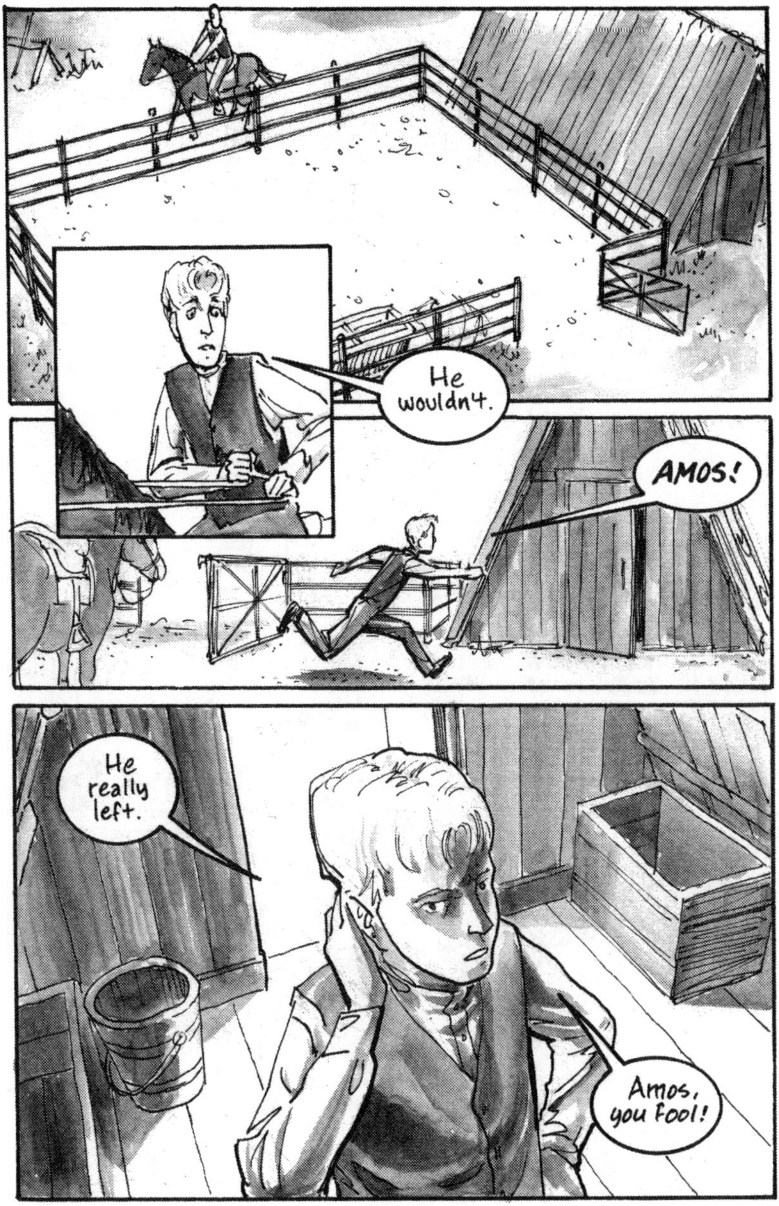
He wouldn't.
AMOS!
He really left.
Amos, you fool!

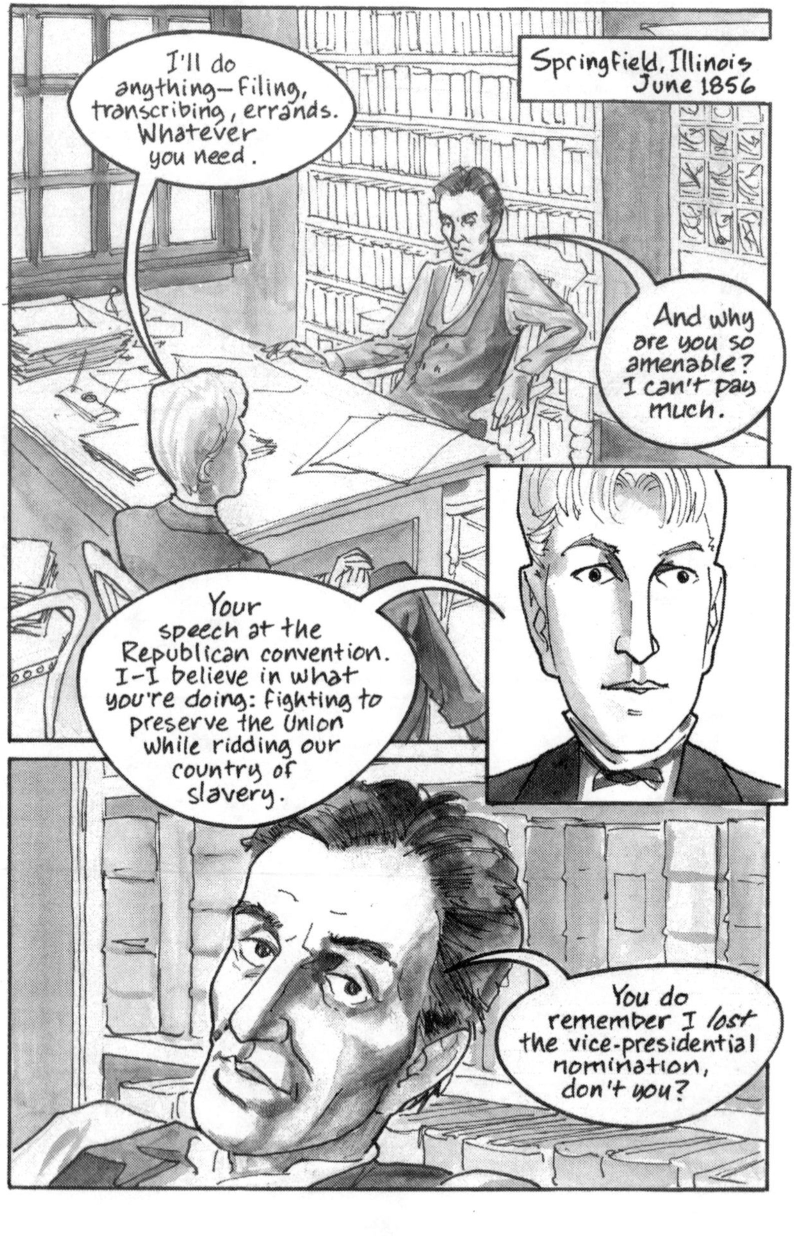
Springfield, Illinois June 1856
I'll do anything—filing, transcribing, errands. Whatever you need.
And why are you so amenable? I can't pay much.
Your speech at the Republican convention. I-I believe in what you're doing: fighting to preserve the Union while ridding our country of slavery.
You do remember I *lost* the vice-presidential nomination, don't you?

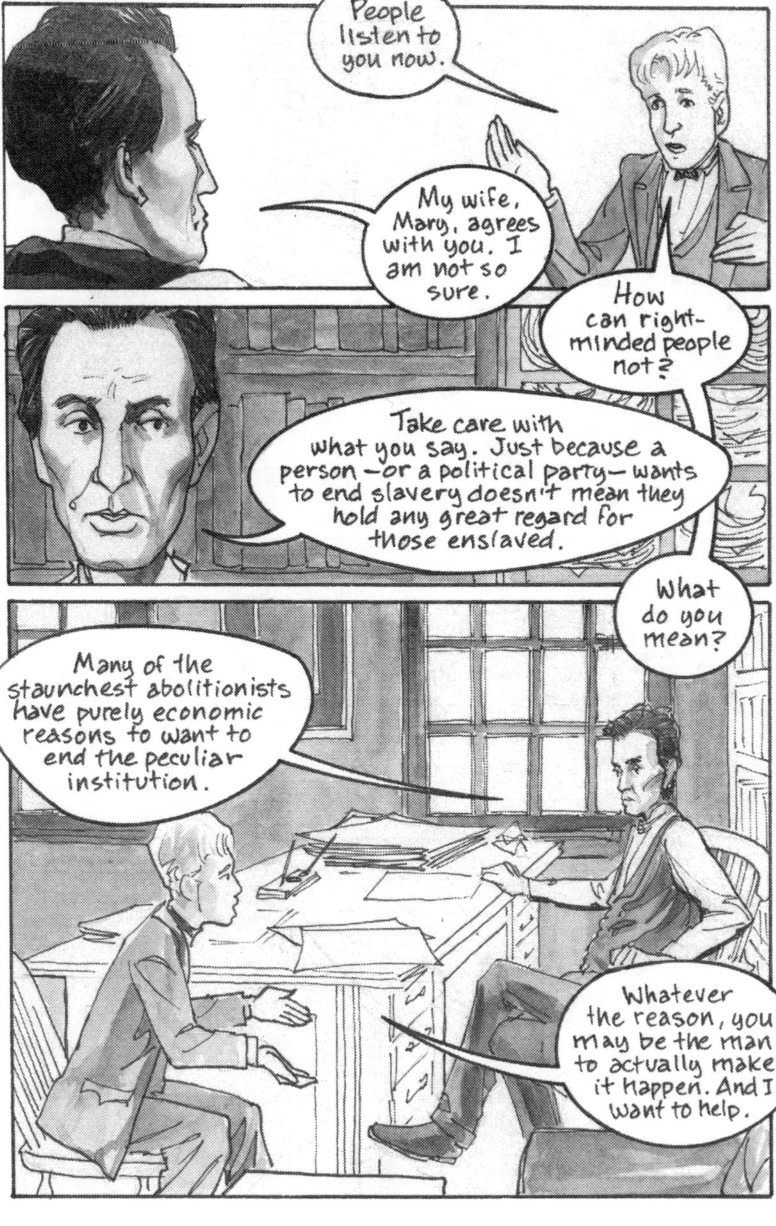
People listen to you now.
My wife, Mary, agrees with you. I am not so sure.
How can right-minded people not?
Take care with what you say. Just because a person —or a political party— wants to end slavery doesn't mean they hold any great regard for those enslaved.
What do you mean?
Many of the staunchest abolitionists have purely economic reasons to want to end the peculiar institution.
Whatever the reason, you may be the man to actually make it happen. And I want to help.

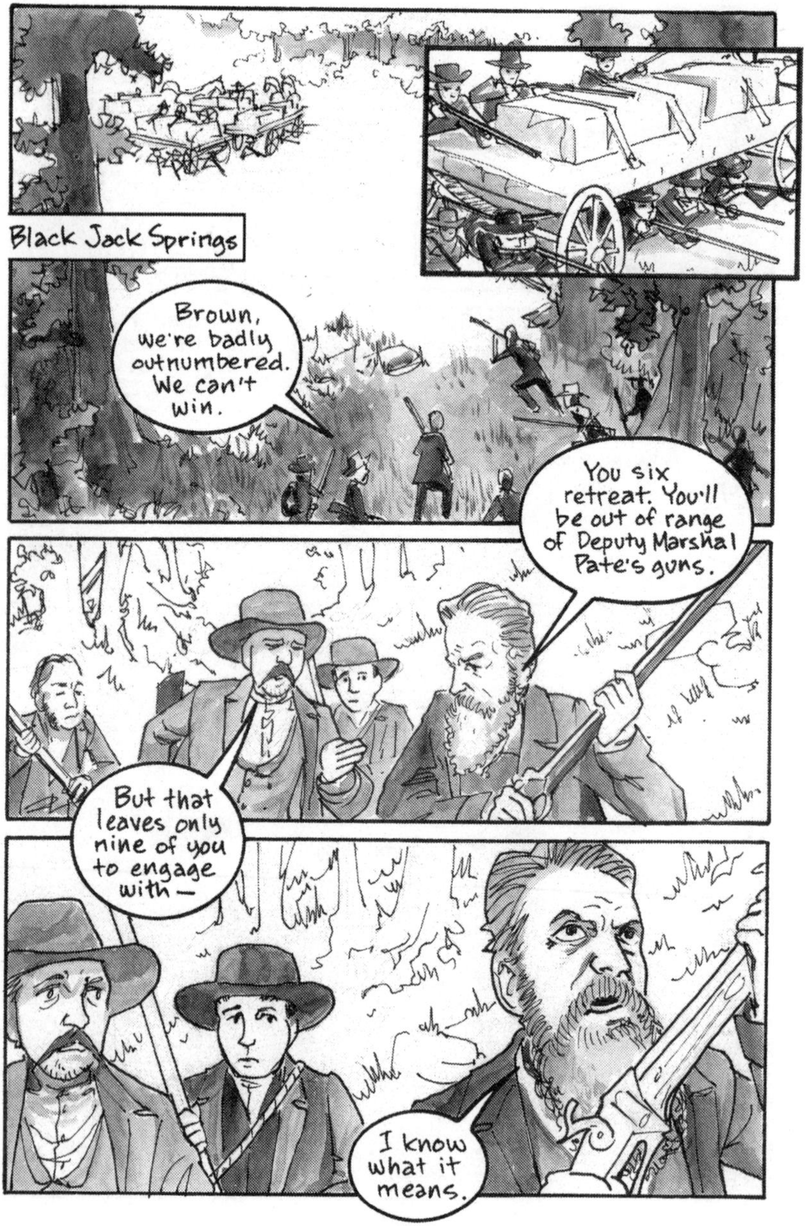
Black Jack Springs
Brown, we're badly outnumbered. We can't win.
You six retreat. You'll be out of range of Deputy Marshal Pate's guns.
But that leaves only nine of you to engage with—
I know what it means.

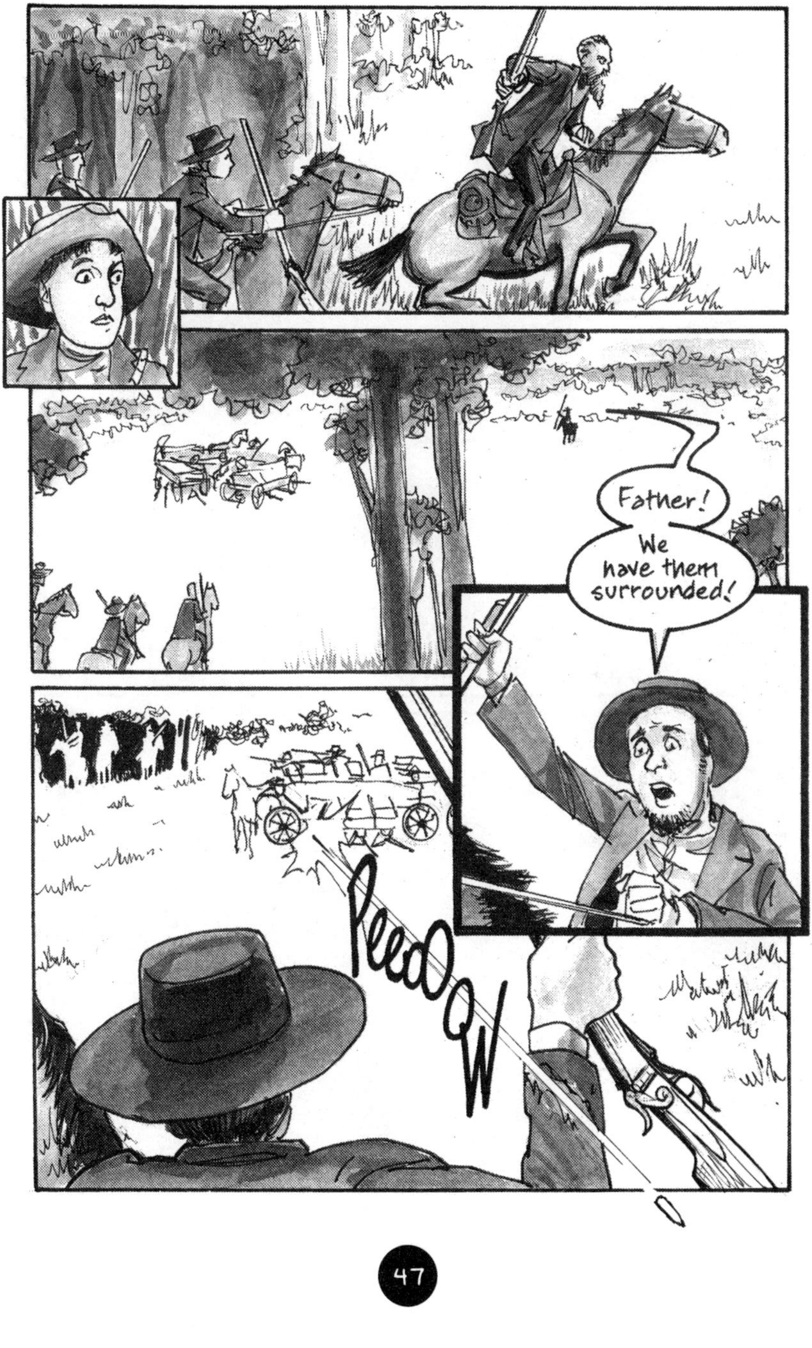
Father!
We have them surrounded!
PEEOOW

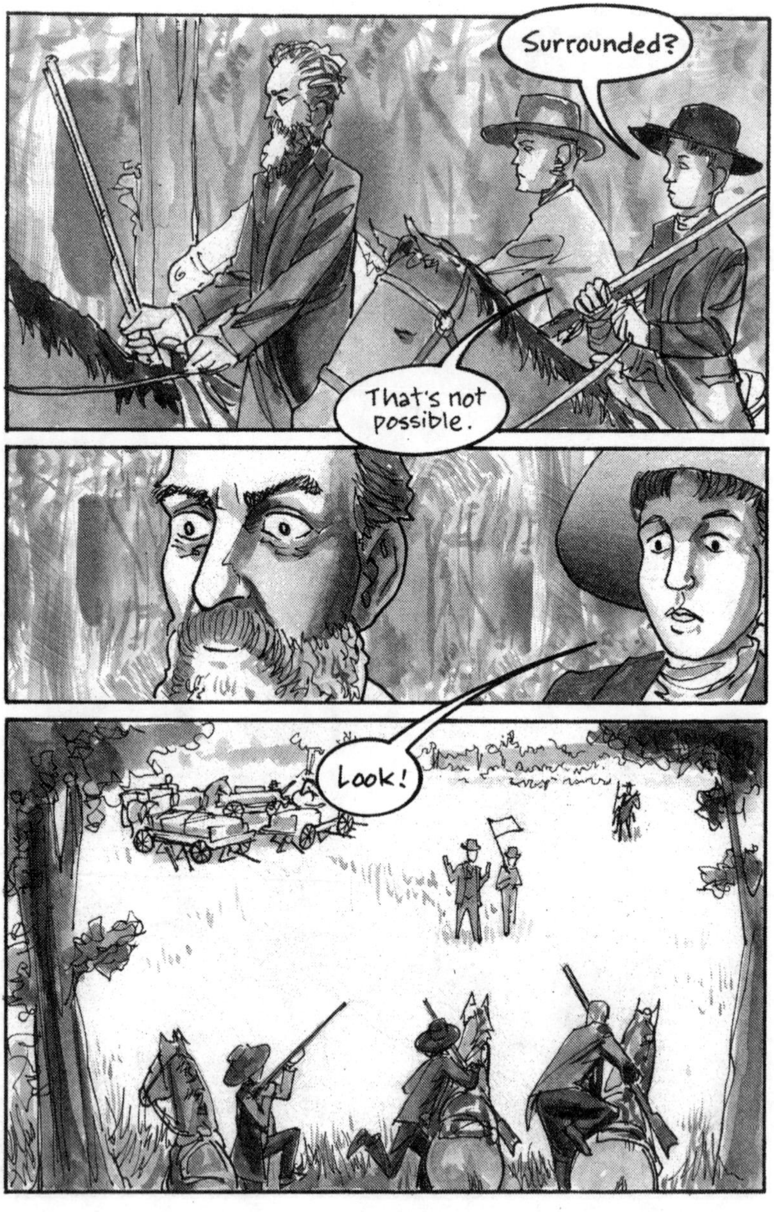
Surrounded?
That's not possible.
Look!

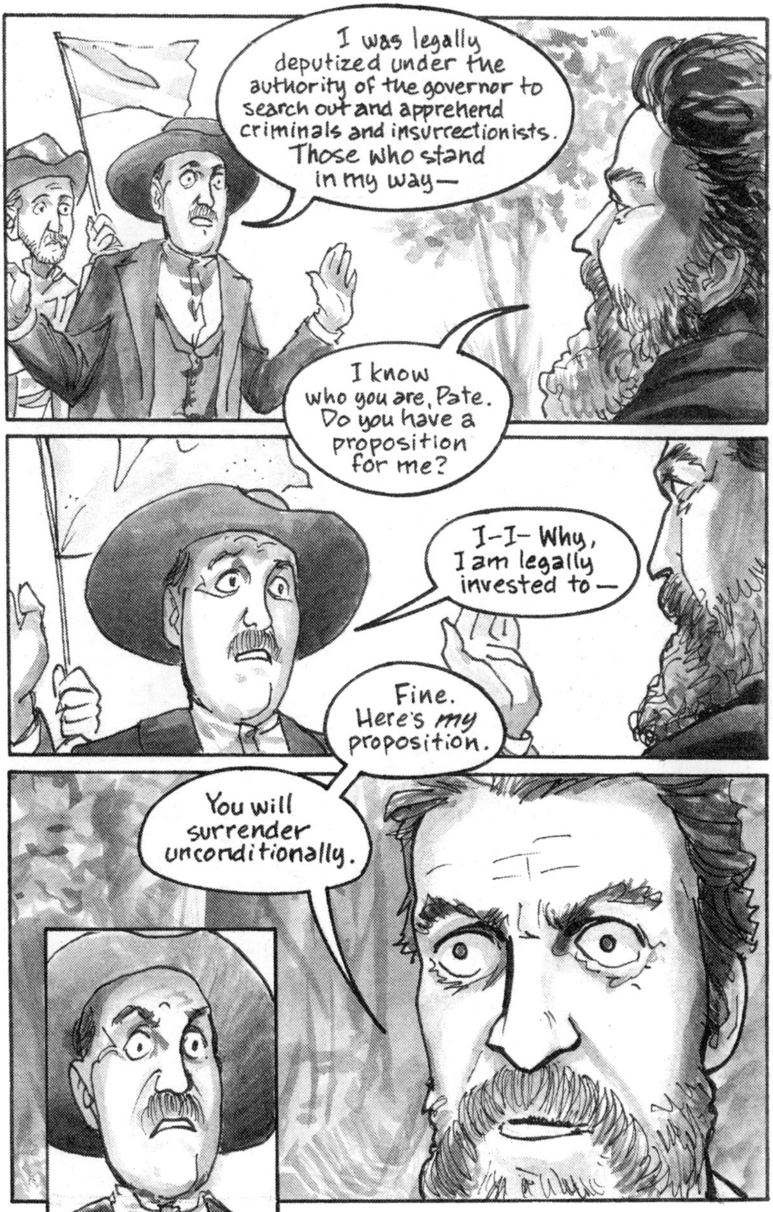
I was legally deputized under the authority of the governor to search out and apprehend criminals and insurrectionists. Those who stand in my way—
I know who you are, Pate. Do you have a proposition for me?
I-I- Why, I am legally invested to—
Fine. Here's *my* proposition.
You will surrender unconditionally.

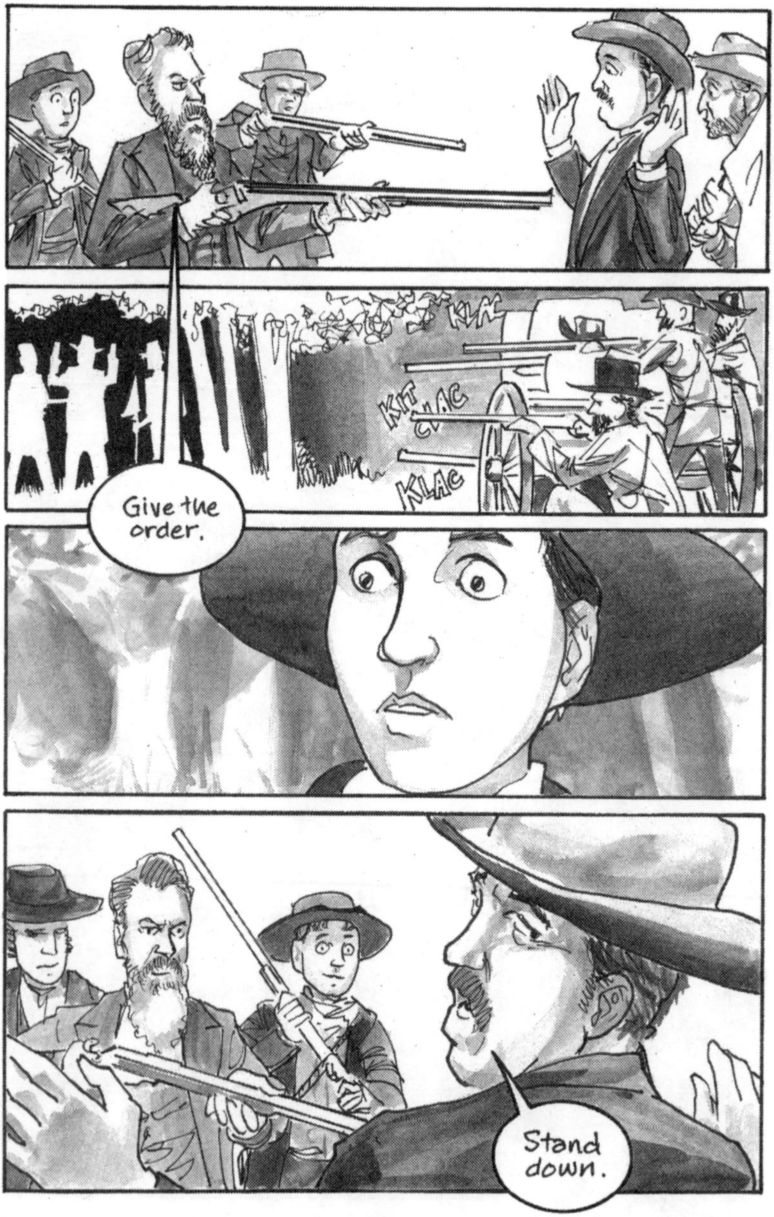
KLAC
KIT
CLAC
KLAC
Give the order.
Stand down.

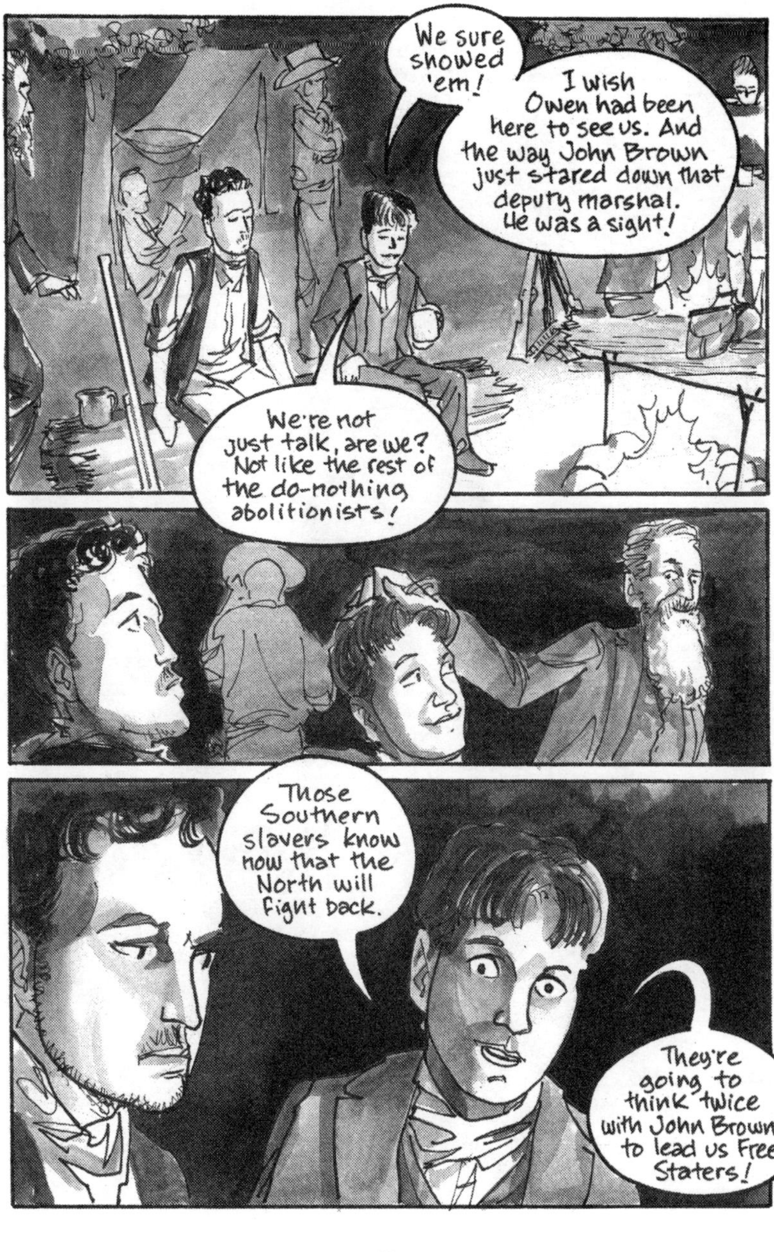
We sure showed 'em!
I wish Owen had been here to see us. And the way John Brown just stared down that deputy marshal. He was a sight!
We're not just talk, are we? Not like the rest of the do-nothing abolitionists!
Those Southern slavers know now that the North will fight back.
They're going to think twice with John Brown to lead us Free Staters!

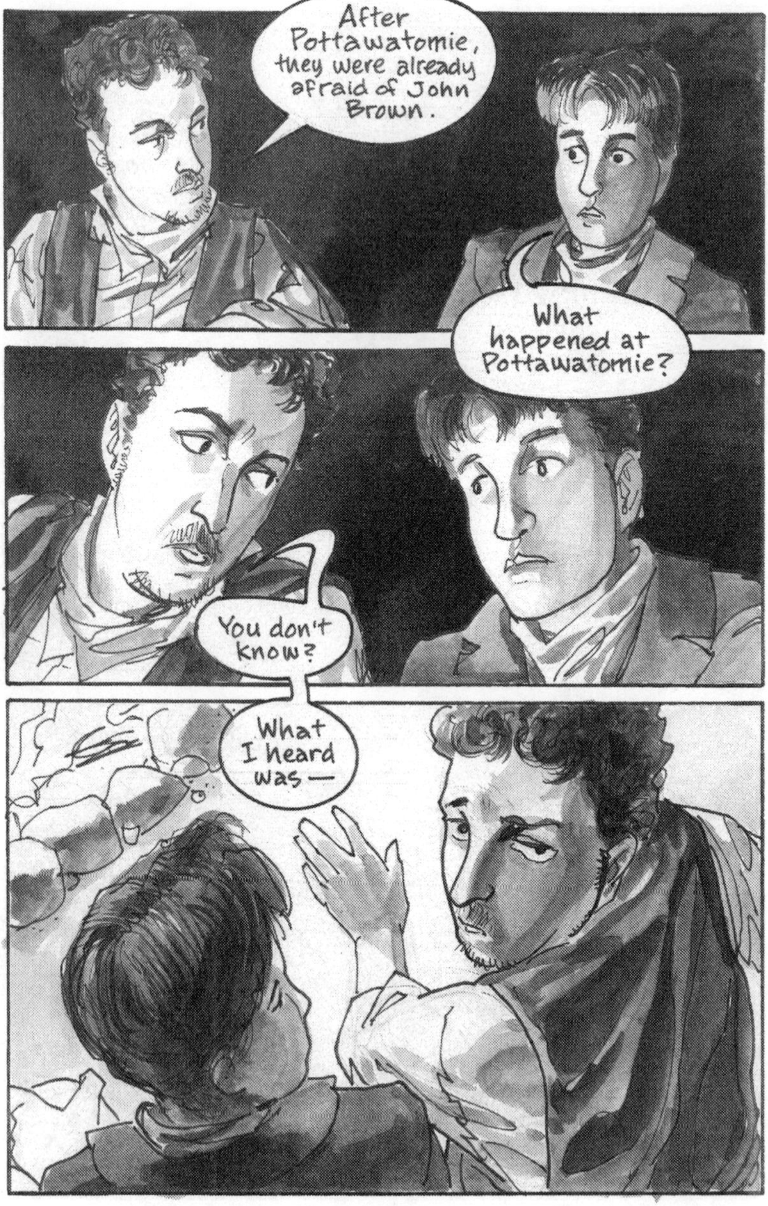
After Pottawatomie, they were already afraid of John Brown.
What happened at Pottawatomie?
You don't know?
What I heard was—

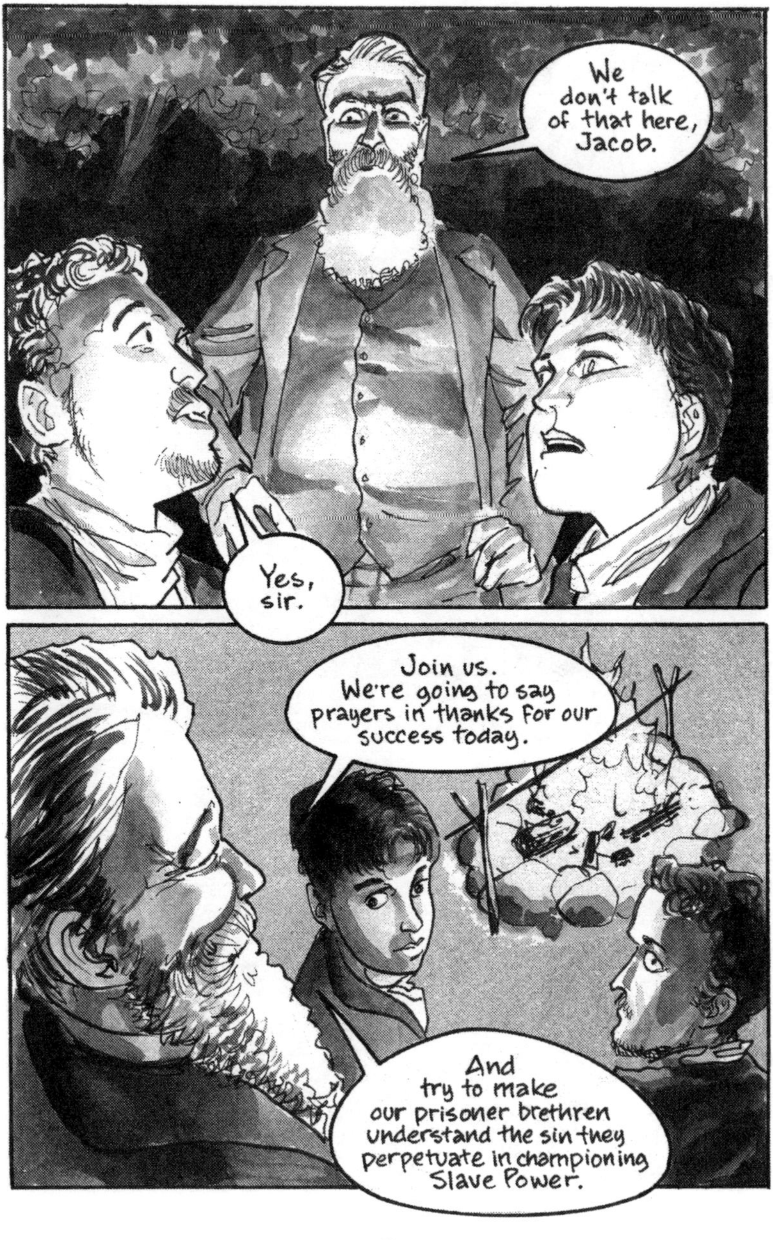
We don't talk of that here, Jacob.
Yes, sir.
Join us. We're going to say prayers in thanks for our success today.
And try to make our prisoner brethren understand the sin they perpetuate in championing Slave Power.

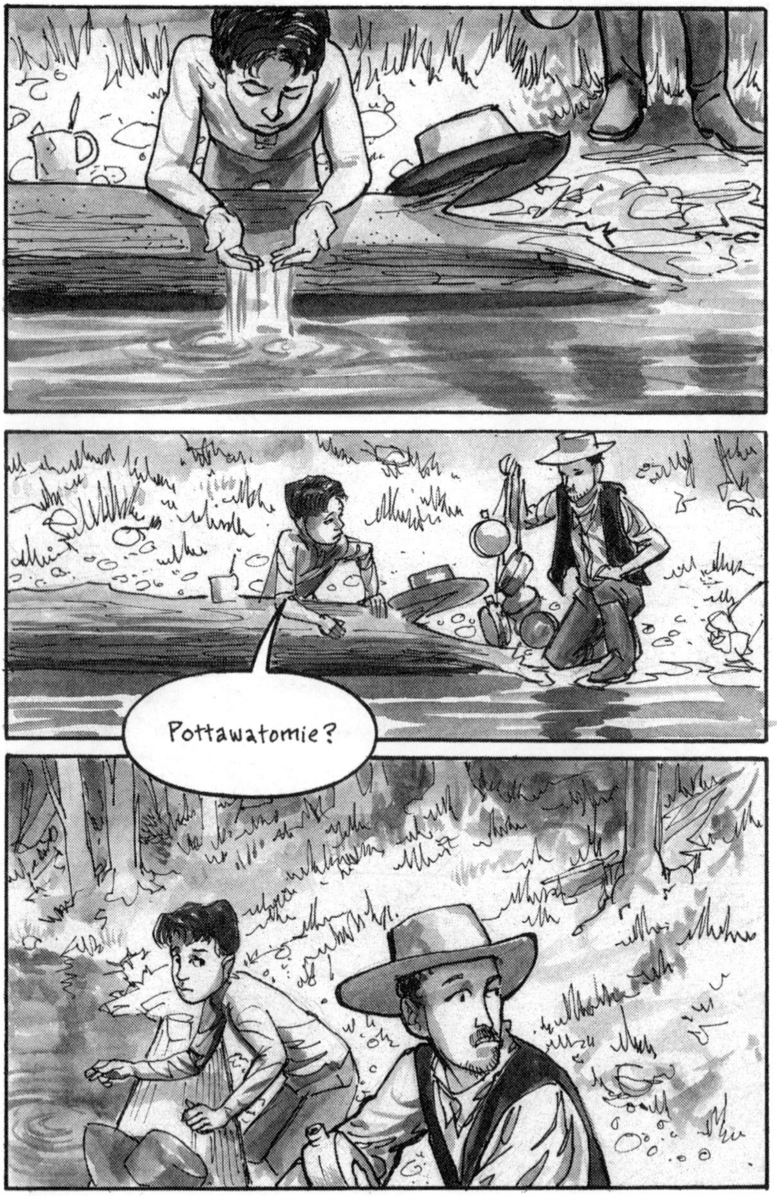
Pottawatomie?

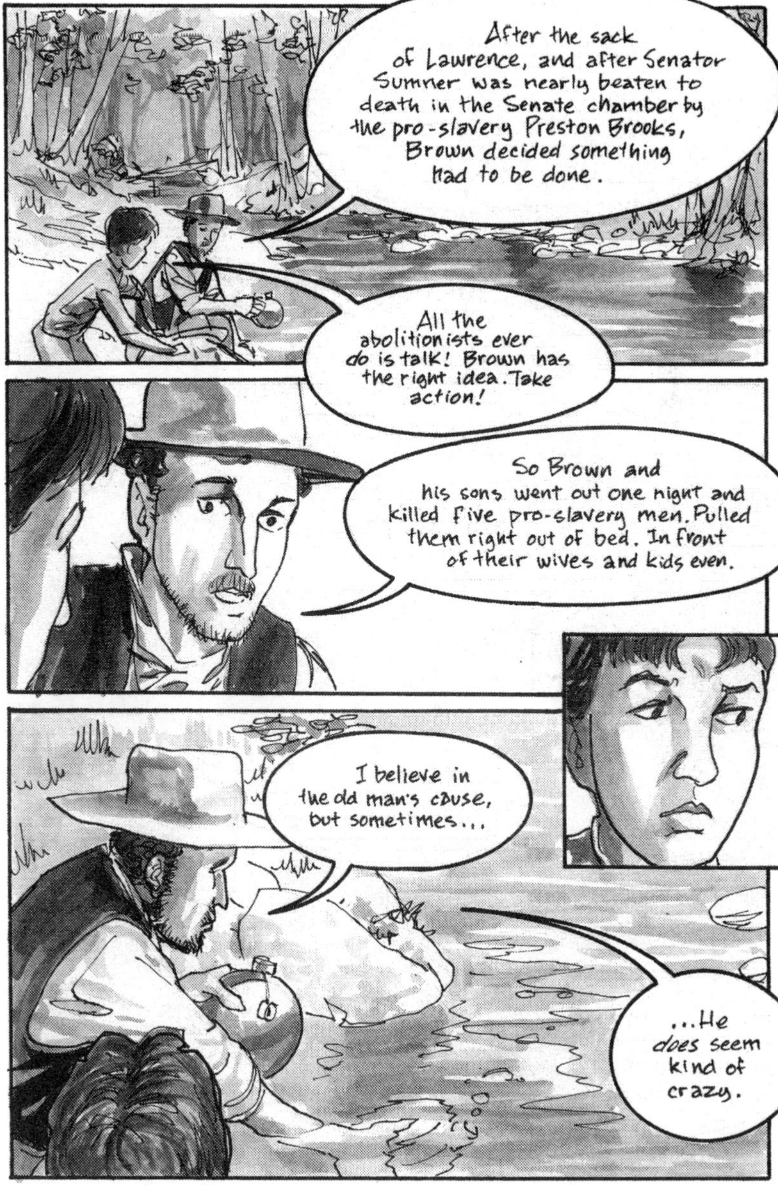
After the sack of Lawrence, and after Senator Sumner was nearly beaten to death in the Senate chamber by the pro-slavery Preston Brooks, Brown decided something had to be done.
All the abolitionists ever do is talk! Brown has the right idea. Take action!
So Brown and his sons went out one night and killed five pro-slavery men. Pulled them right out of bed. In front of their wives and kids even.
I believe in the old man's cause, but sometimes...
...He *does* seem kind of crazy.

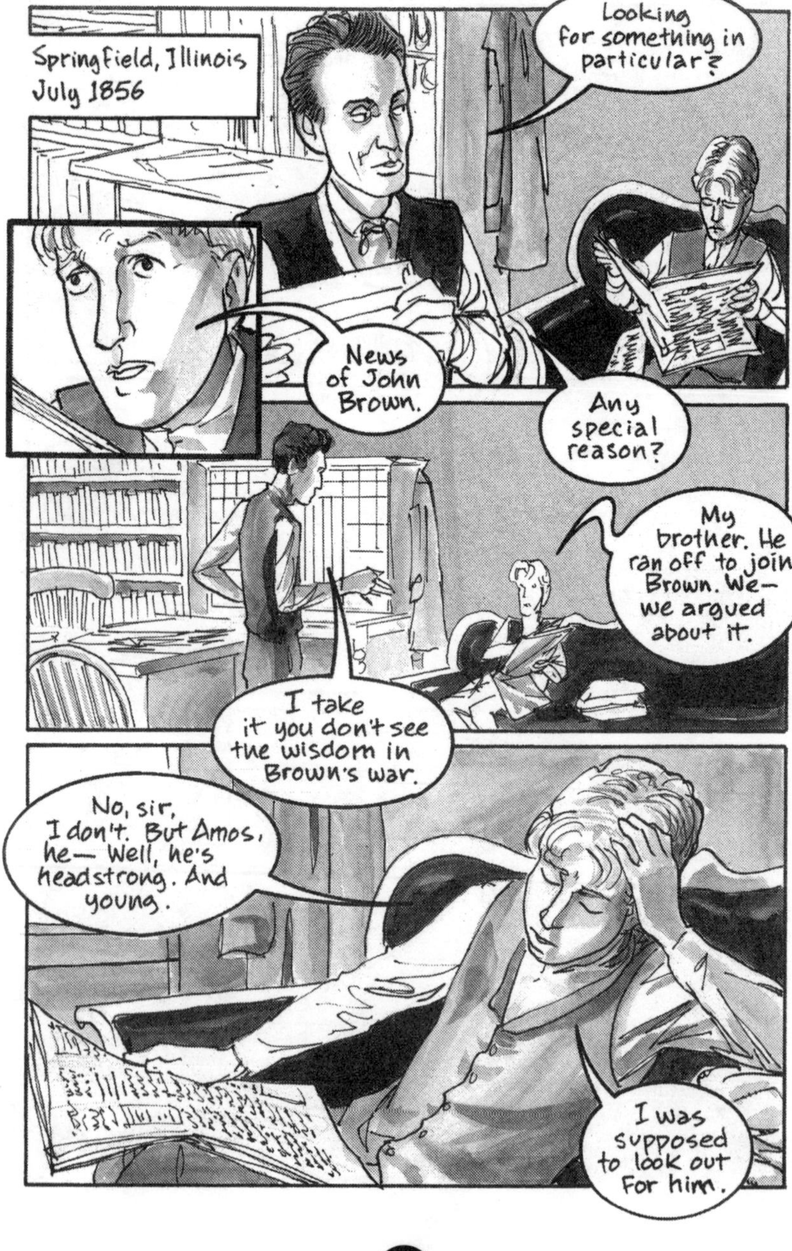
Springfield, Illinois July 1856
Looking for something in particular?
News of John Brown.
Any special reason?
My brother. He ran off to join Brown. We— we argued about it.
I take it you don't see the wisdom in Brown's war.
No, sir, I don't. But Amos, he— Well, he's headstrong. And young.
I was supposed to look out for him.

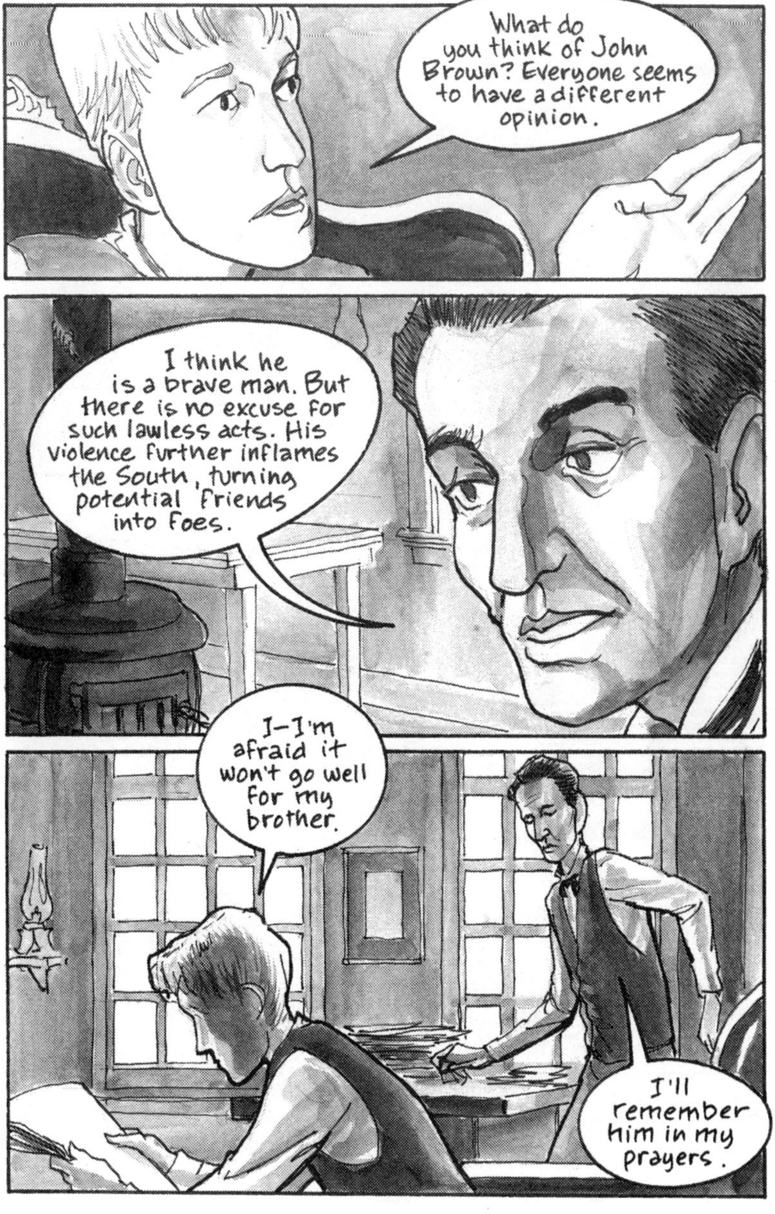
What do you think of John Brown? Everyone seems to have a different opinion.
I think he is a brave man. But there is no excuse for such lawless acts. His violence further inflames the South, turning potential friends into foes.
I-I'm afraid it won't go well for my brother.
I'll remember him in my prayers.

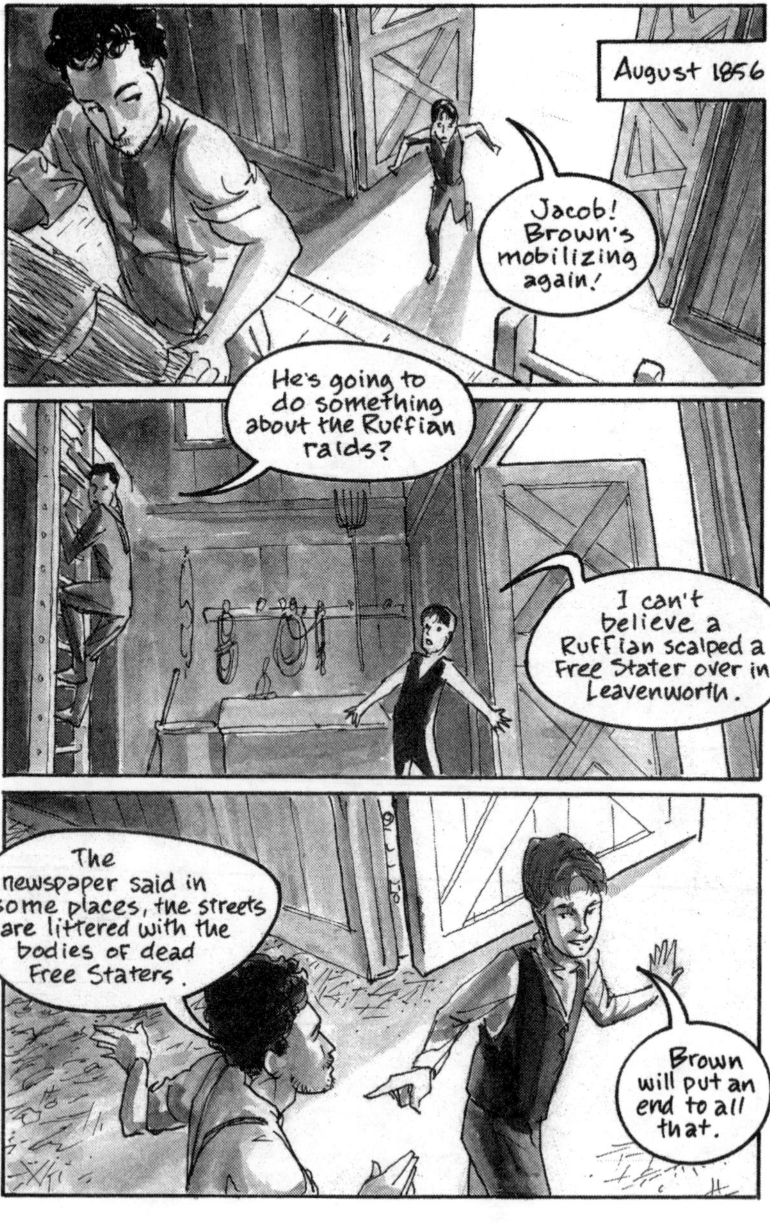
August 1856
Jacob! Brown's mobilizing again!
He's going to do something about the Ruffian raids?
I can't believe a Ruffian scalped a Free Stater over in Leavenworth.
The newspaper said in some places, the streets are littered with the bodies of dead Free Staters.
Brown will put an end to all that.

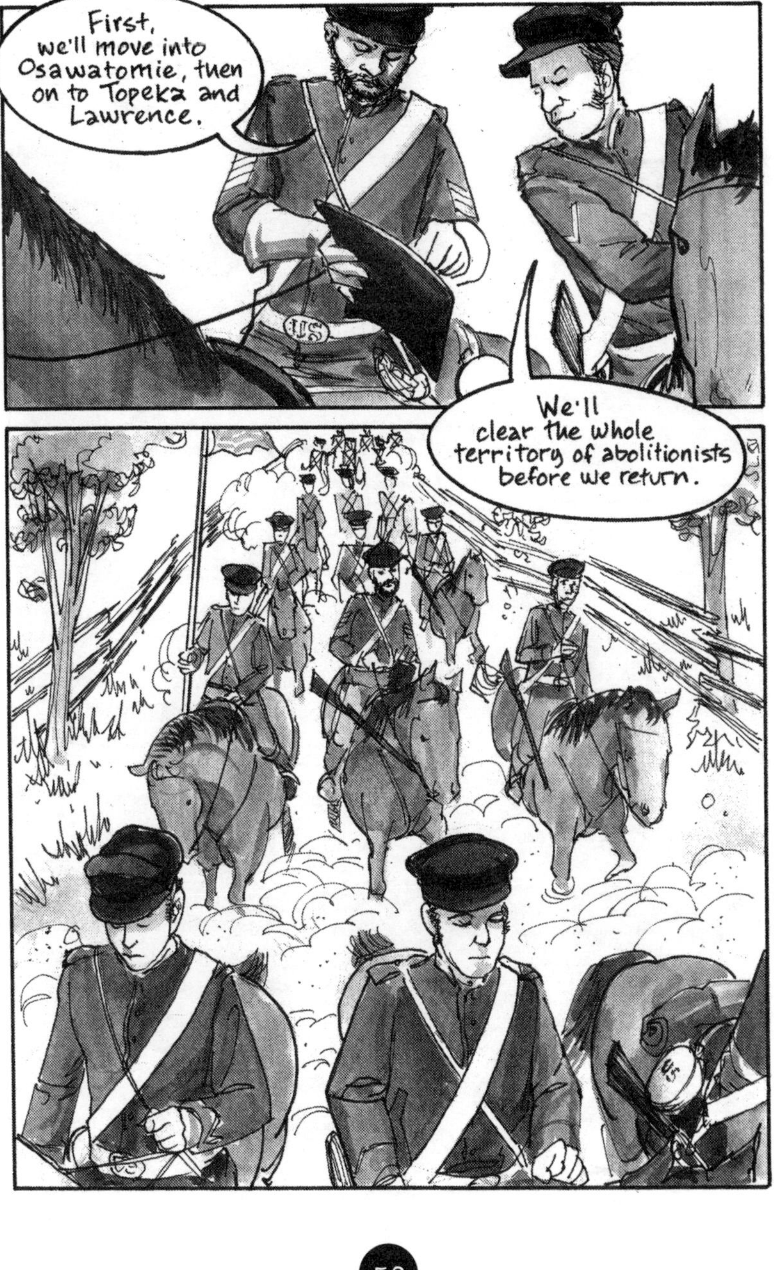
First, we'll move into Osawatomie, then on to Topeka and Lawrence.
We'll clear the whole territory of abolitionists before we return.

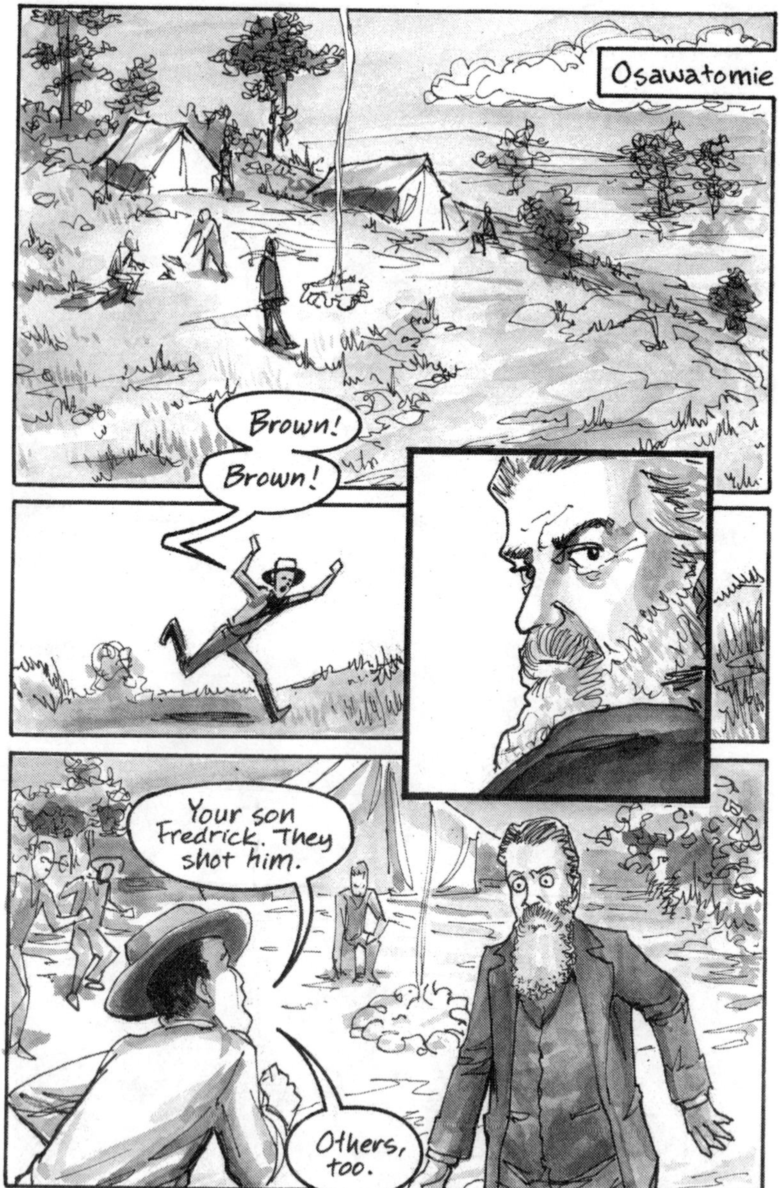
Osawatomie
Brown!
Brown!
Your son Fredrick. They shot him.
Others, too.

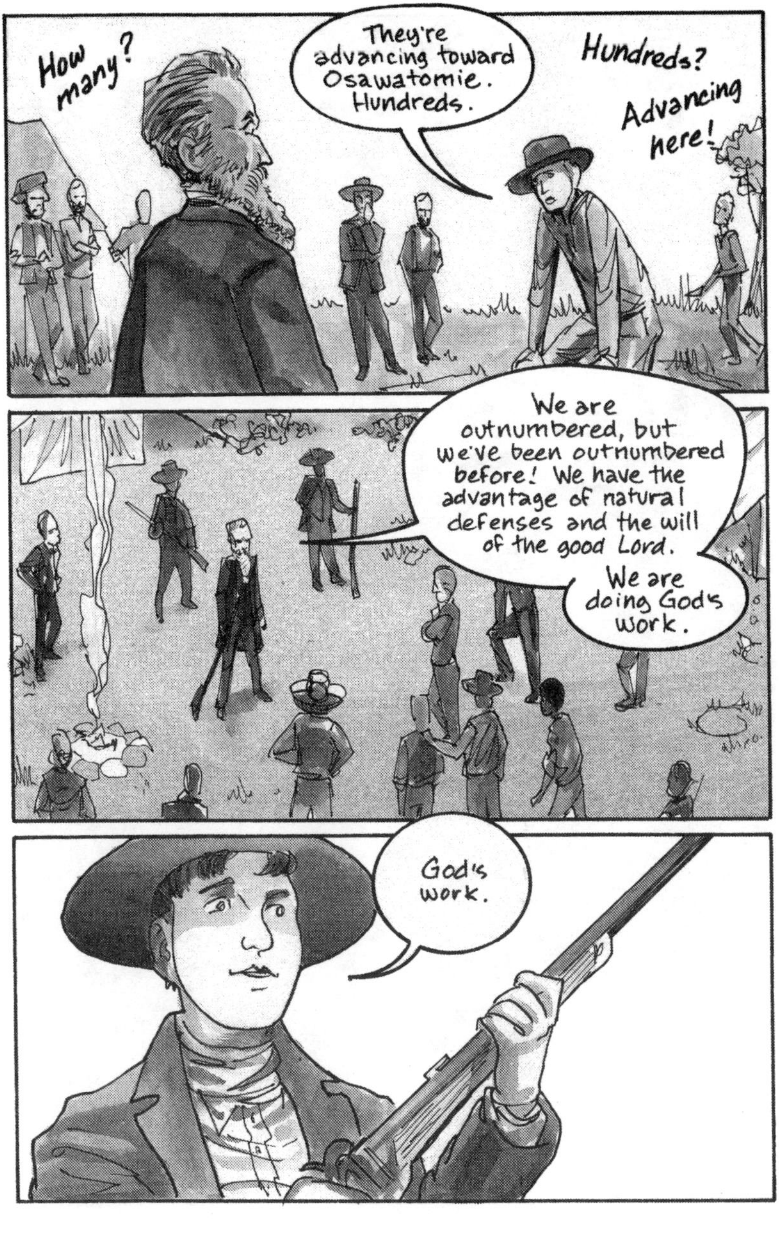
How many?
They're advancing toward Osawatomie. Hundreds.
Hundreds?
Advancing here!
We are outnumbered, but we've been outnumbered before! We have the advantage of natural defenses and the will of the good Lord.
We are doing God's work.
God's work.

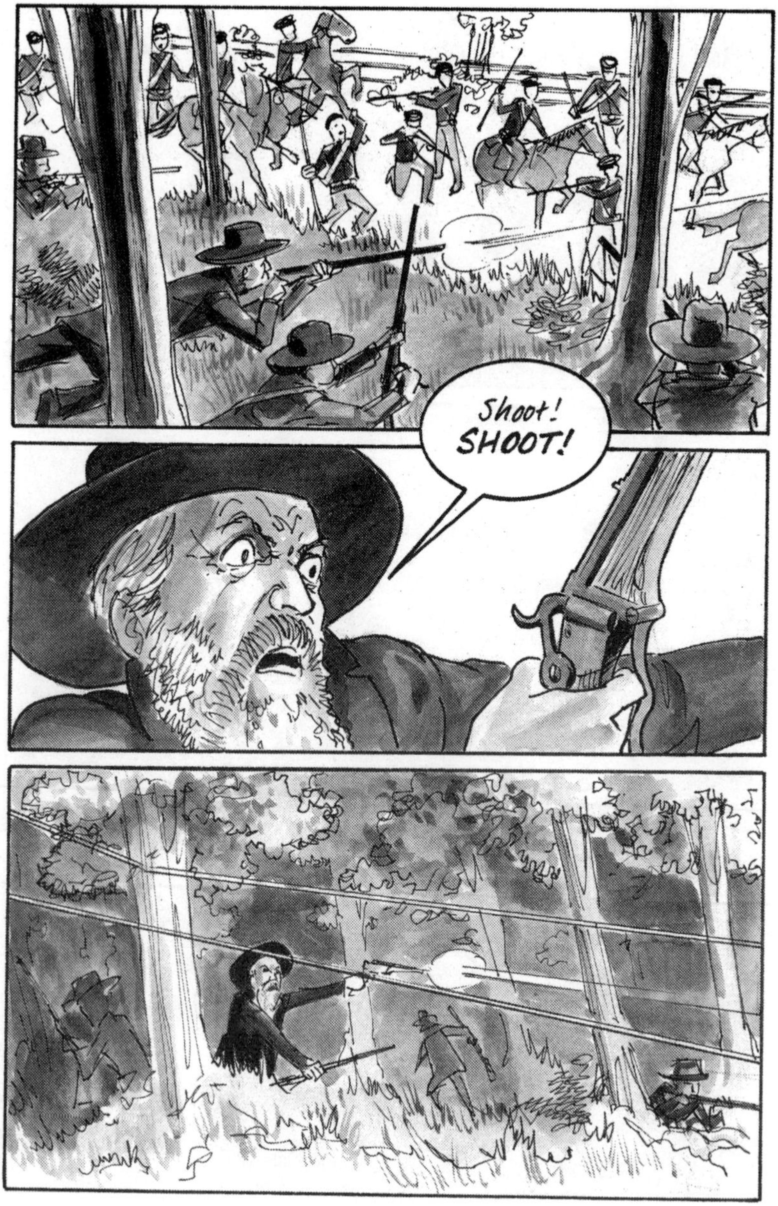
Shoot!
SHOOT!

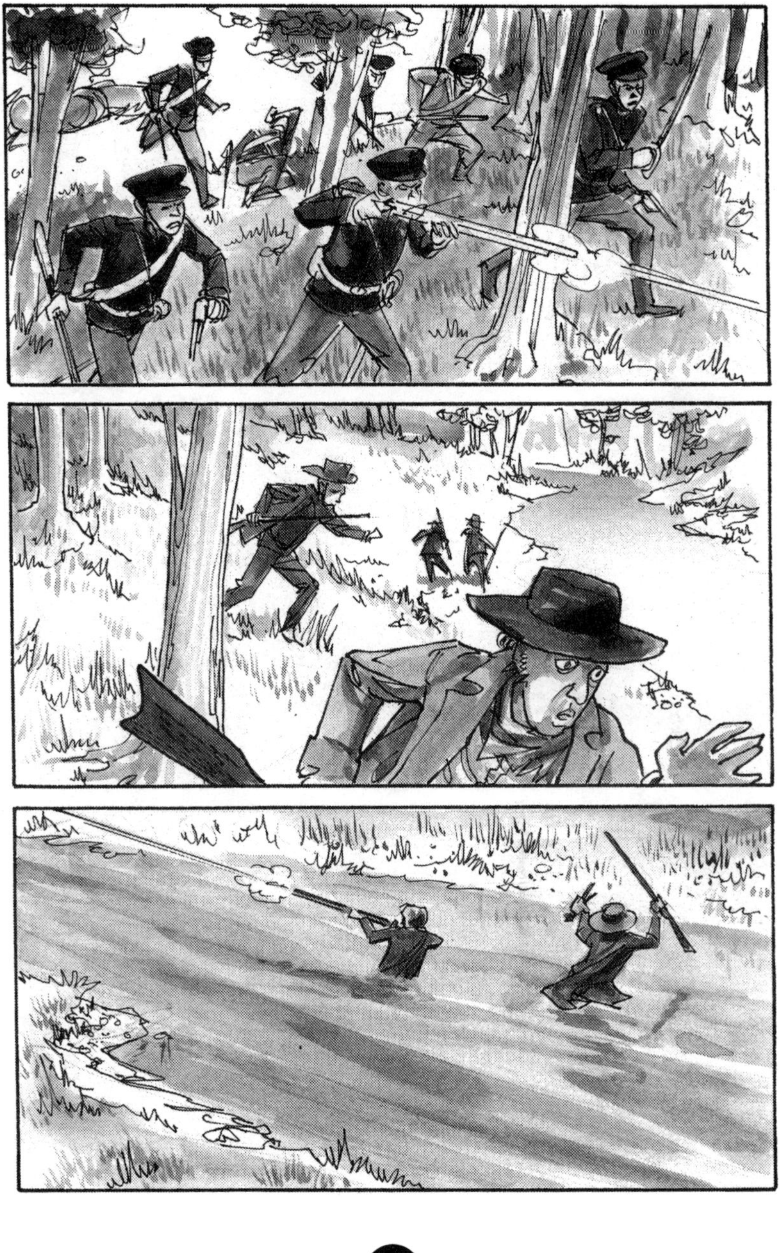

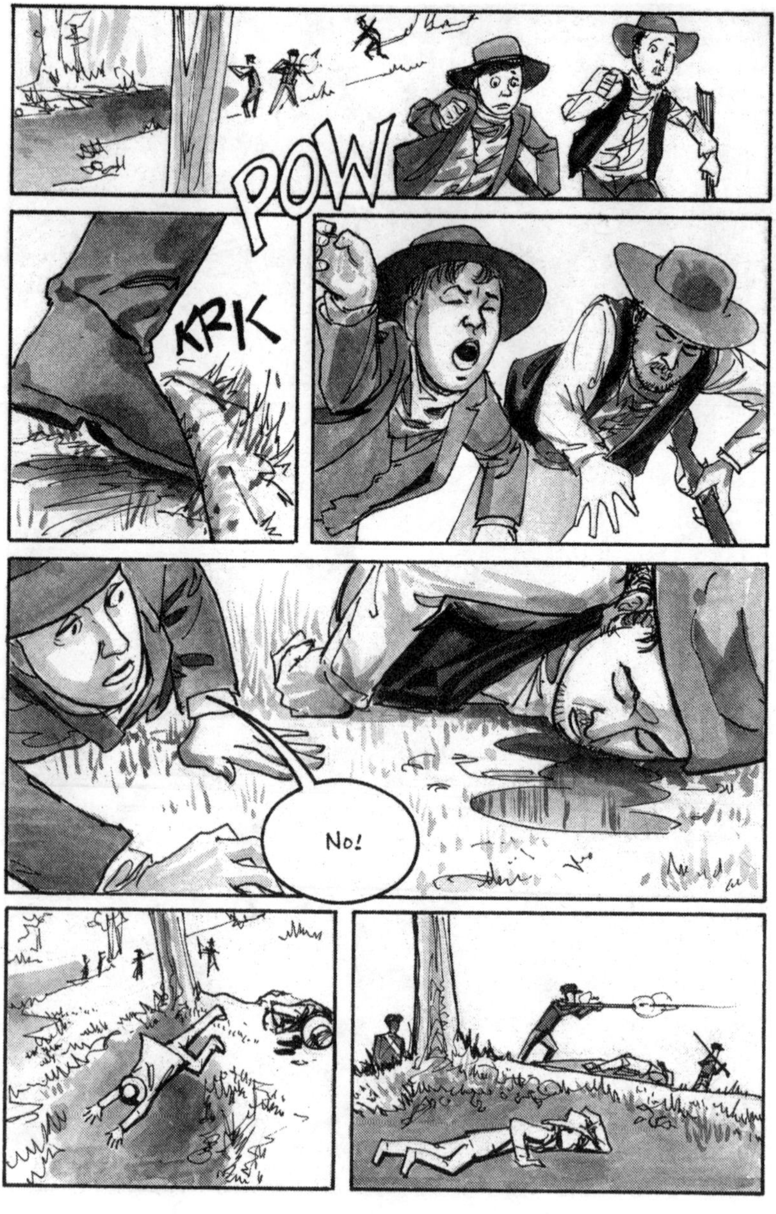
POW
KRK
No!

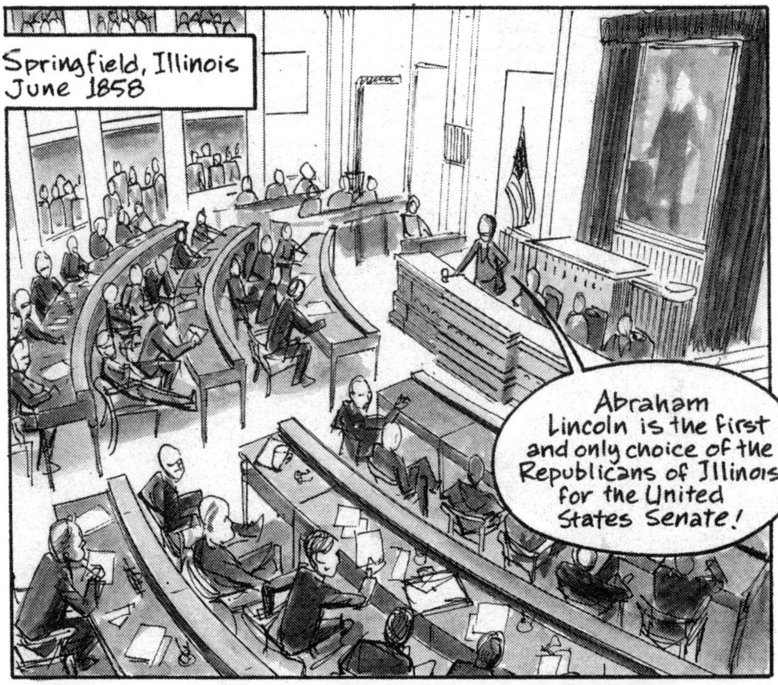
Springfield, Illinois
June 1858
Abraham Lincoln is the first and only choice of the Republicans of Illinois for the United States Senate!

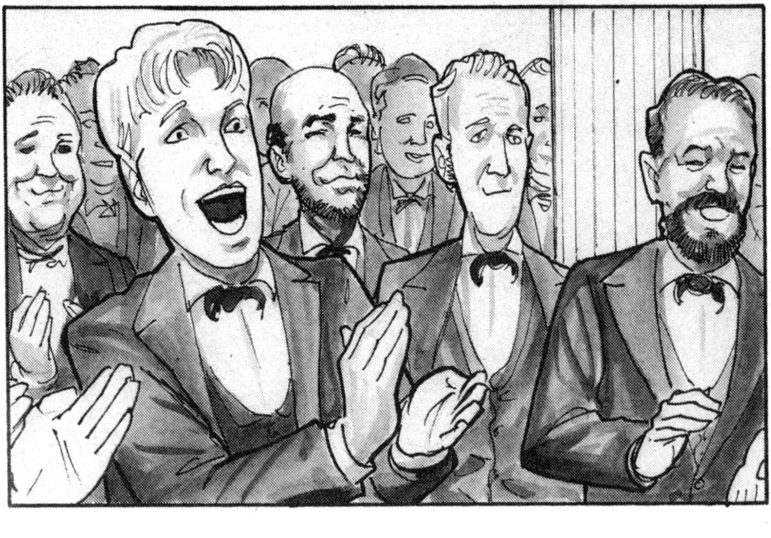

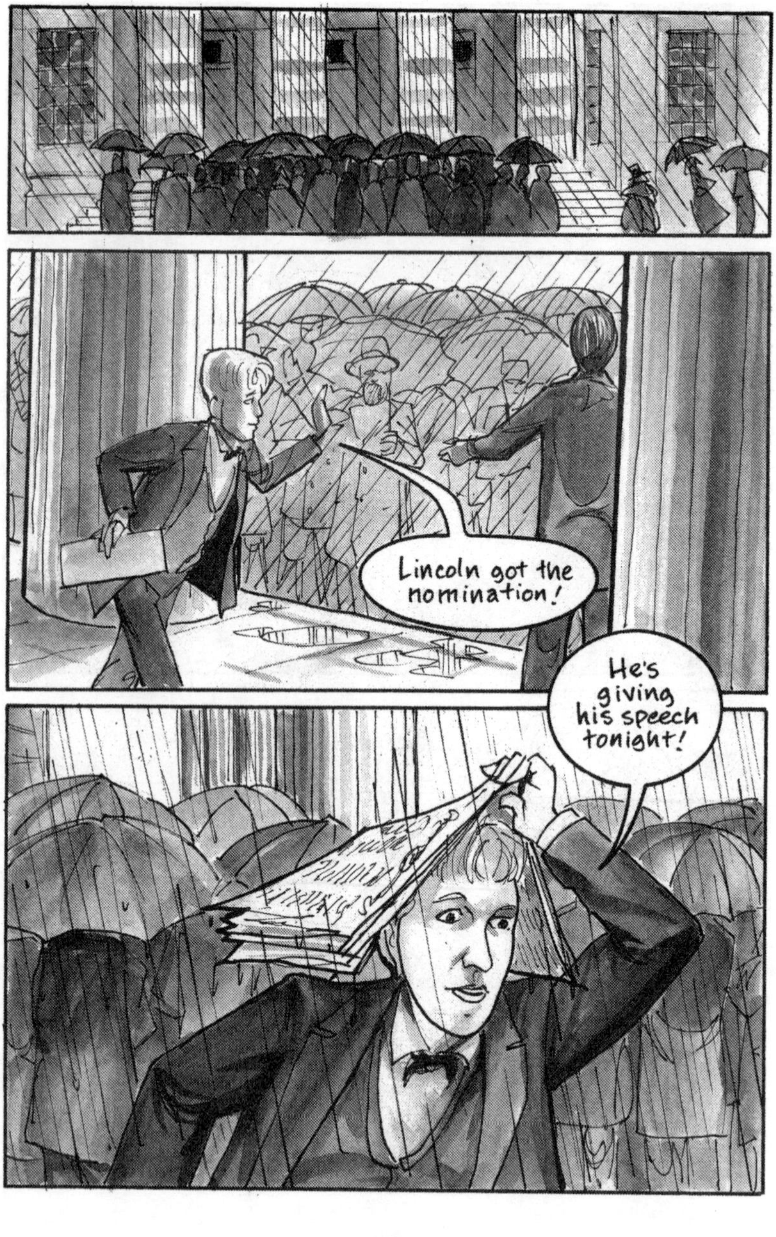
Lincoln got the nomination!
He's giving his speech tonight!

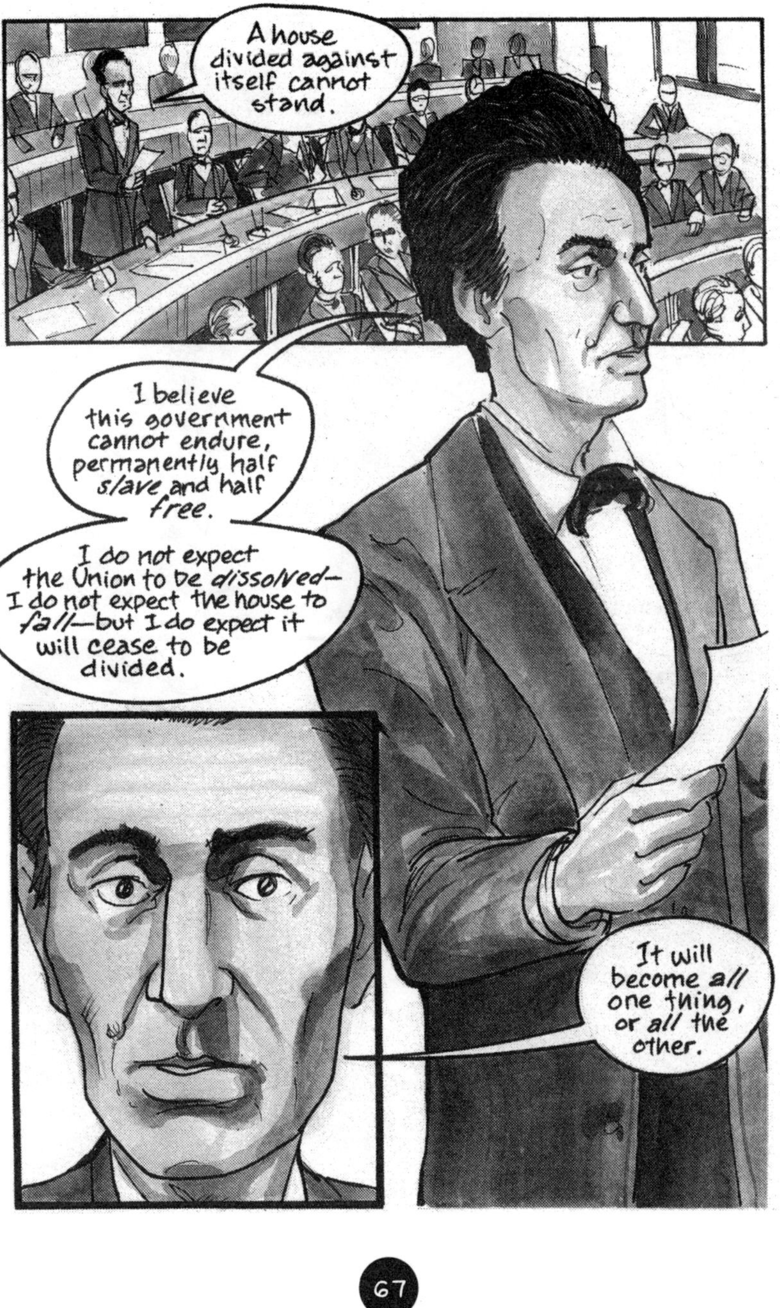
A house divided against itself cannot stand.
I believe this government cannot endure, permanently half *slave* and half *free*.
I do not expect the Union to be *dissolved*—I do not expect the house to *fall*—but I do expect it will cease to be divided.
It will become *all* one thing, or *all* the other.

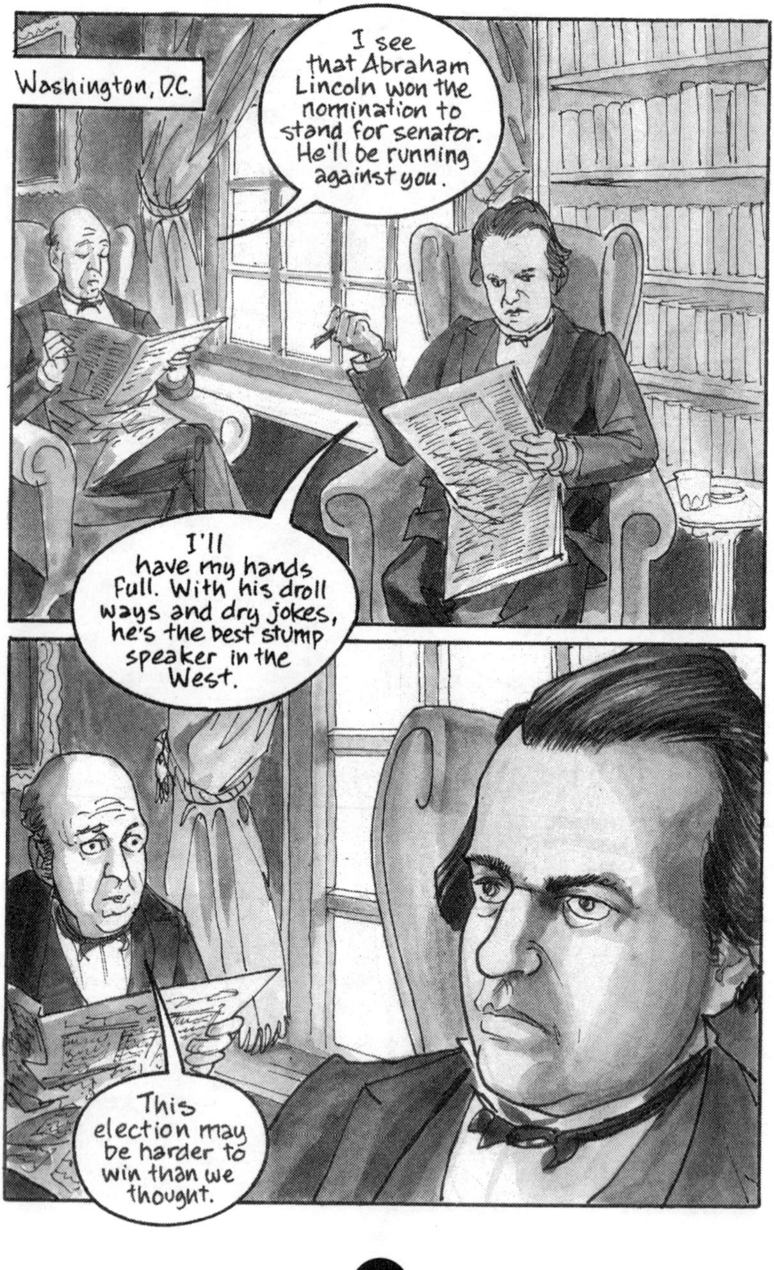
Washington, D.C.
I see that Abraham Lincoln won the nomination to stand for senator. He'll be running against you.
I'll have my hands full. With his droll ways and dry jokes, he's the best stump speaker in the West.
This election may be harder to win than we thought.

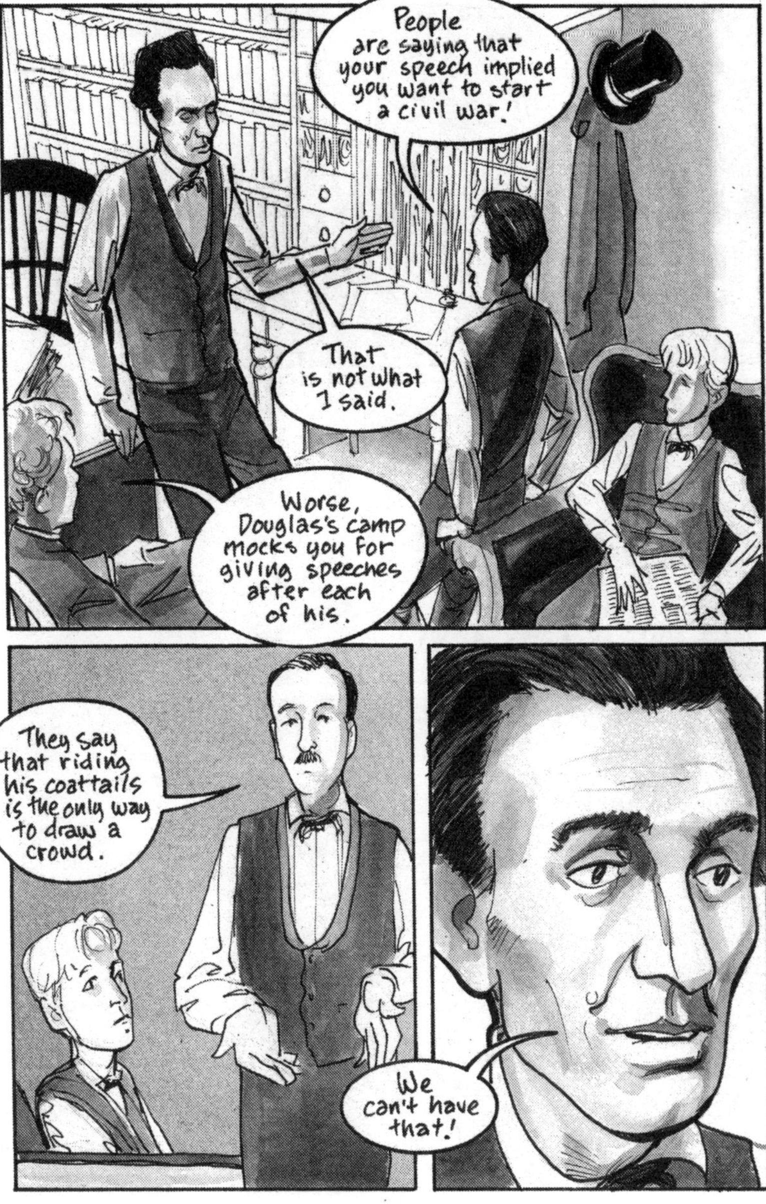
People are saying that your speech implied you want to start a civil war!
That is not what I said.
Worse, Douglas's camp mocks you for giving speeches after each of his.
They say that riding his coattails is the only way to draw a crowd.
We can't have that!

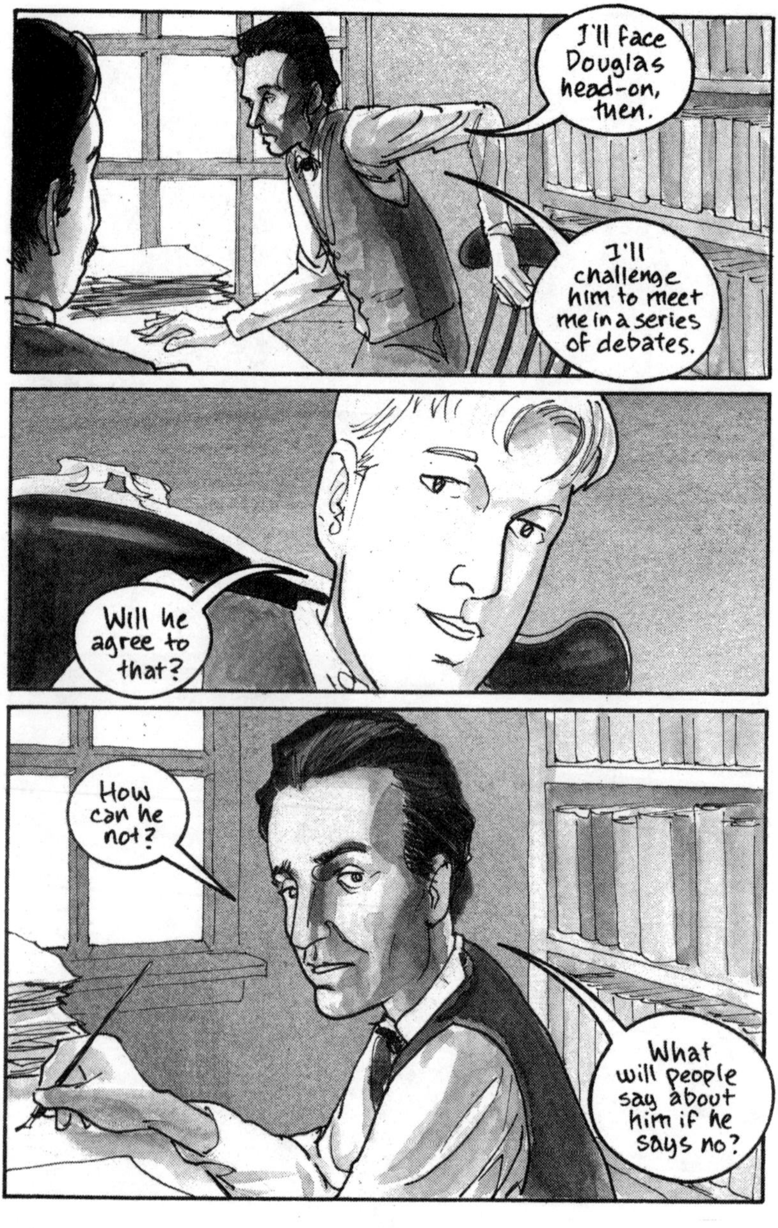
I'll face Douglas head-on, then.
I'll challenge him to meet me in a series of debates.
Will he agree to that?
How can he not?
What will people say about him if he says no?

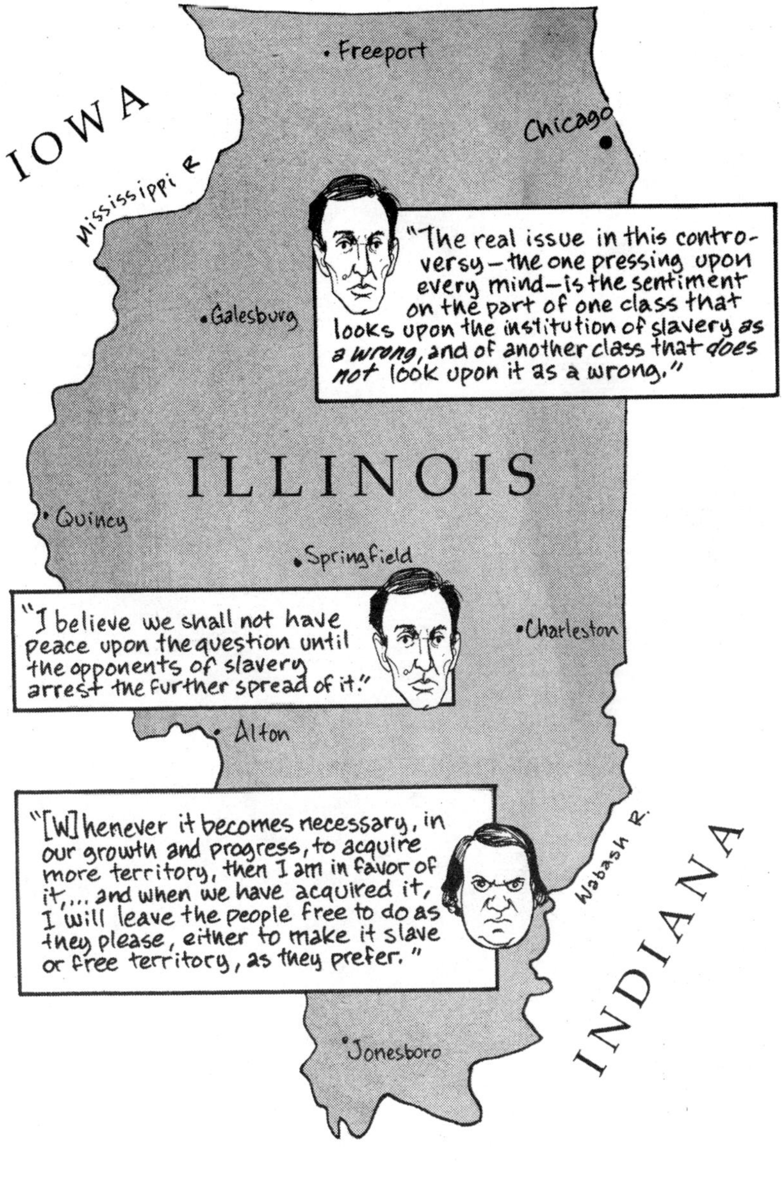
Freeport
IOWA
Chicago
Mississippi R
"The real issue in this controversy—the one pressing upon every mind—is the sentiment on the part of one class that looks upon the institution of slavery as *a wrong*, and of another class that *does not* look upon it as a wrong."
Galesburg
ILLINOIS
Quincy
Springfield
"I believe we shall not have peace upon the question until the opponents of slavery arrest the further spread of it."
Charleston
Alton
"[W]henever it becomes necessary, in our growth and progress, to acquire more territory, then I am in favor of it,... and when we have acquired it, I will leave the people free to do as they please, either to make it slave or free territory, as they prefer."
Wabash R.
INDIANA
Jonesboro

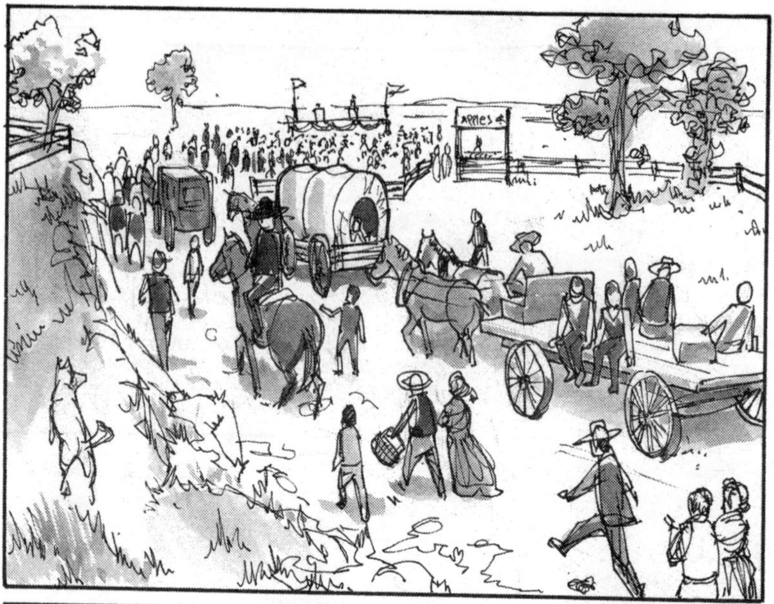
APPLES

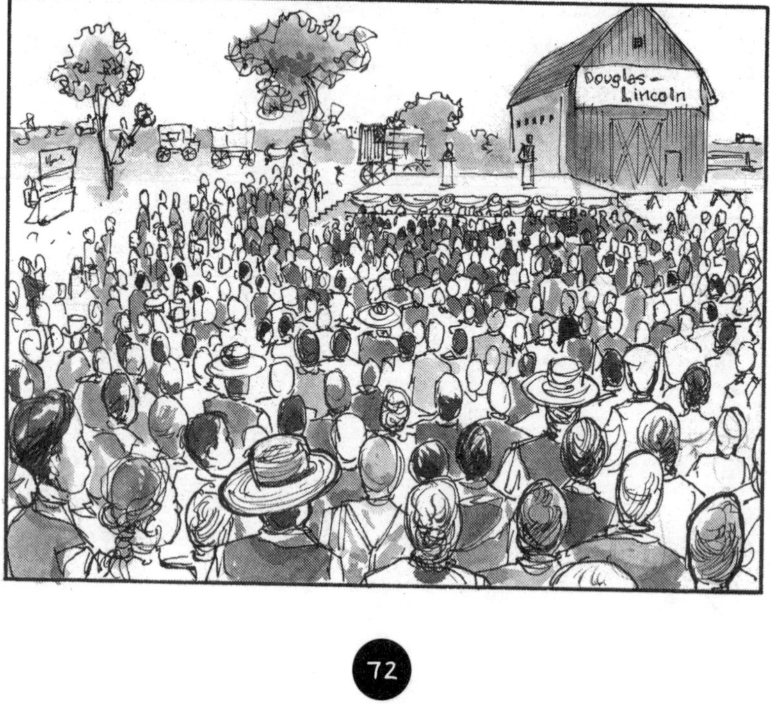
Douglas -
Lincoln

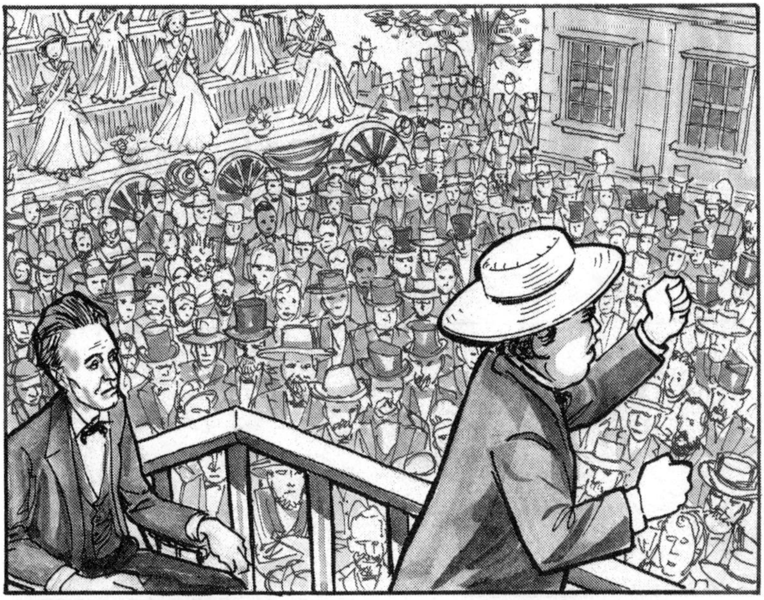

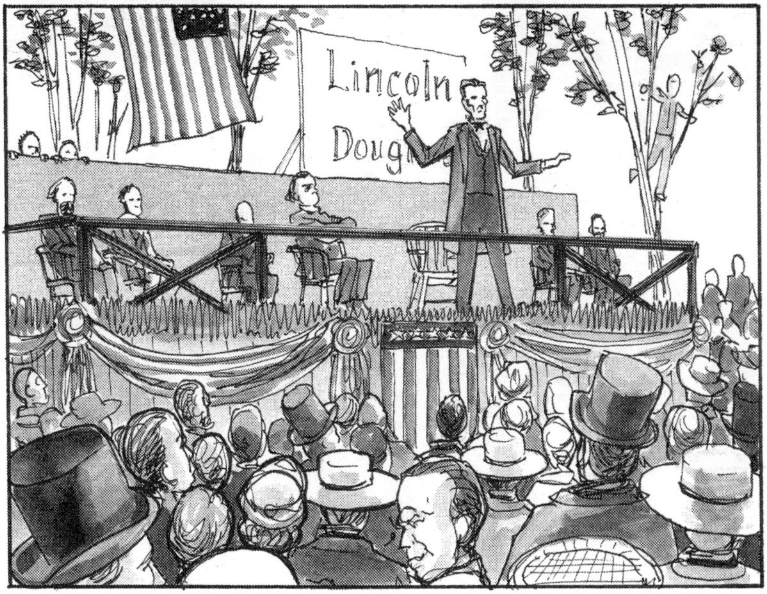
Lincoln

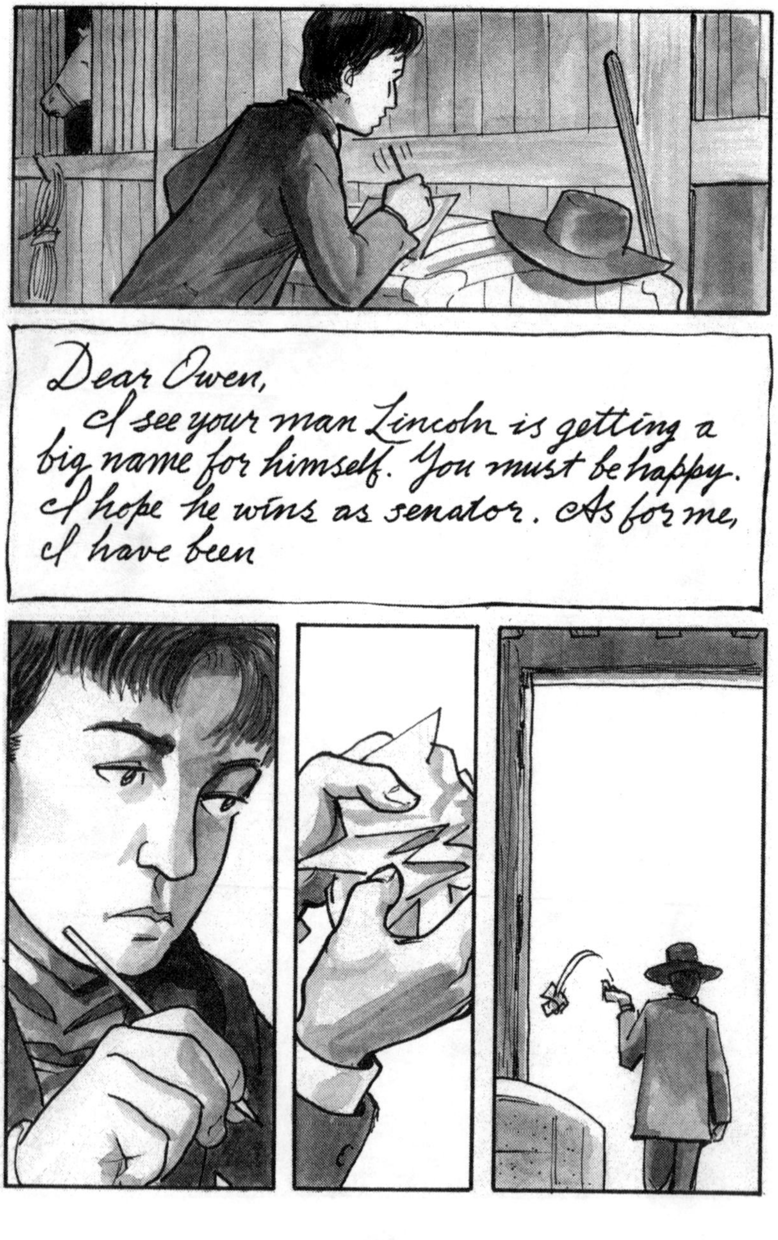
Dear Owen,
I see your man Lincoln is getting a big name for himself. You must be happy. I hope he wins as senator. As for me, I have been

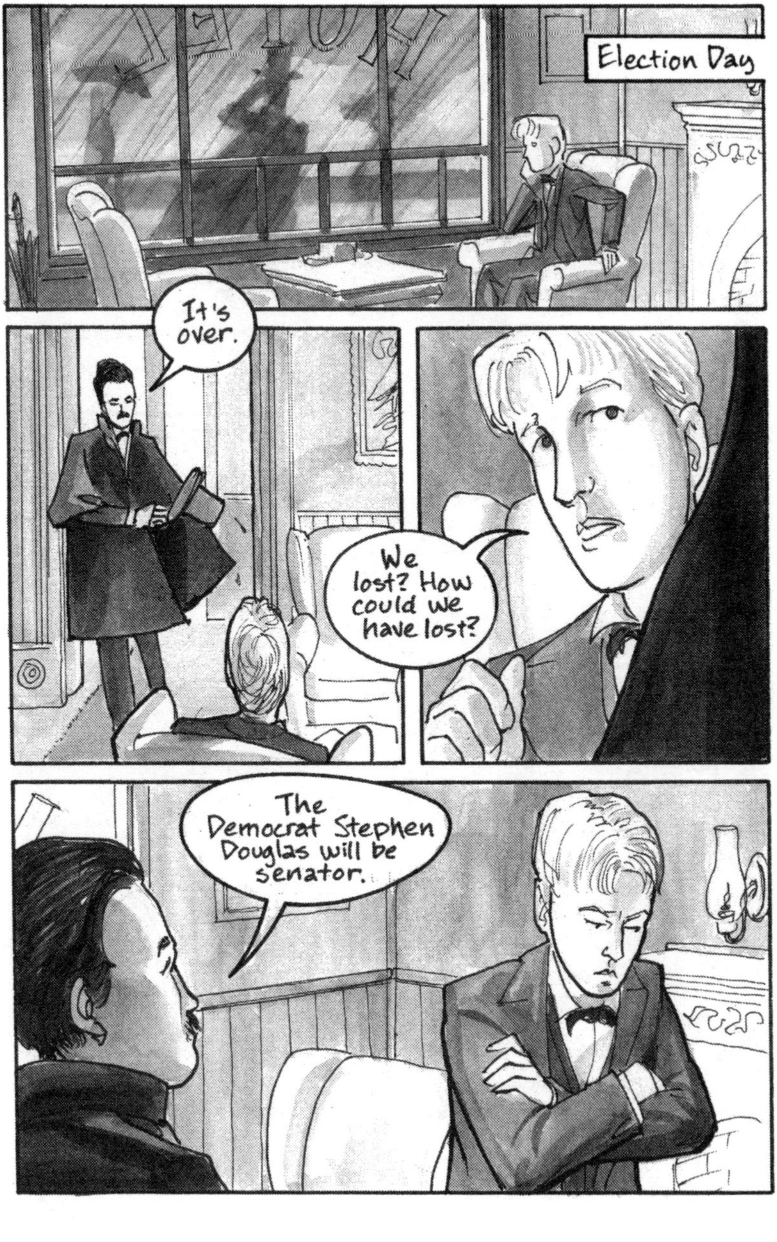
Election Day
It's over.
We lost? How could we have lost?
The Democrat Stephen Douglas will be senator.

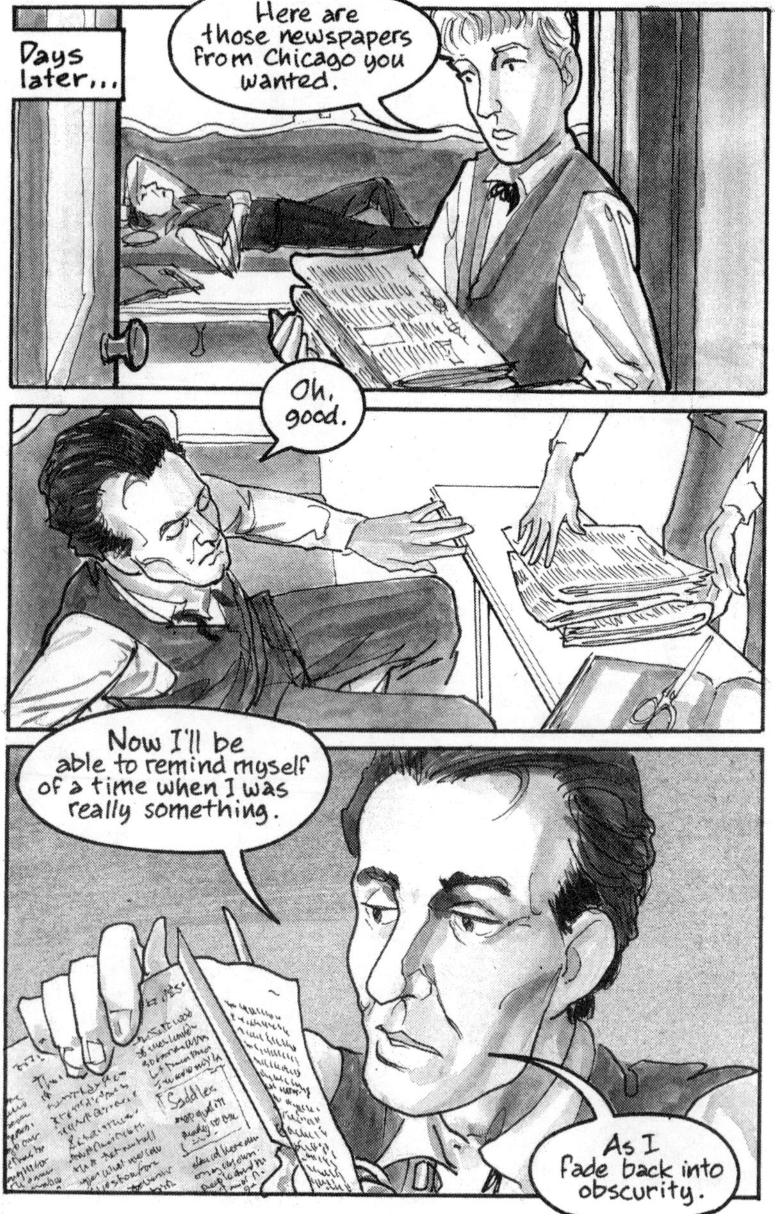
Days later...
Here are those newspapers from Chicago you wanted.
Oh, good.
Now I'll be able to remind myself of a time when I was really something.
Saddles
As I fade back into obscurity.

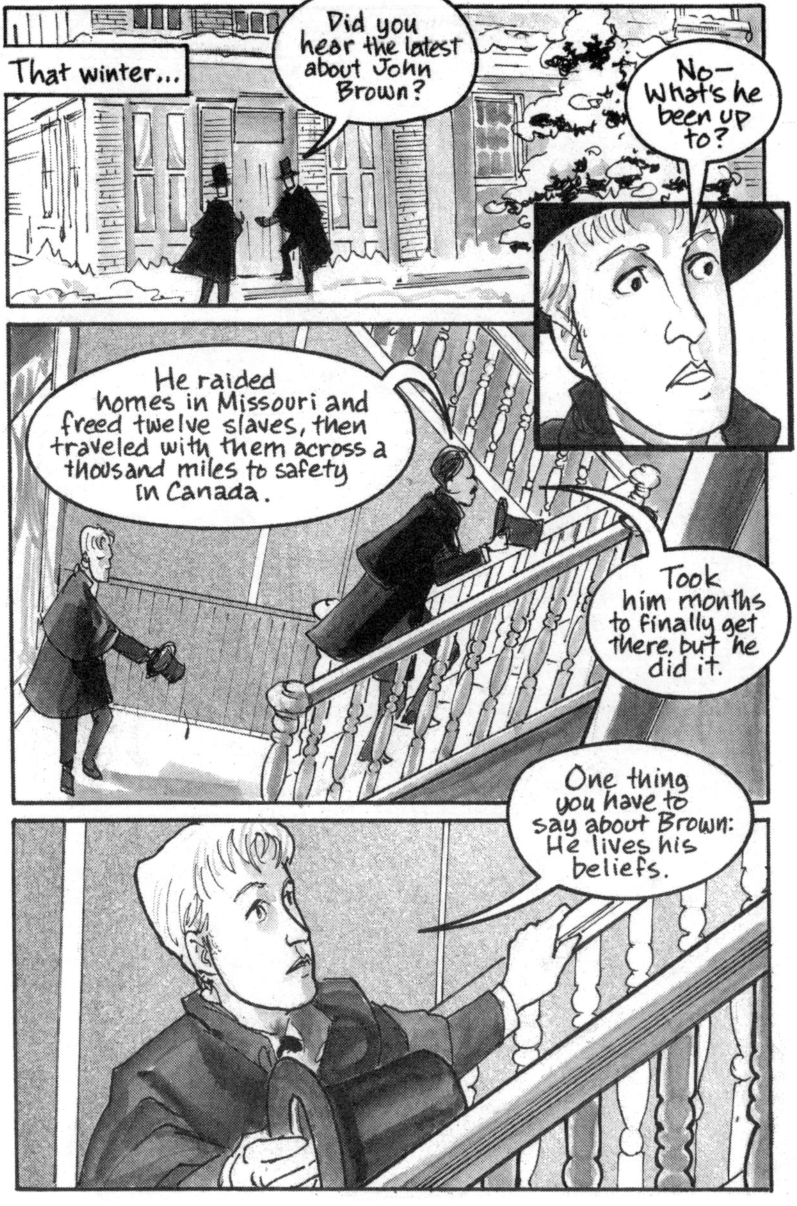
That winter...
Did you hear the latest about John Brown?
No— What's he been up to?
He raided homes in Missouri and freed twelve slaves, then traveled with them across a thousand miles to safety in Canada.
Took him months to finally get there, but he did it.
One thing you have to say about Brown: He lives his beliefs.

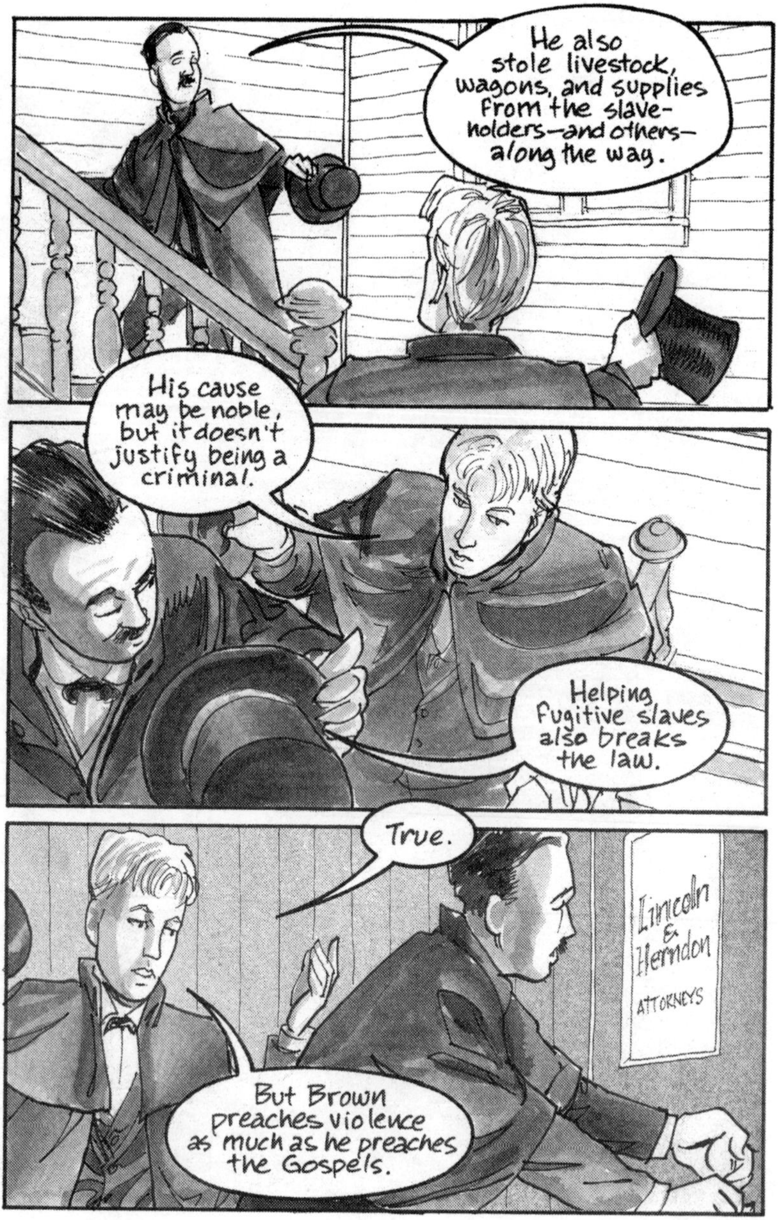
He also stole livestock, wagons, and supplies from the slave-holders—and others—along the way.
His cause may be noble, but it doesn't justify being a criminal.
Helping fugitive slaves also breaks the law.
True.
Lincoln & Herndon ATTORNEYS
But Brown preaches violence as much as he preaches the Gospels.

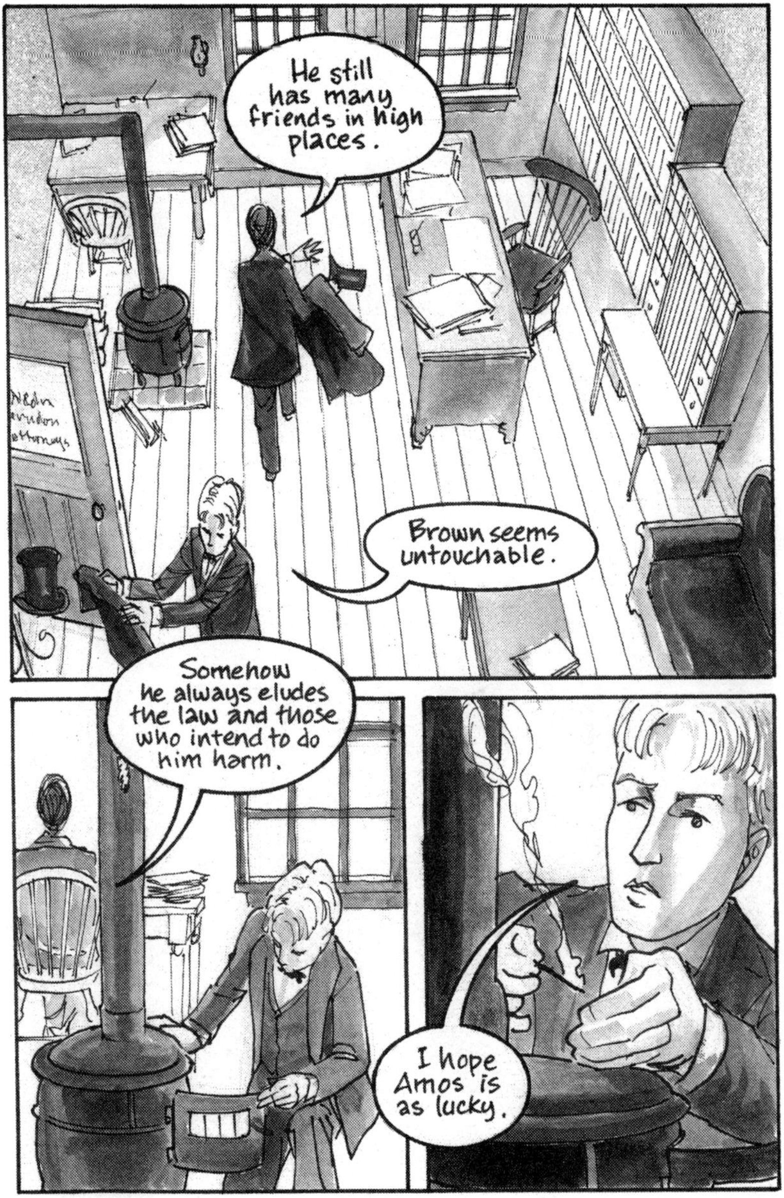
He still has many friends in high places.
Brown seems untouchable.
Somehow he always eludes the law and those who intend to do him harm.
I hope Amos is as lucky.

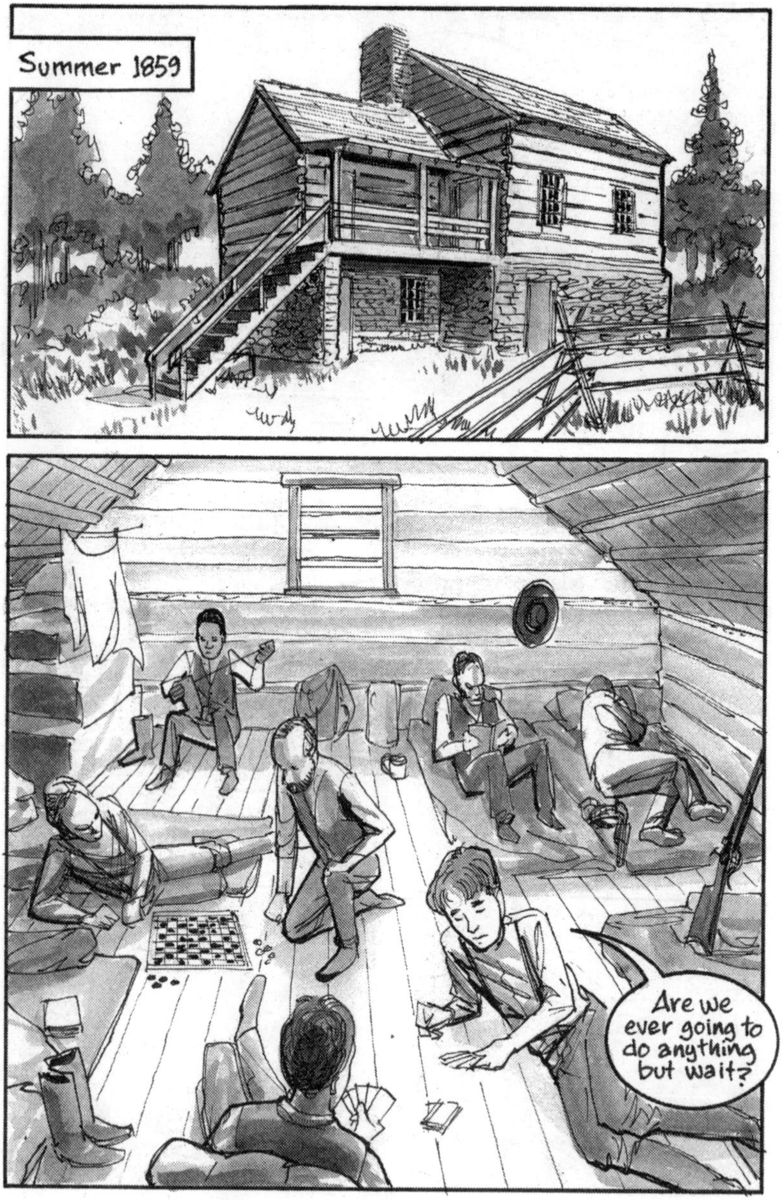
Summer 1859
Are we ever going to do anything but wait?

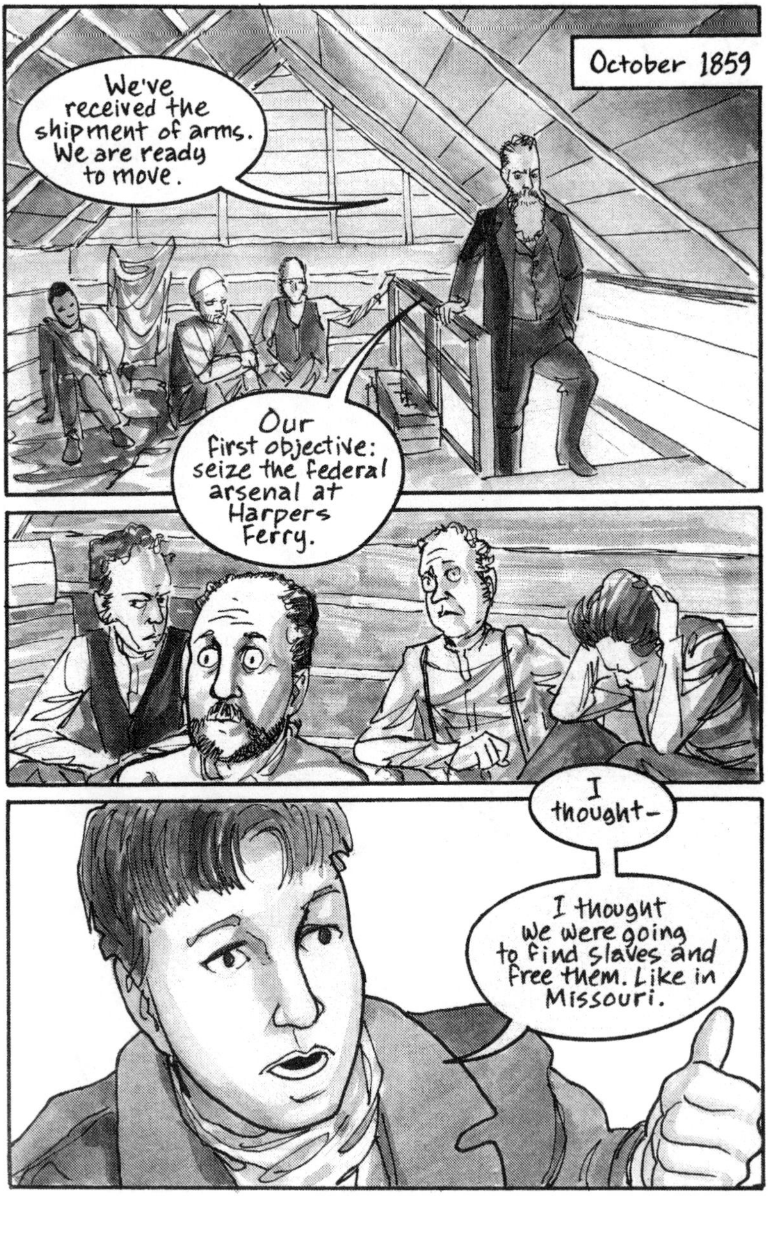
October 1859
We've received the shipment of arms. We are ready to move.
Our first objective: seize the federal arsenal at Harpers Ferry.
I thought-
I thought we were going to find slaves and free them. Like in Missouri.

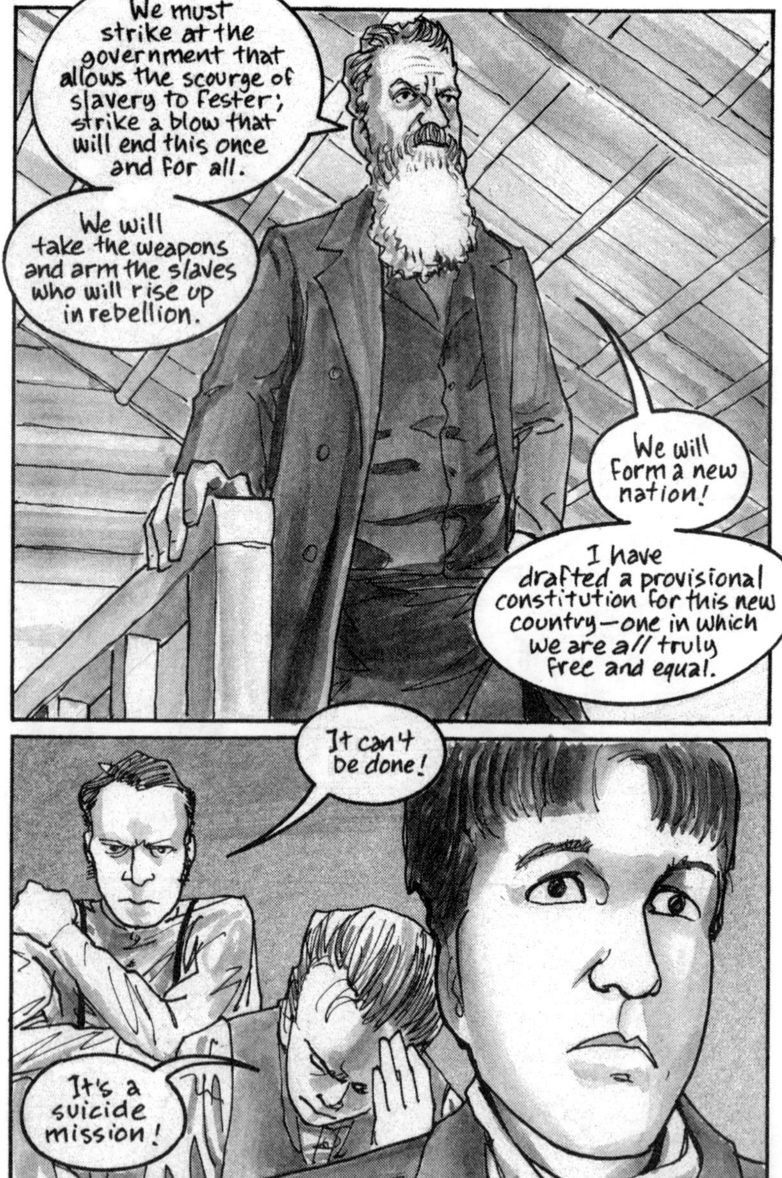
We must strike at the government that allows the scourge of slavery to fester; strike a blow that will end this once and for all.
We will take the weapons and arm the slaves who will rise up in rebellion.
We will form a new nation!
I have drafted a provisional constitution for this new country—one in which we are all truly free and equal.
It can't be done!
It's a suicide mission!

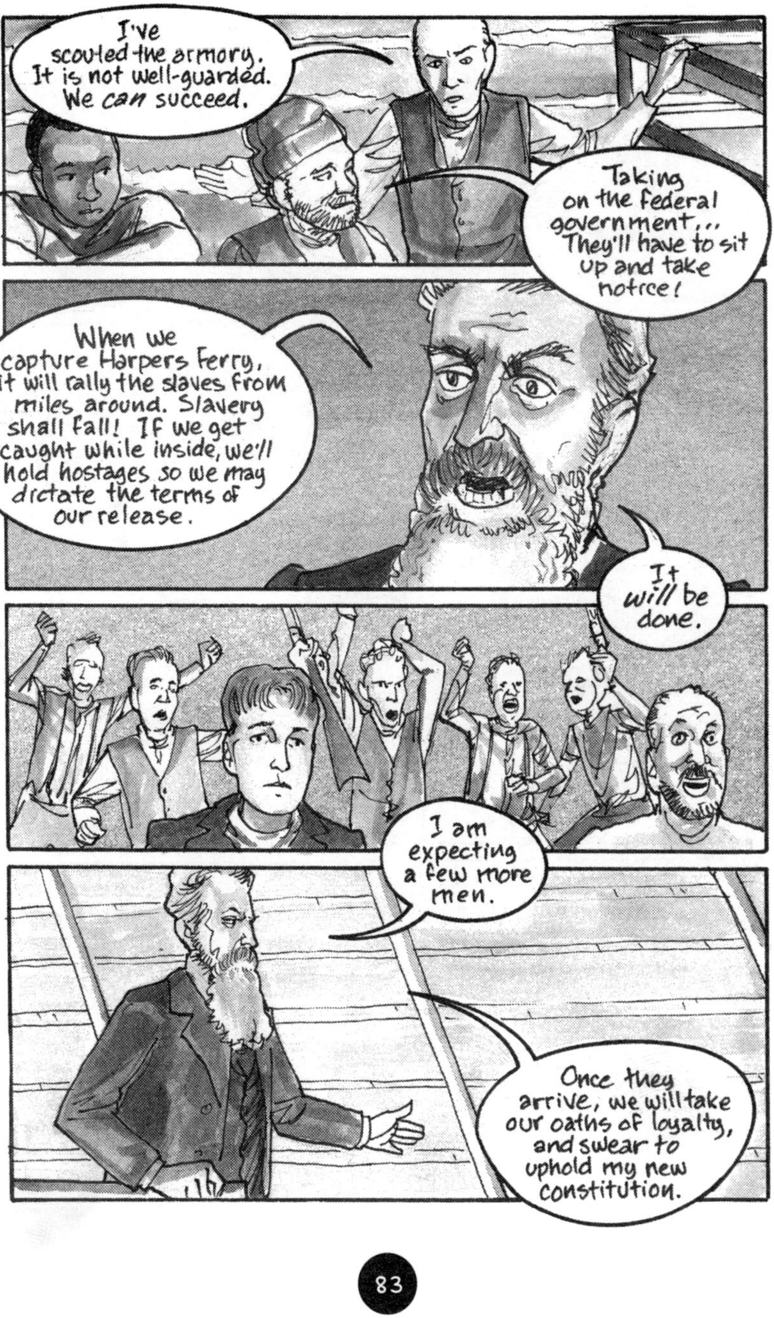
I've scouted the armory. It is not well-guarded. We *can* succeed.
Taking on the federal government... They'll have to sit up and take notice!
When we capture Harpers Ferry, it will rally the slaves from miles around. Slavery shall fall! If we get caught while inside, we'll hold hostages so we may dictate the terms of our release.
It *will* be done.
I am expecting a few more men.
Once they arrive, we will take our oaths of loyalty, and swear to uphold my new constitution.

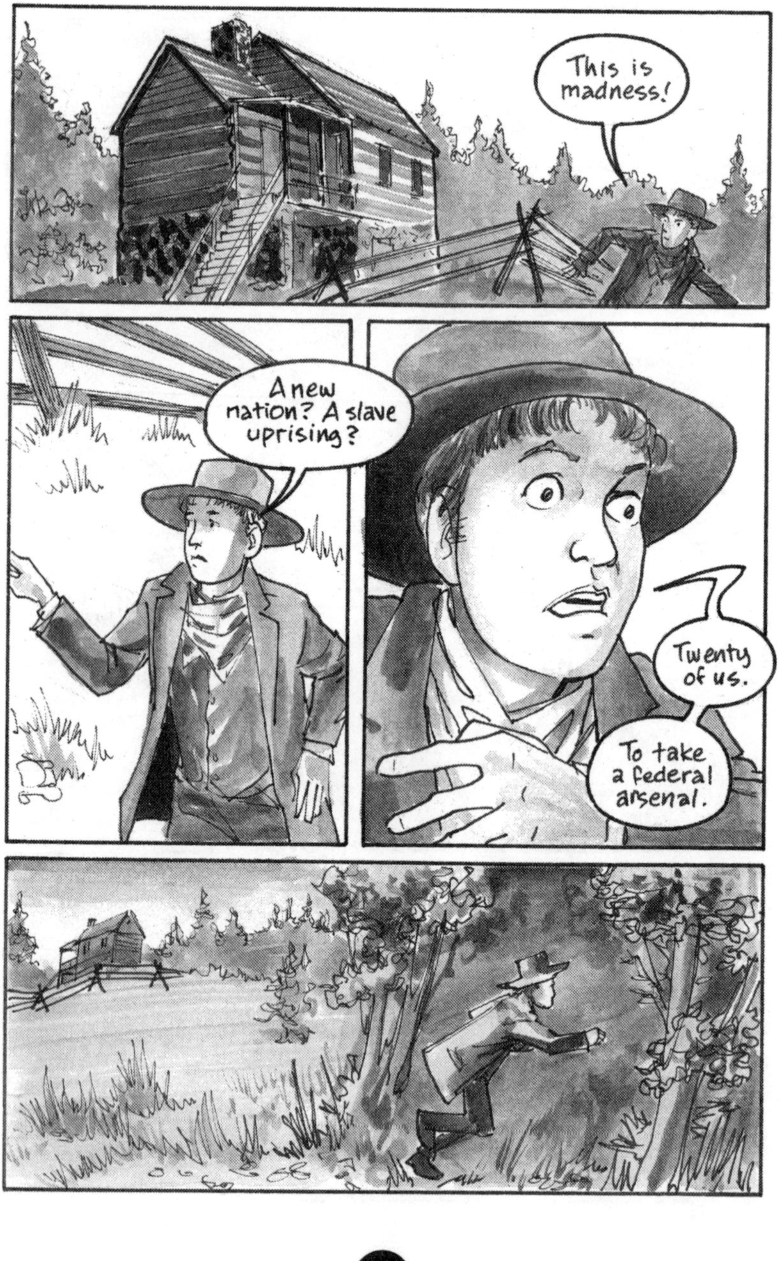
This is madness!
A new nation? A slave uprising?
Twenty of us.
To take a federal arsenal.

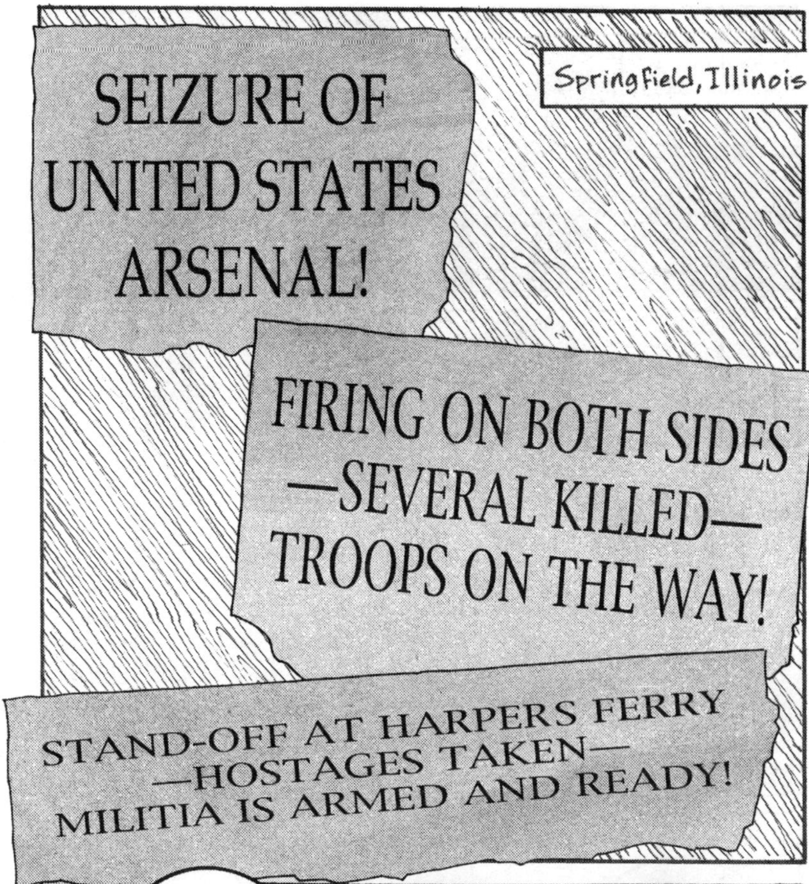
SEIZURE OF UNITED STATES ARSENAL!
Springfield, Illinois
FIRING ON BOTH SIDES —SEVERAL KILLED— TROOPS ON THE WAY!
STAND-OFF AT HARPERS FERRY —HOSTAGES TAKEN— MILITIA IS ARMED AND READY!

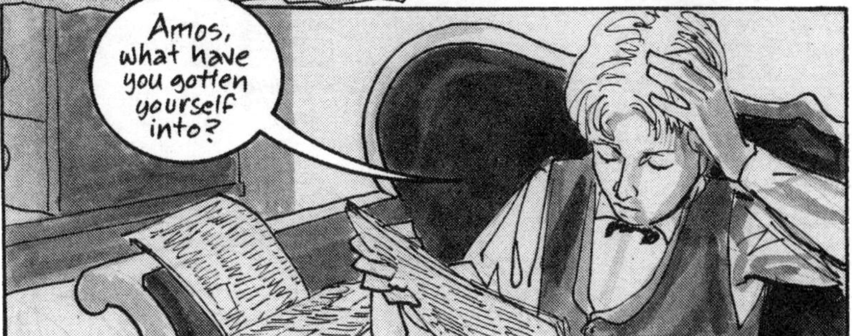
Amos, what have you gotten yourself into?

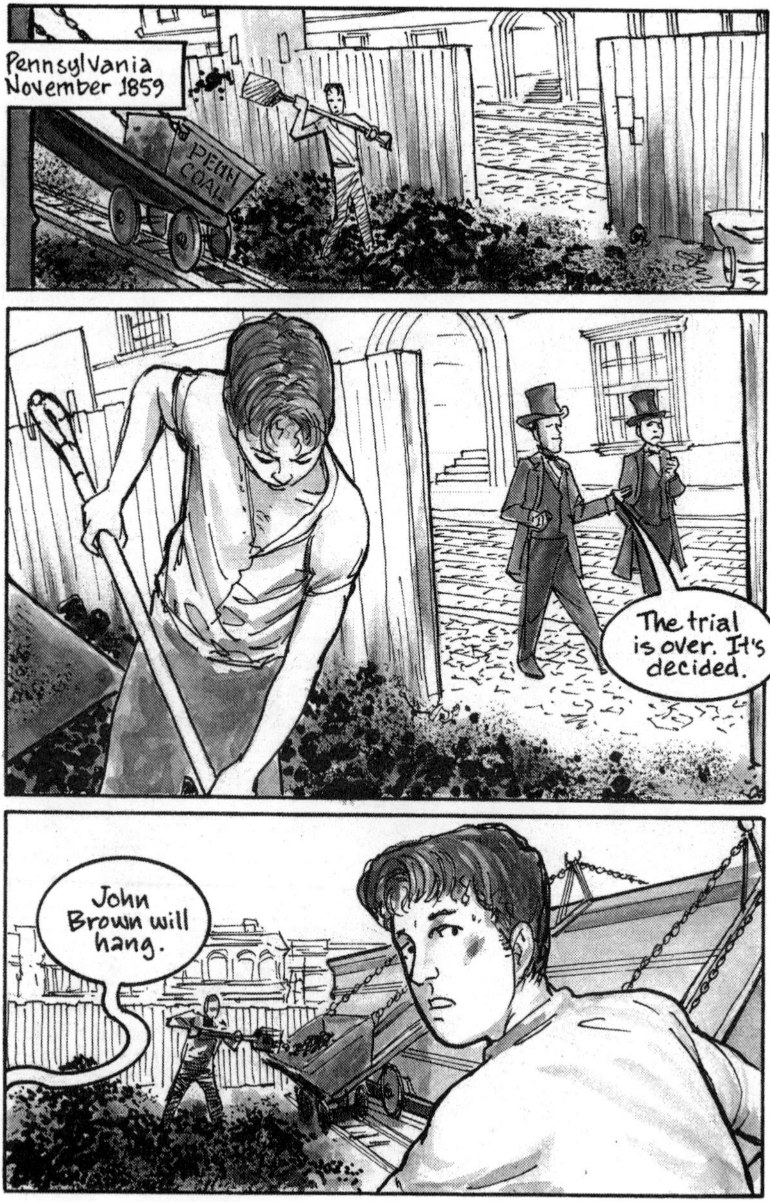
Pennsylvania
November 1859
PENN COAL
The trial is over. It's decided.
John Brown will hang.

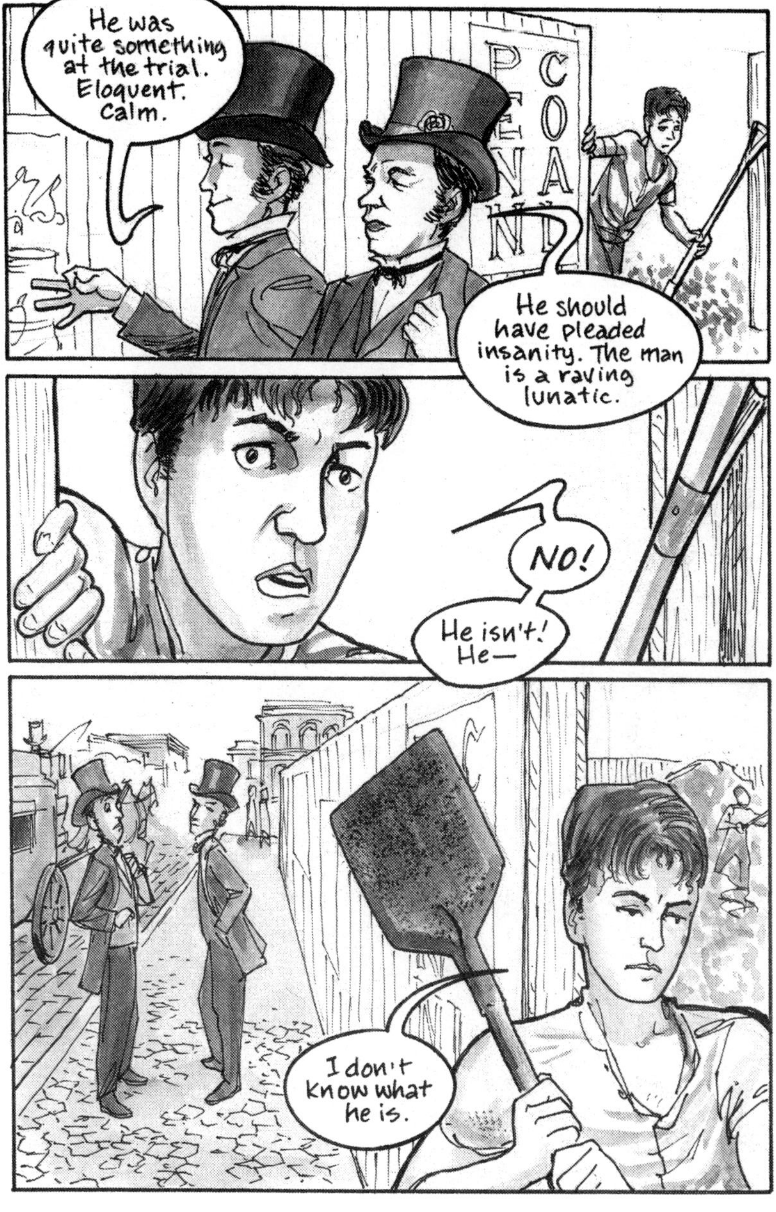
He was quite something at the trial. Eloquent. Calm.
He should have pleaded insanity. The man is a raving lunatic.
NO!
He isn't! He—
I don't know what he is.

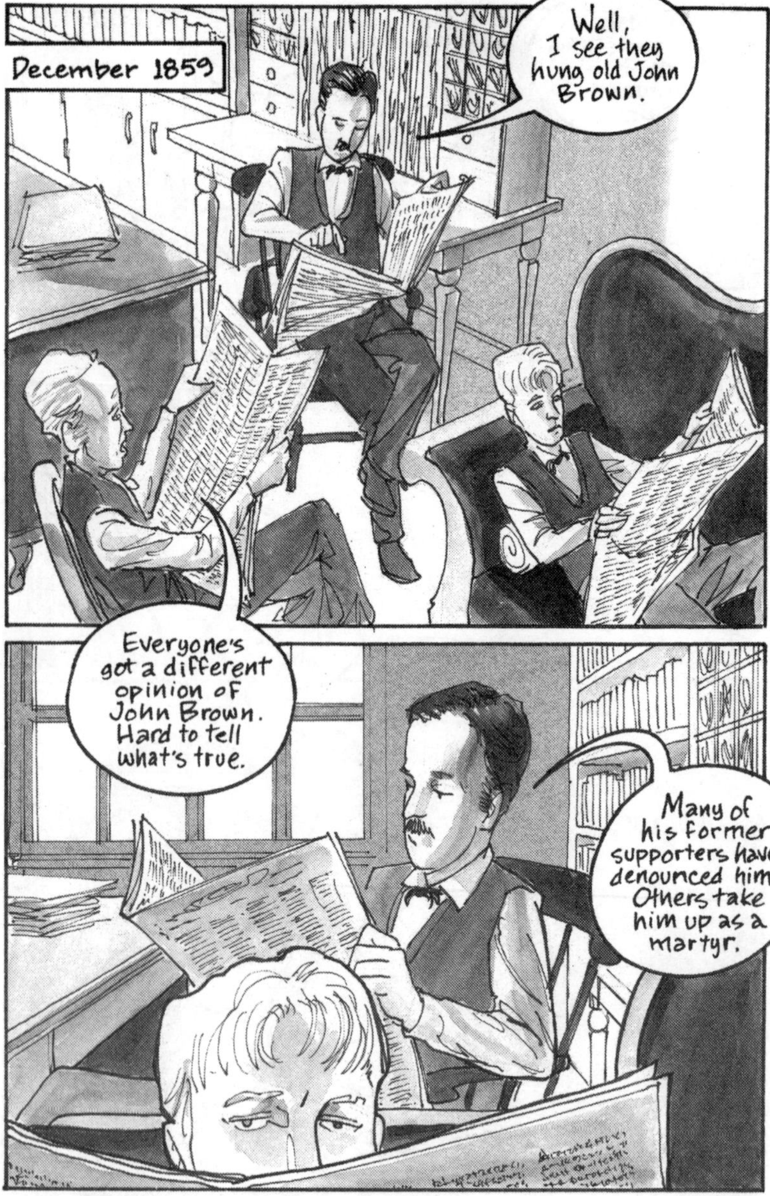
December 1859
Well, I see they hung old John Brown.
Everyone's got a different opinion of John Brown. Hard to tell what's true.
Many of his former supporters have denounced him. Others take him up as a martyr.

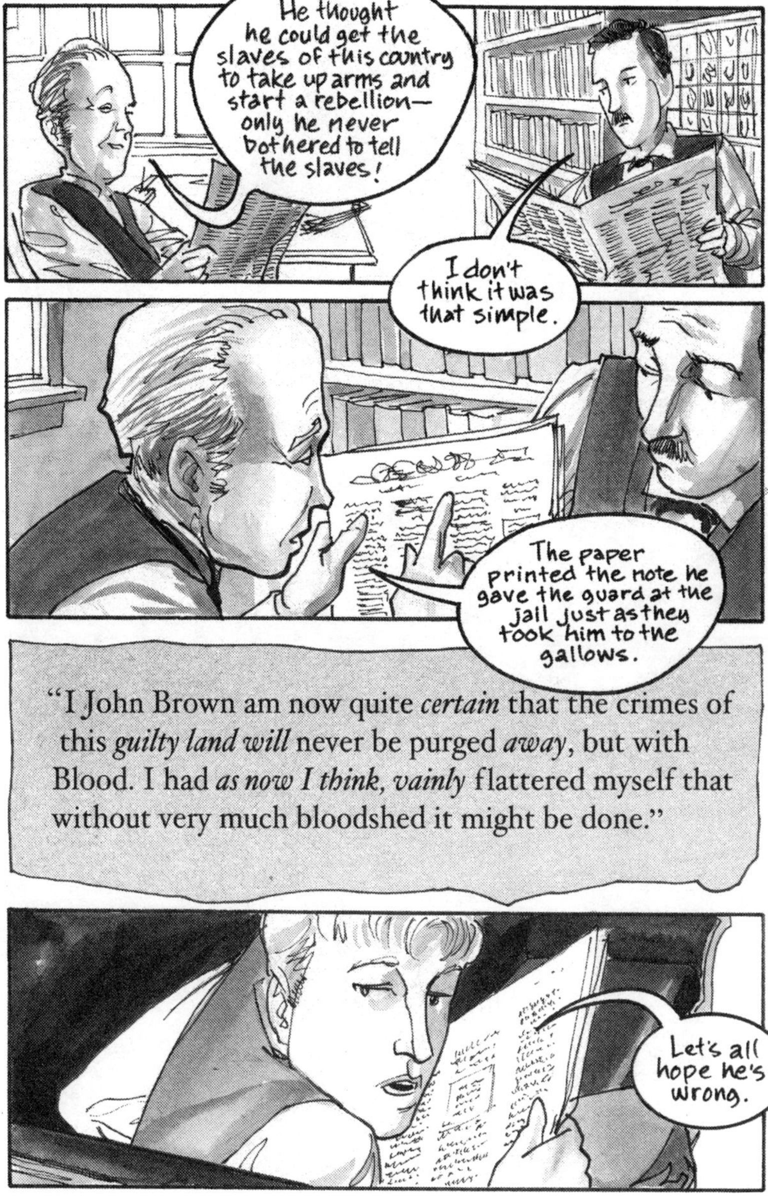
He thought he could get the slaves of this country to take up arms and start a rebellion— only he never bothered to tell the slaves!
I don't think it was that simple.
The paper printed the note he gave the guard at the jail just as they took him to the gallows.
"I John Brown am now quite *certain* that the crimes of this *guilty land will* never be purged *away*, but with Blood. I had *as now I think, vainly* flattered myself that without very much bloodshed it might be done."
Let's all hope he's wrong.

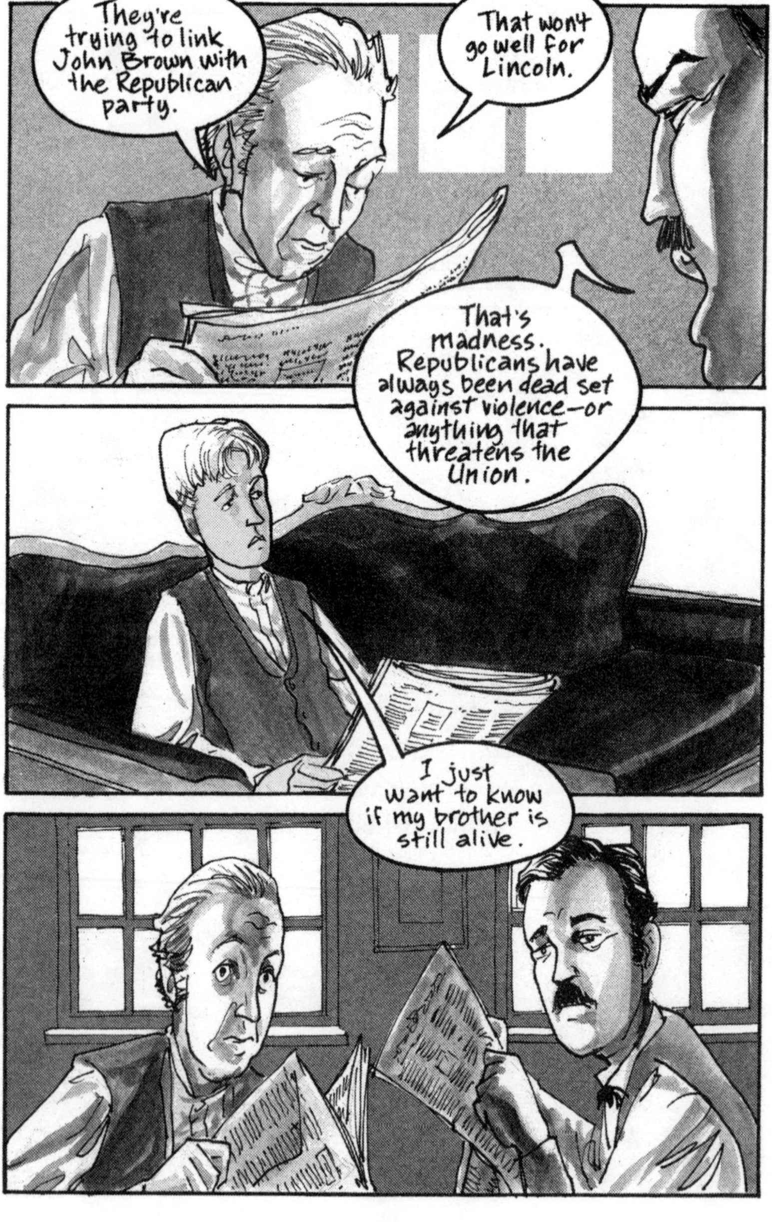
They're trying to link John Brown with the Republican party.
That won't go well for Lincoln.
That's madness. Republicans have always been dead set against violence—or anything that threatens the Union.
I just want to know if my brother is still alive.

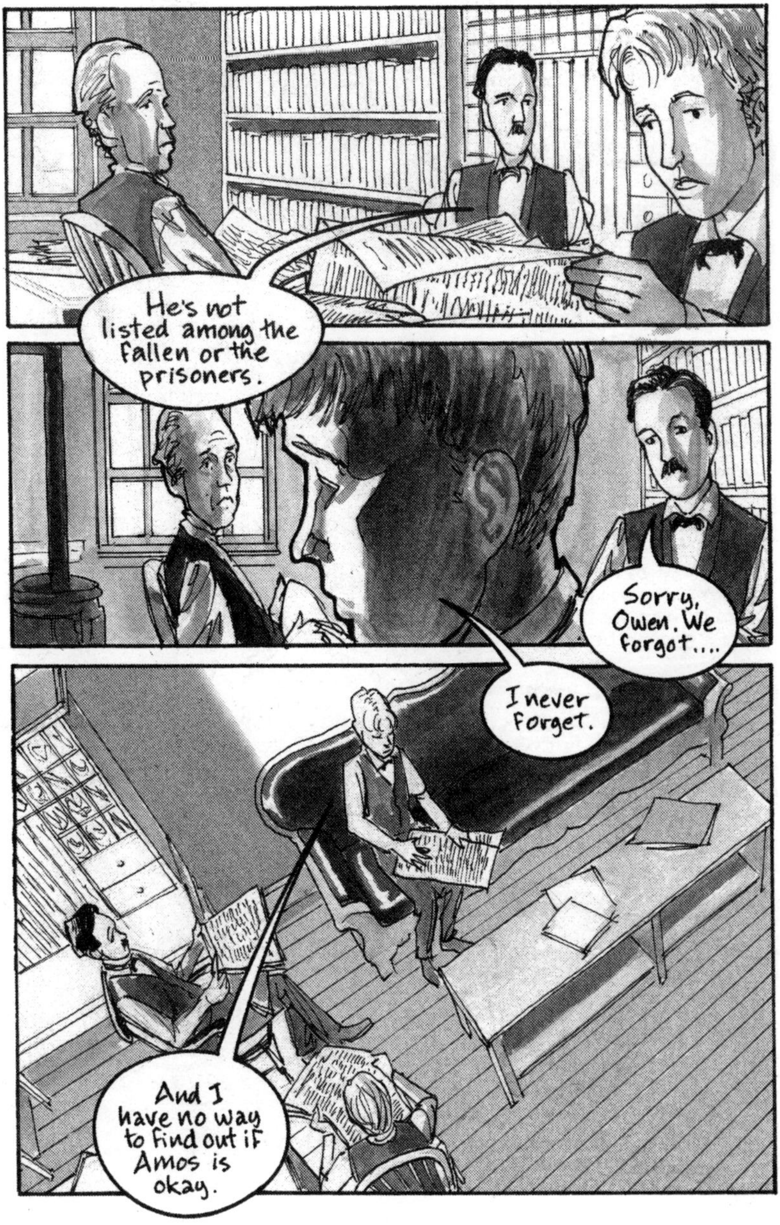
He's not listed among the fallen or the prisoners.
Sorry, Owen. We forgot....
I never forget.
And I have no way to find out if Amos is okay.

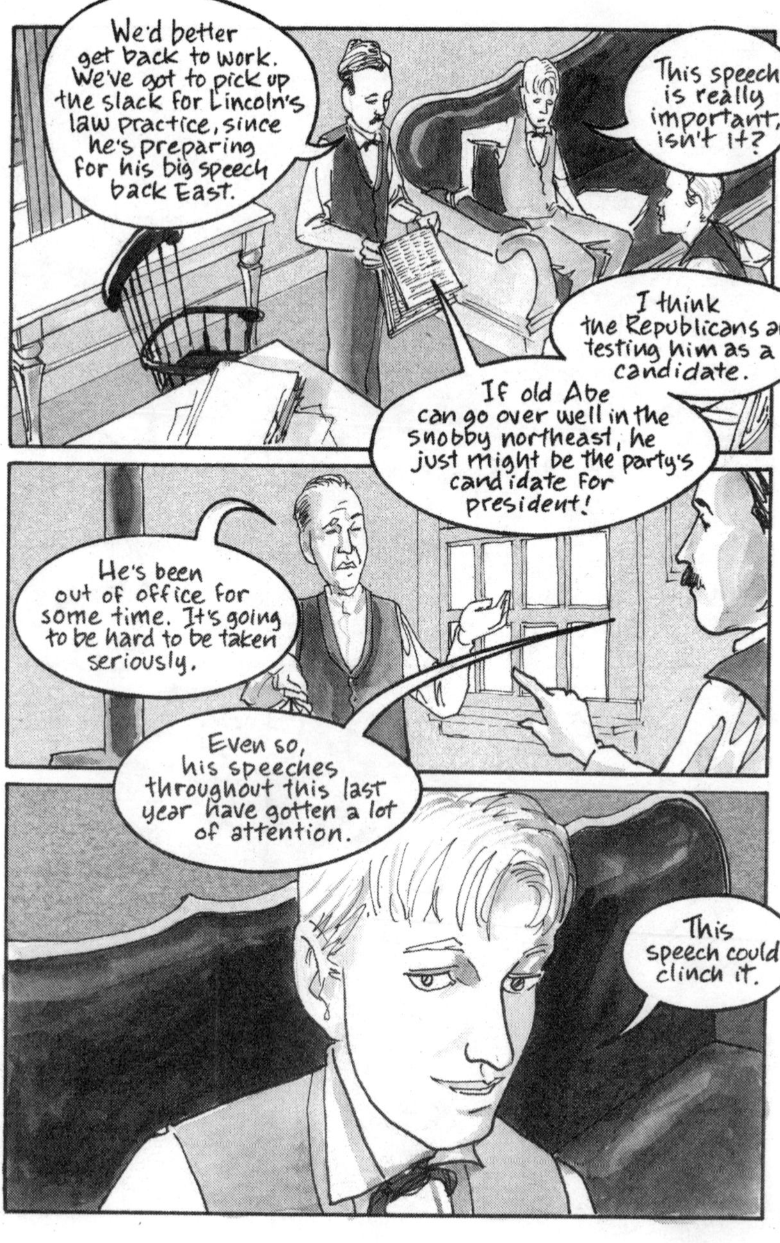
We'd better get back to work. We've got to pick up the slack for Lincoln's law practice, since he's preparing for his big speech back East.
This speech is really important, isn't it?
I think the Republicans are testing him as a candidate.
If old Abe can go over well in the snobby northeast, he just might be the party's candidate for president!
He's been out of office for some time. It's going to be hard to be taken seriously.
Even so, his speeches throughout this last year have gotten a lot of attention.
This speech could clinch it.

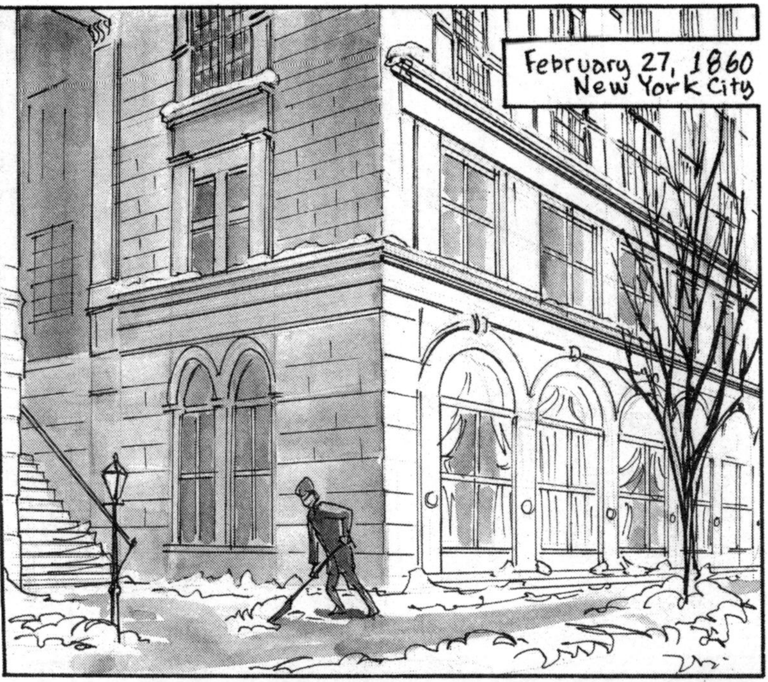
February 27, 1860
New York City

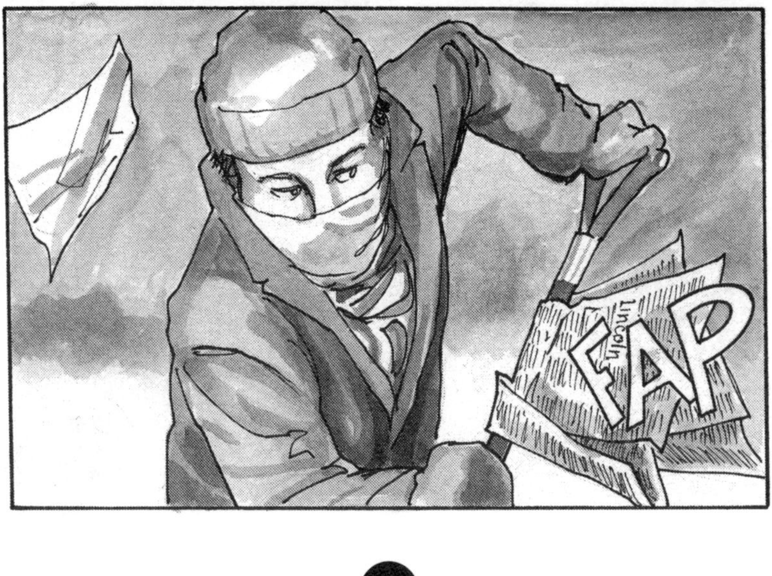
Lincoln
FAP

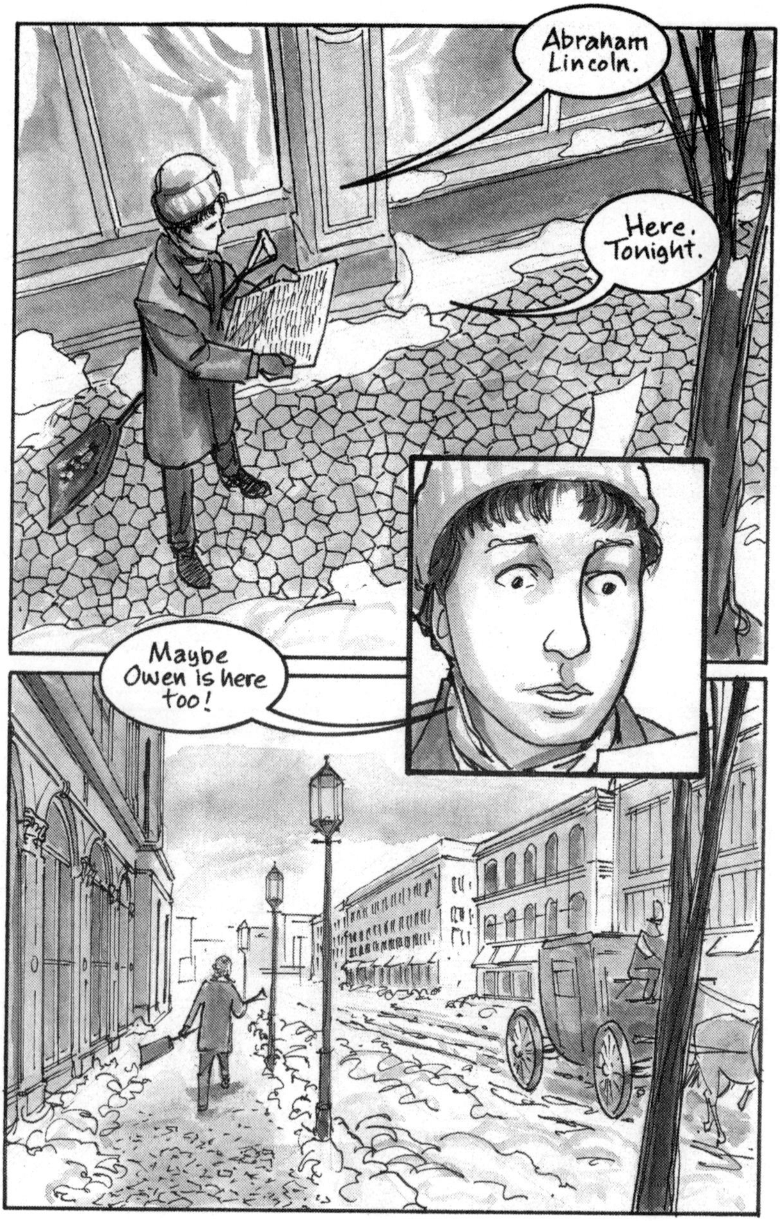
Abraham Lincoln.
Here. Tonight.
Maybe Owen is here too!

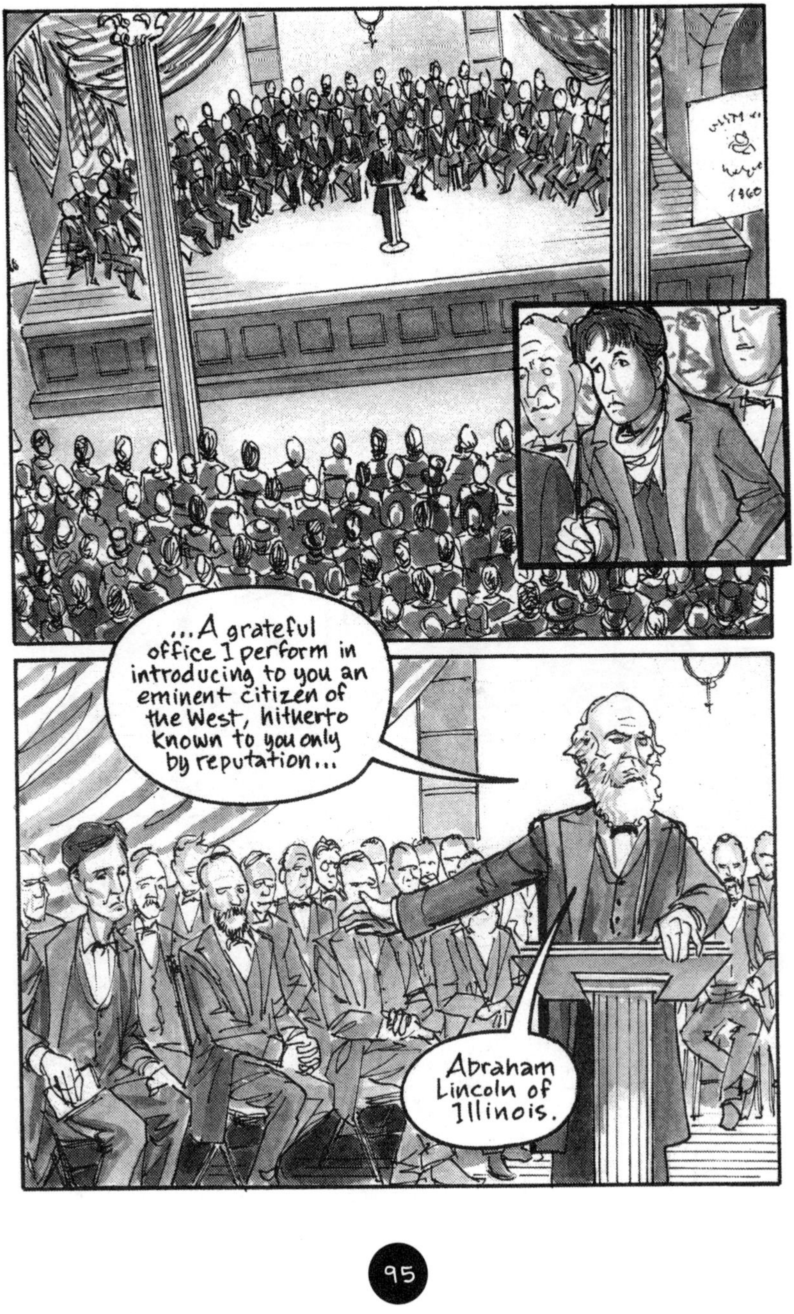
...A grateful office I perform in introducing to you an eminent citizen of the West, hitherto known to you only by reputation...
Abraham Lincoln of Illinois.

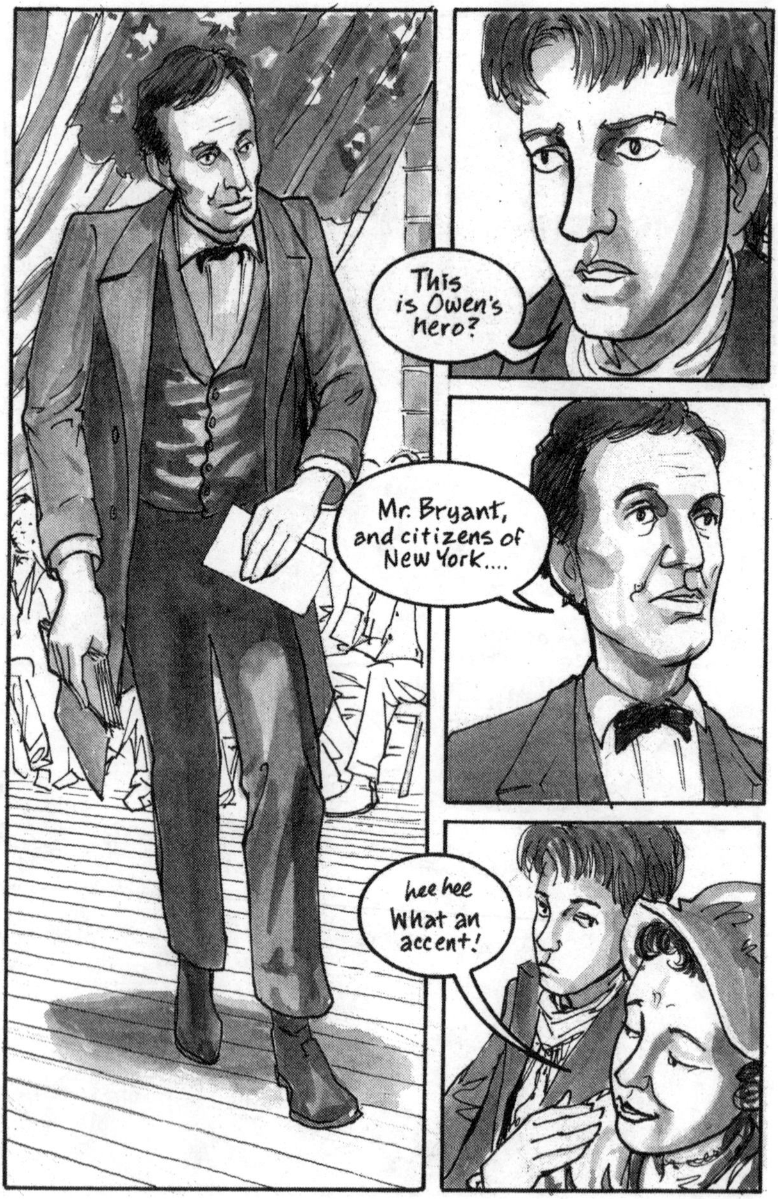
This is Owen's hero?
Mr. Bryant, and citizens of New York....
hee hee What an accent!

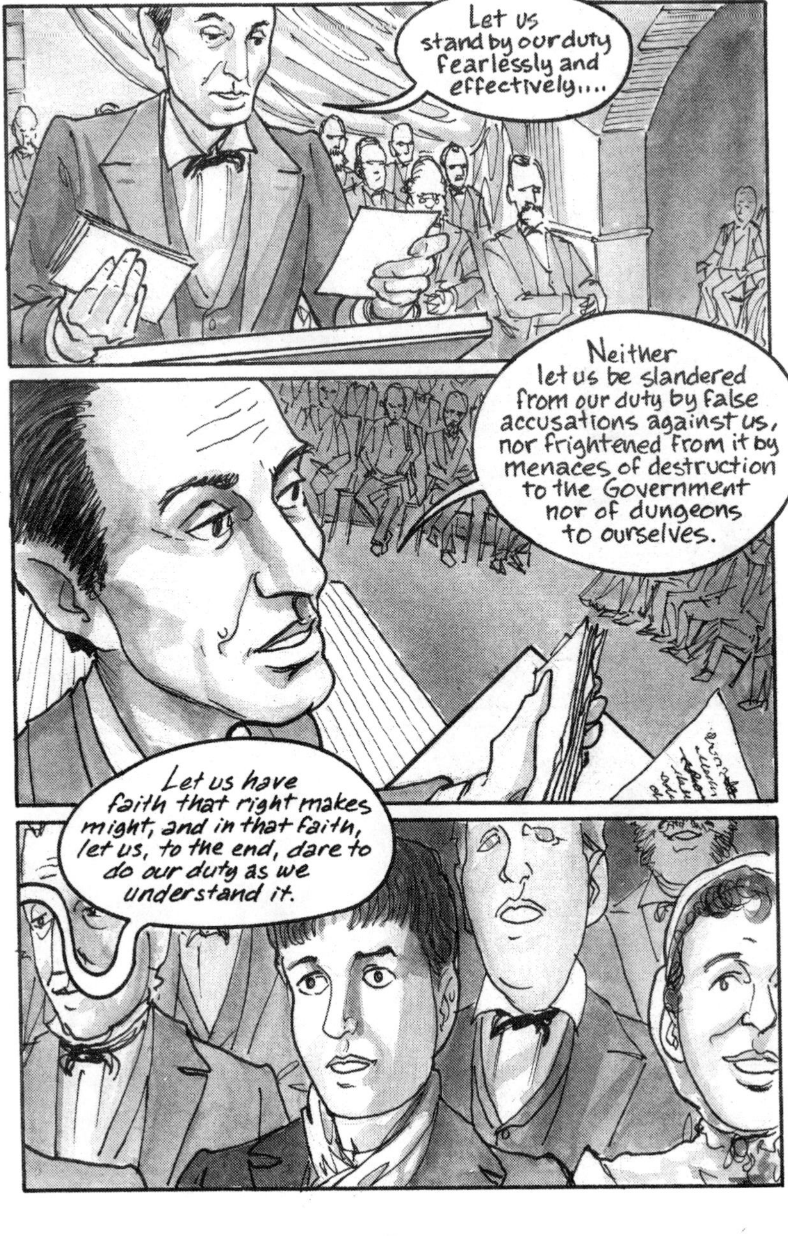
Let us stand by our duty fearlessly and effectively....
Neither let us be slandered from our duty by false accusations against us, nor frightened from it by menaces of destruction to the Government nor of dungeons to ourselves.
Let us have faith that right makes might, and in that faith, let us, to the end, dare to do our duty as we understand it.

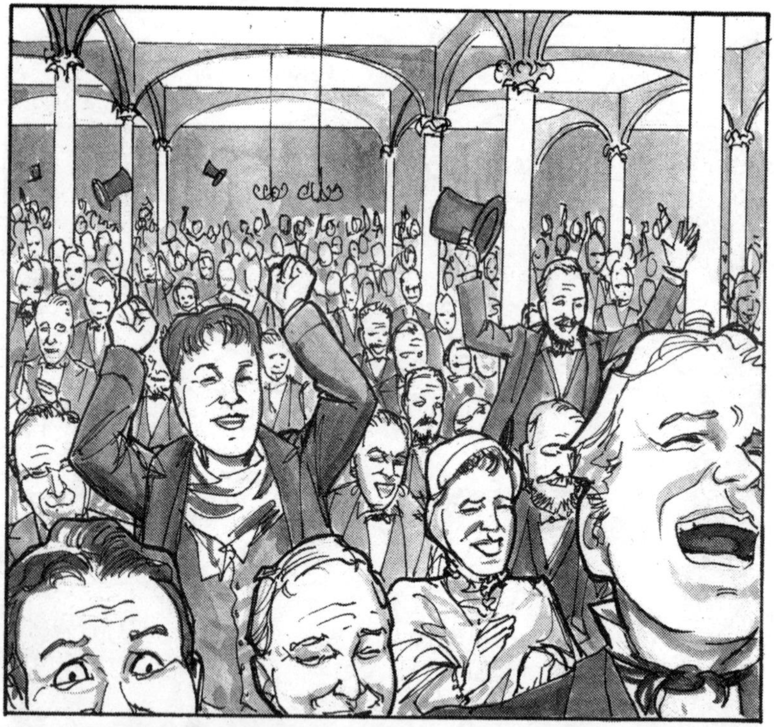

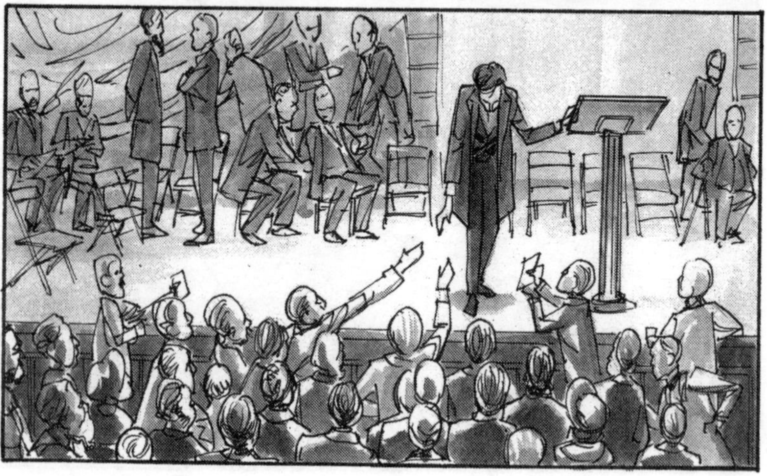

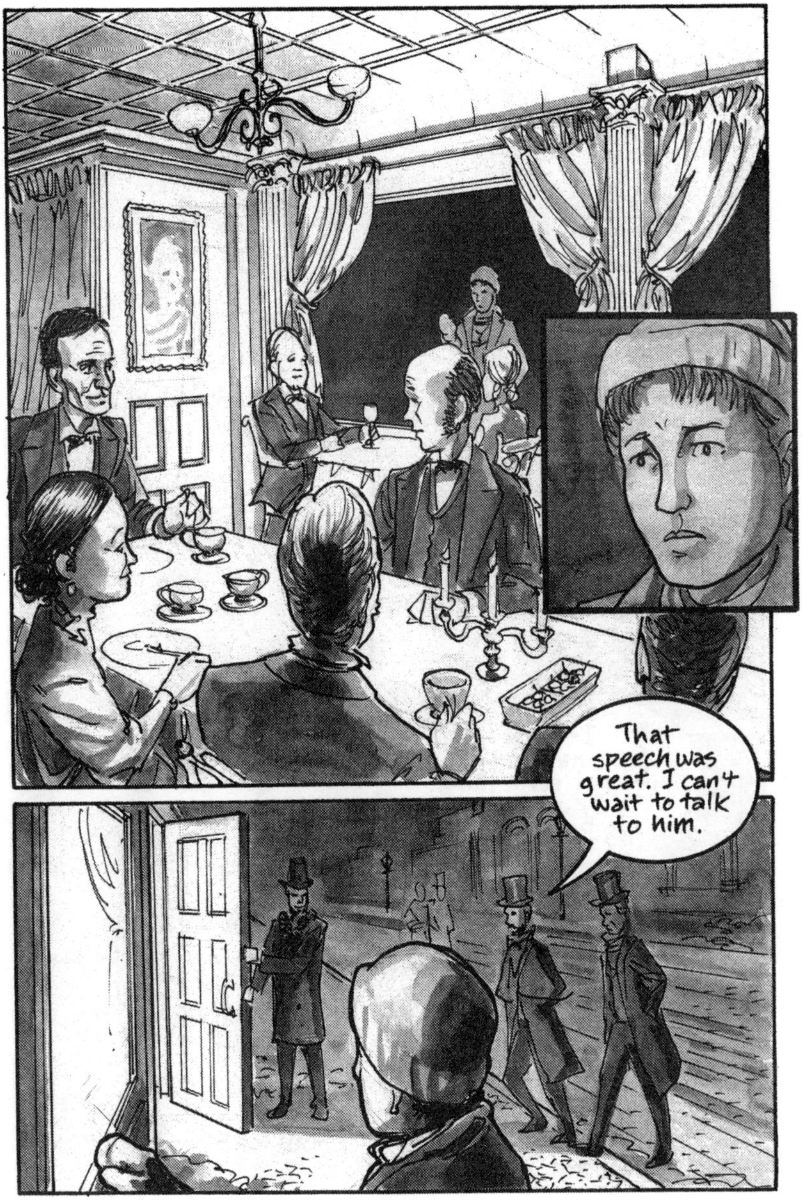
That speech was great. I can't wait to talk to him.

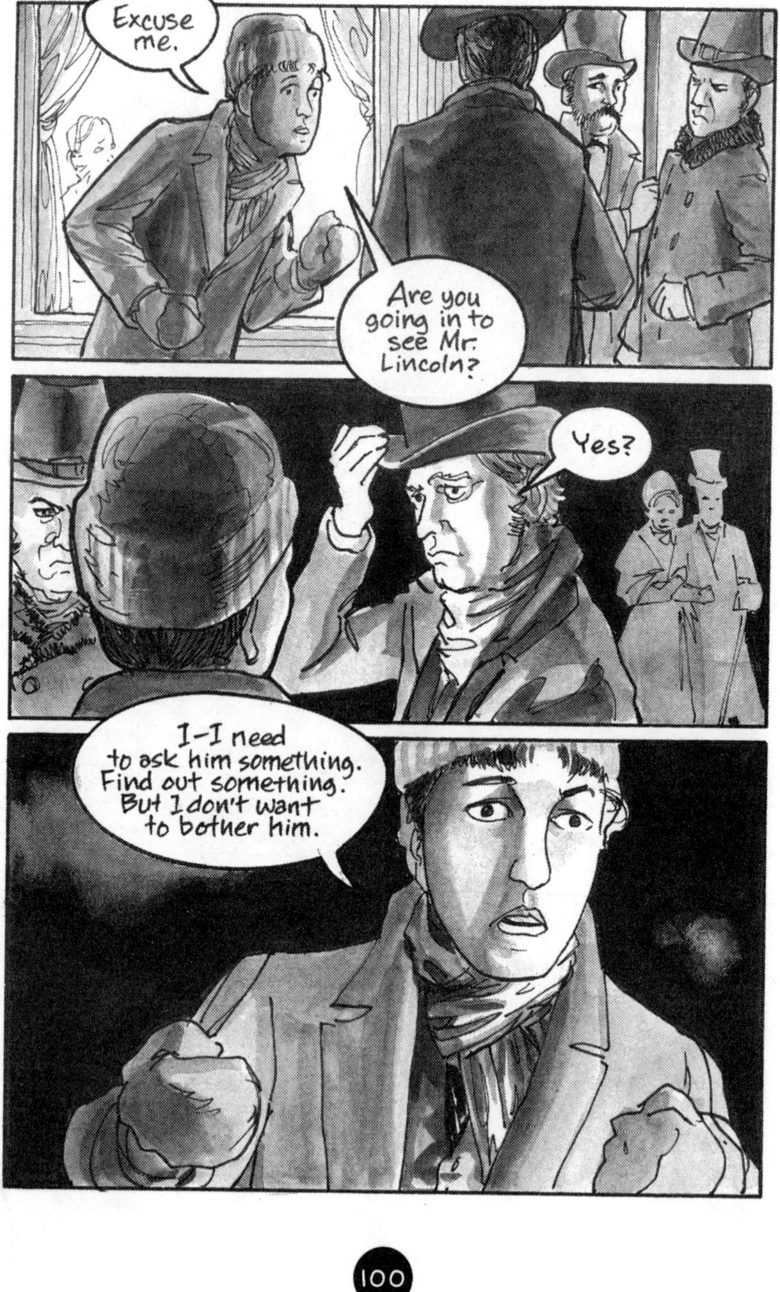
Excuse me.
Are you going in to see Mr. Lincoln?
Yes?
I—I need to ask him something. Find out something. But I don't want to bother him.

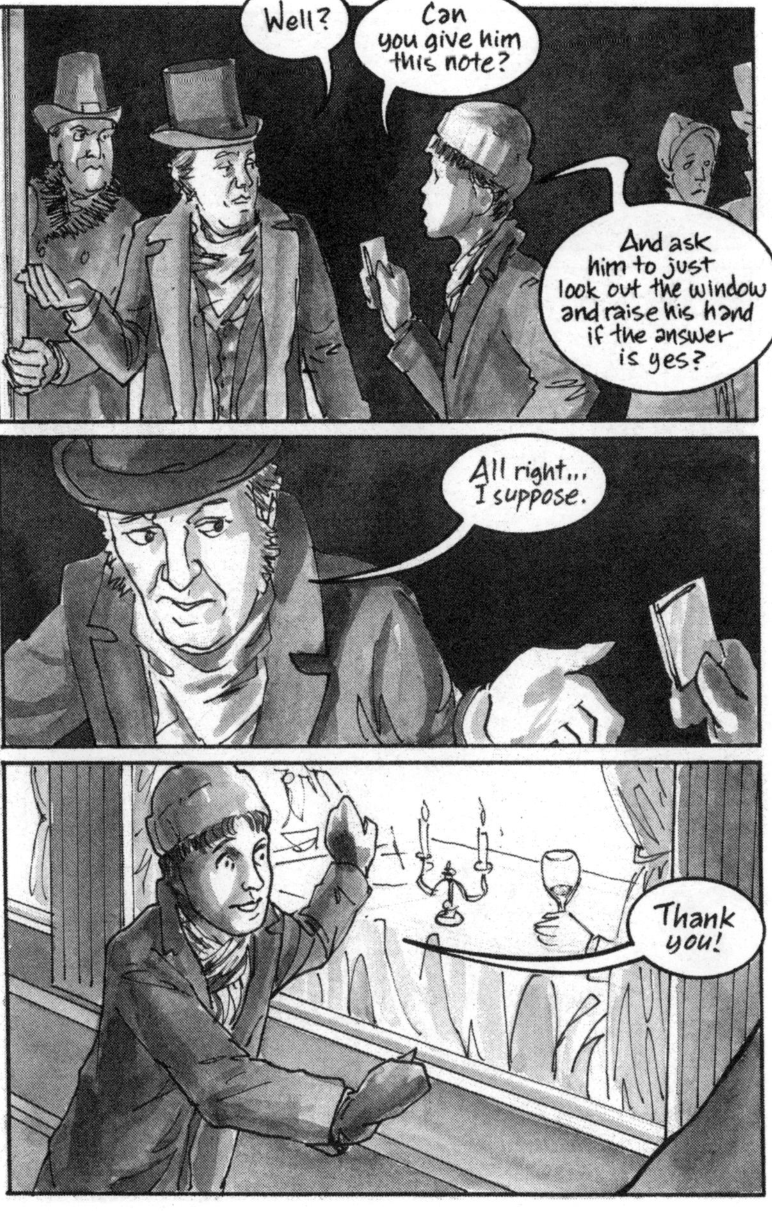
Well?
Can you give him this note?
And ask him to just look out the window and raise his hand if the answer is yes?
All right... I suppose.
Thank you!

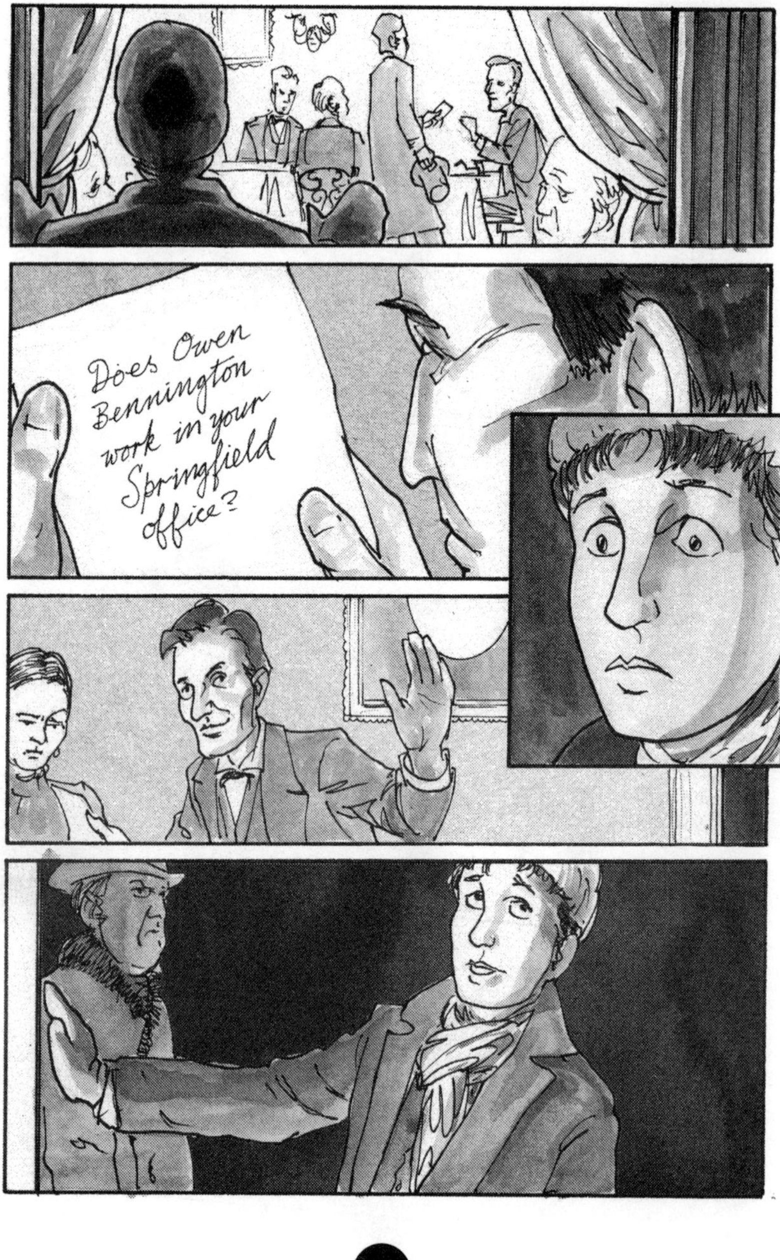
Does Owen Bennington work in your Springfield office?

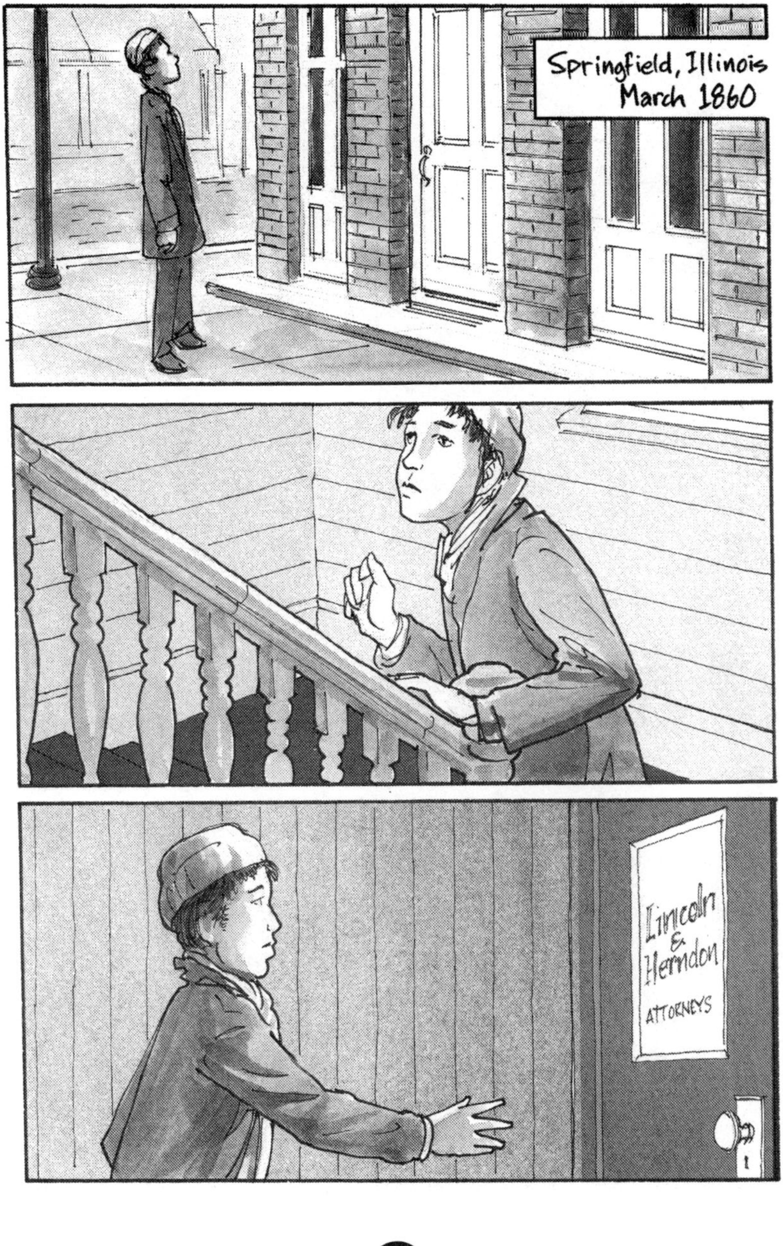
Springfield, Illinois
March 1860
Lincoln
&
Herndon
ATTORNEYS

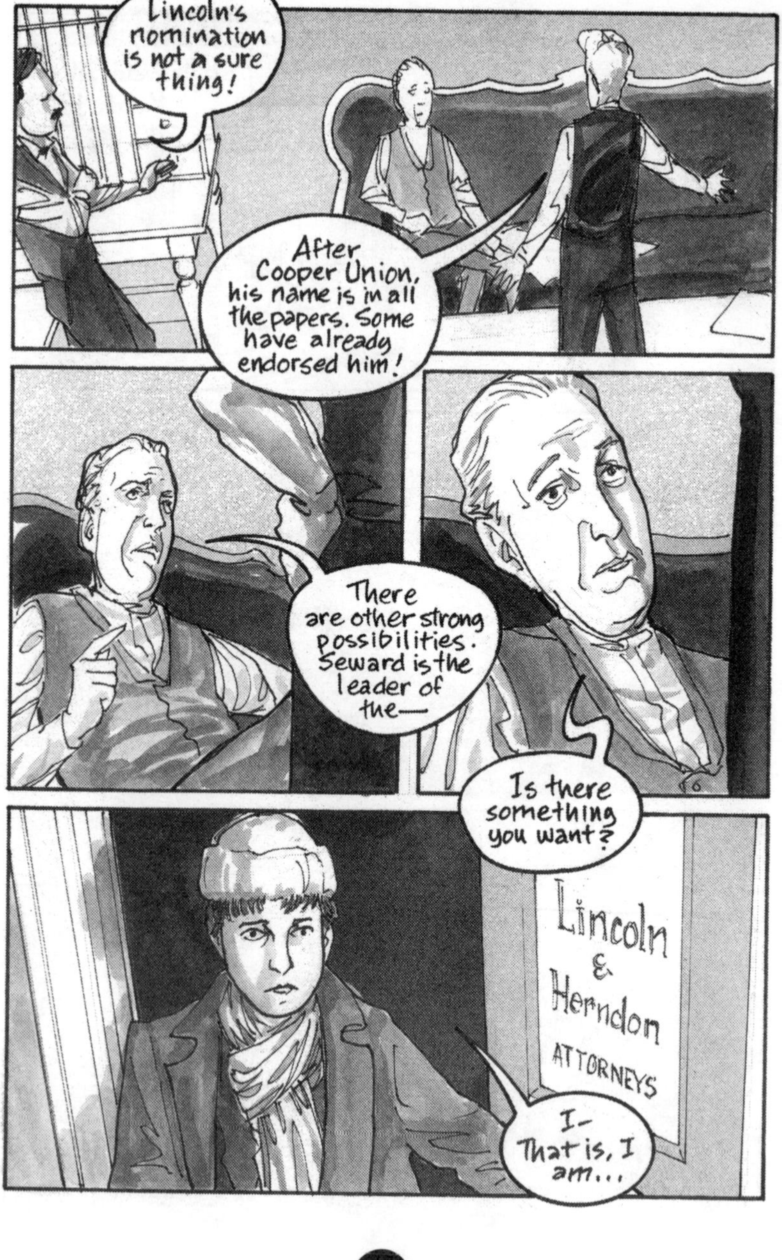
Lincoln's nomination is not a sure thing!
After Cooper Union, his name is in all the papers. Some have already endorsed him!
There are other strong possibilities. Seward is the leader of the—
Is there something you want?
Lincoln & Herndon ATTORNEYS
I— That is, I am...

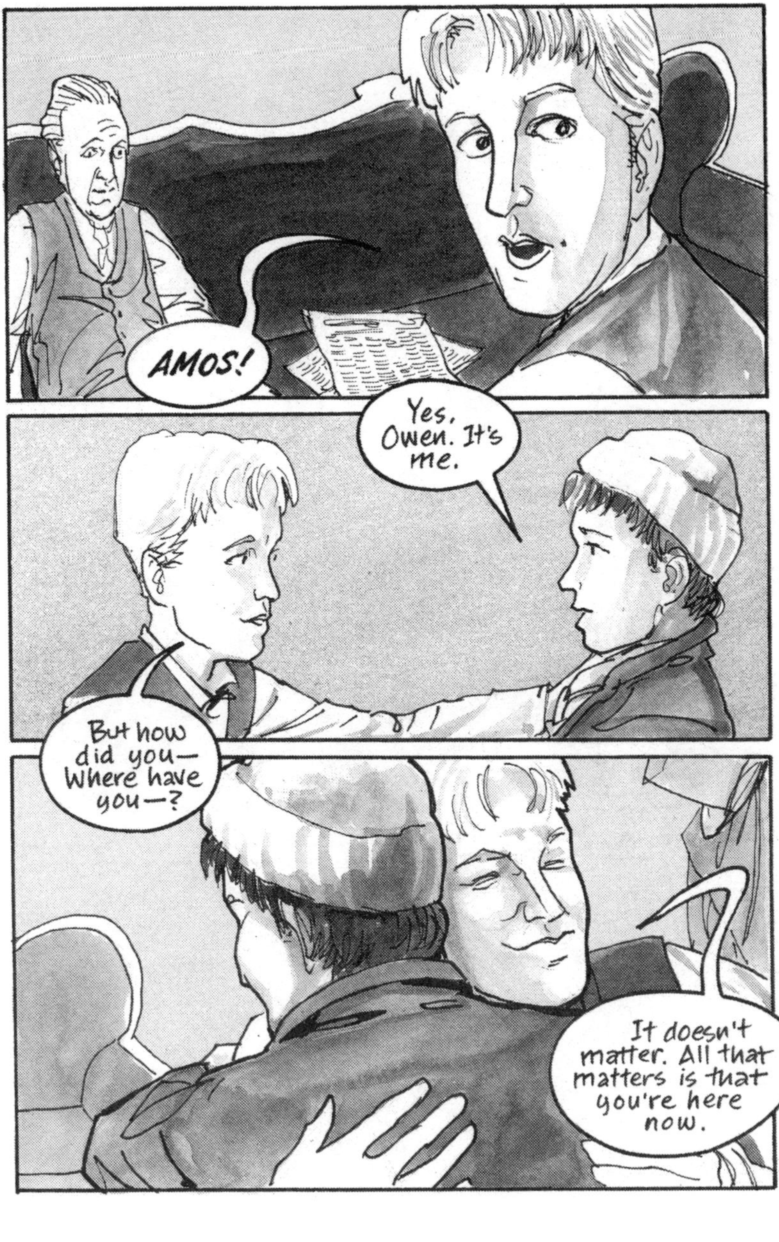
AMOS!
Yes, Owen. It's me.
But how did you— Where have you—?
It doesn't matter. All that matters is that you're here now.

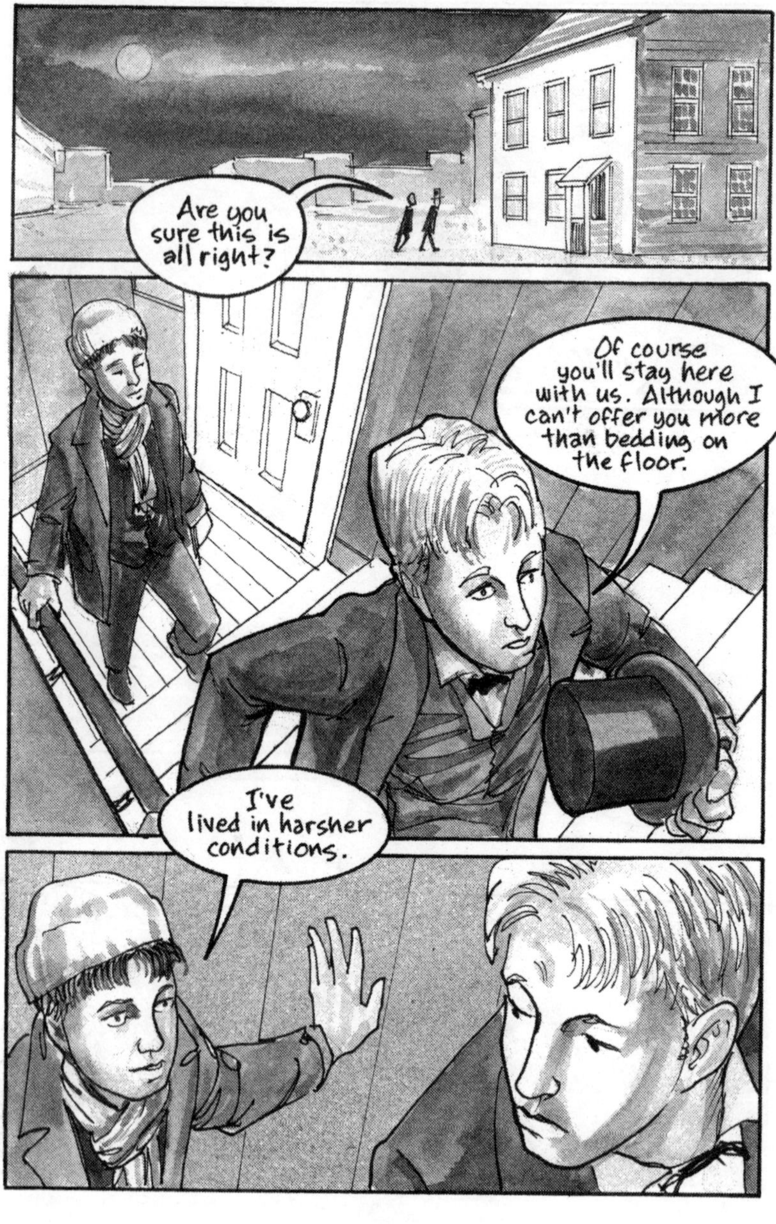
Are you sure this is all right?
Of course you'll stay here with us. Although I can't offer you more than bedding on the floor.
I've lived in harsher conditions.

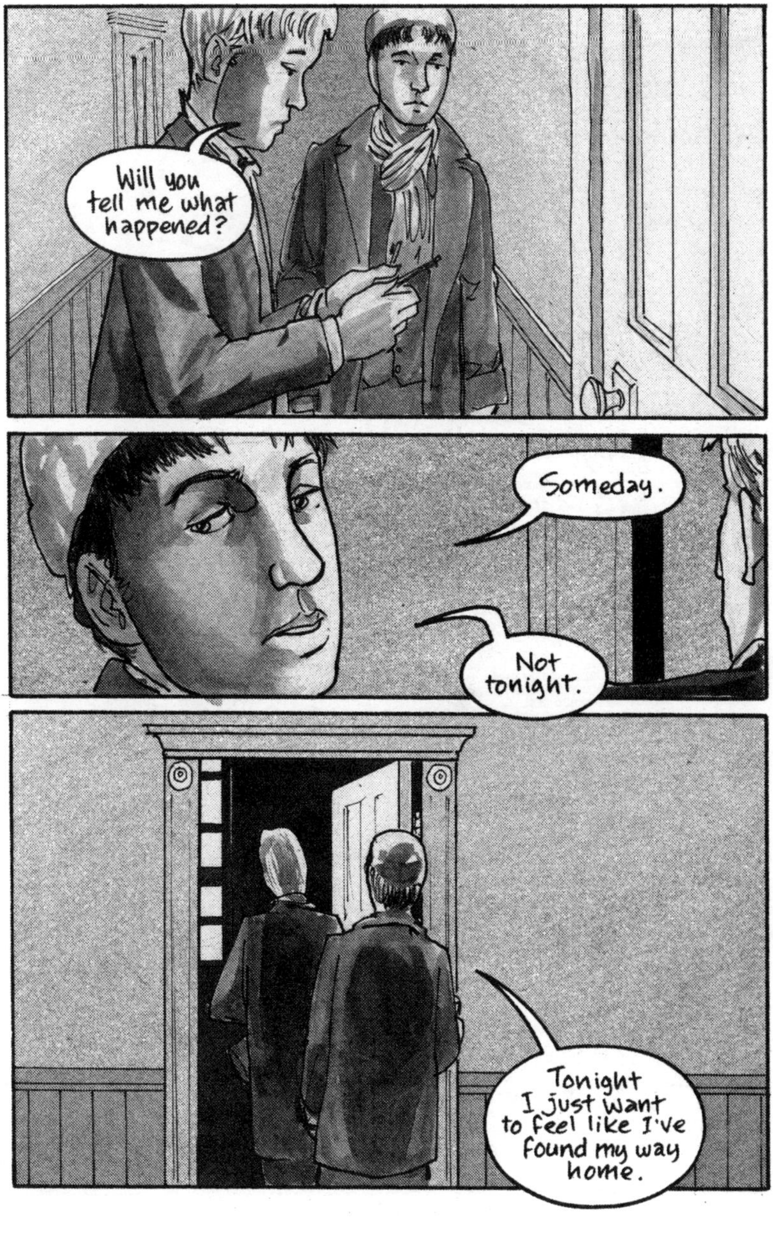
Will you tell me what happened?
Someday.
Not tonight.
Tonight I just want to feel like I've found my way home.

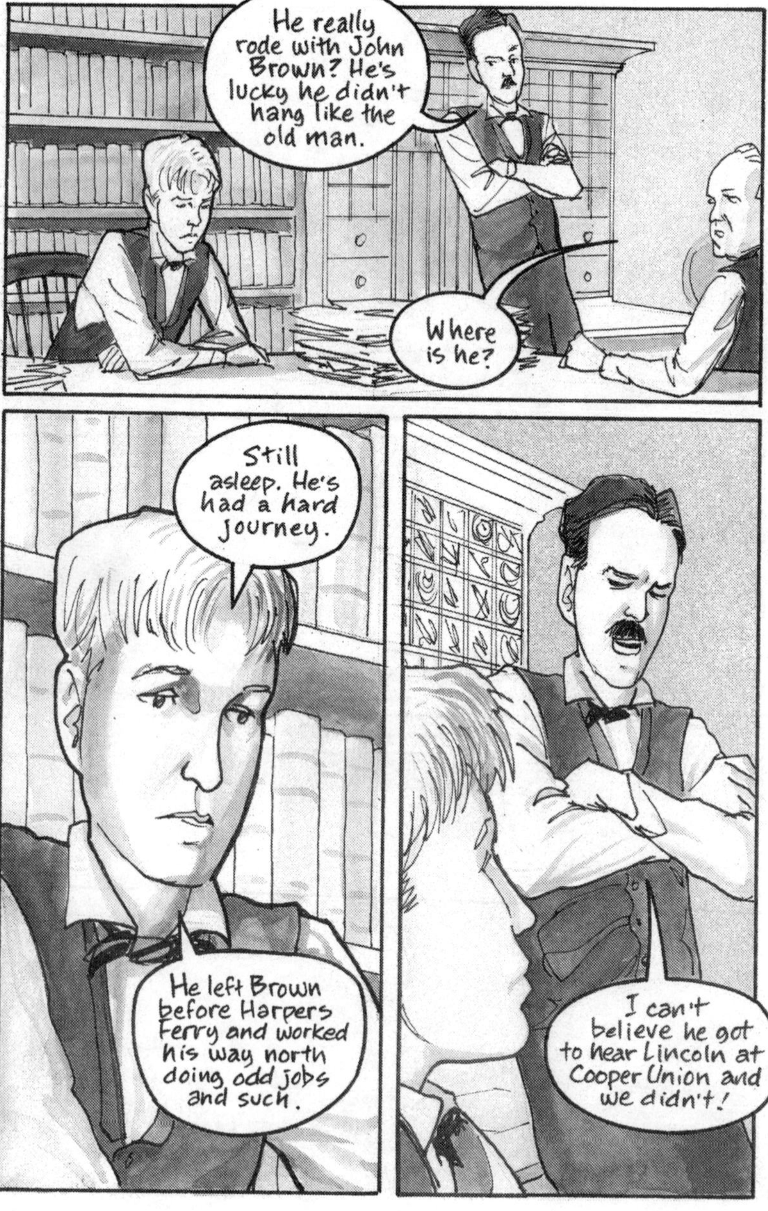
He really rode with John Brown? He's lucky he didn't hang like the old man.
Where is he?
Still asleep. He's had a hard journey.
He left Brown before Harpers Ferry and worked his way north doing odd jobs and such.
I can't believe he got to hear Lincoln at Cooper Union and we didn't!

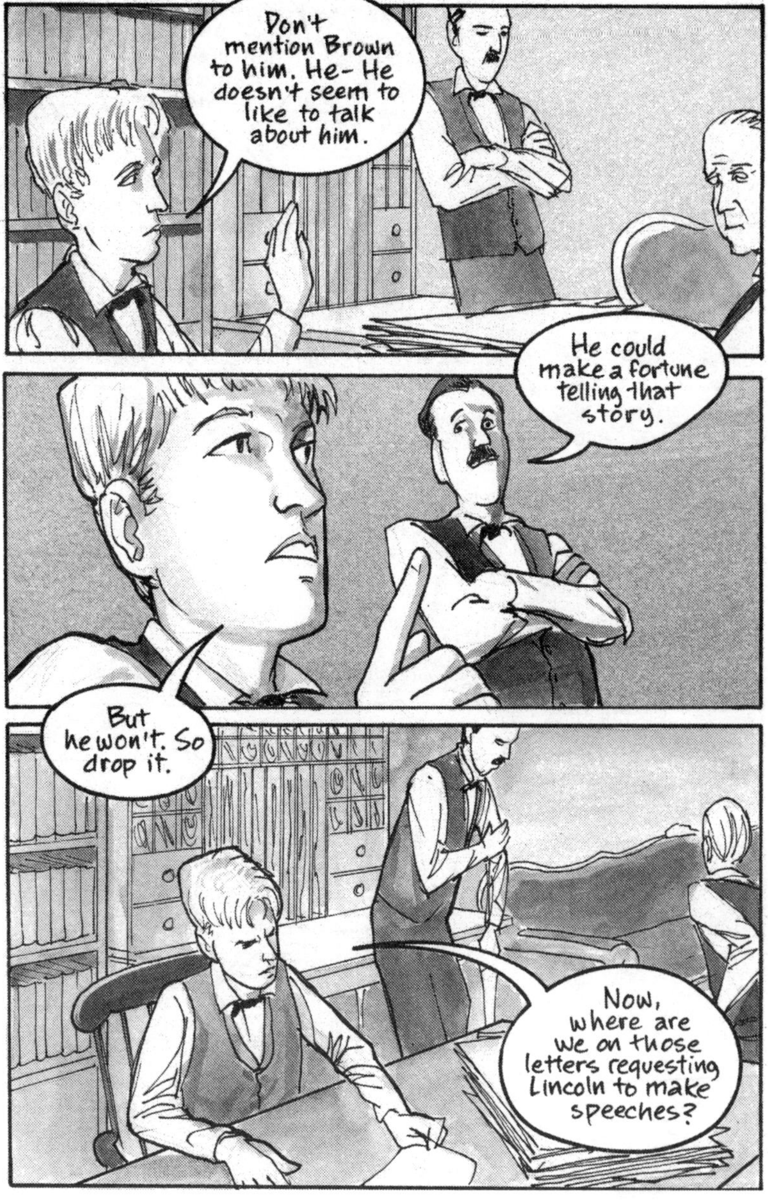
Don't mention Brown to him. He- He doesn't seem to like to talk about him.
He could make a fortune telling that story.
But he won't. So drop it.
Now, where are we on those letters requesting Lincoln to make speeches?

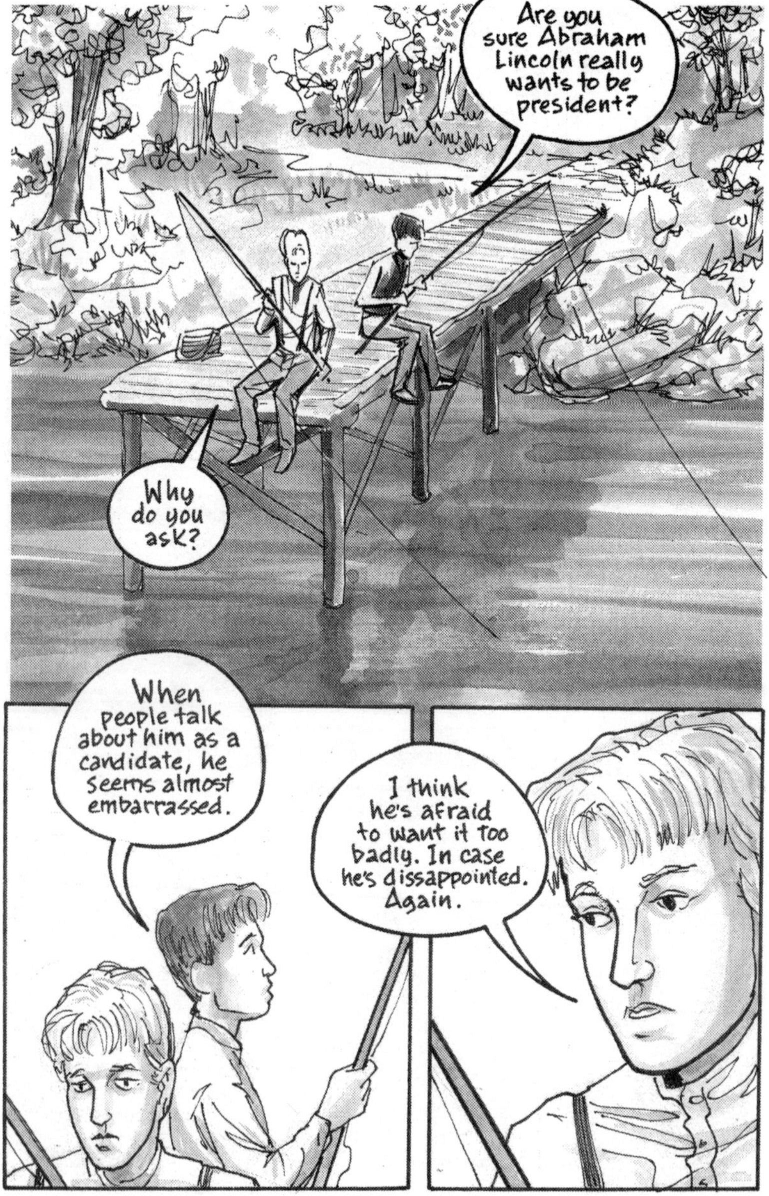
Are you sure Abraham Lincoln really wants to be president?
Why do you ask?
When people talk about him as a candidate, he seems almost embarrassed.
I think he's afraid to want it too badly. In case he's dissappointed. Again.

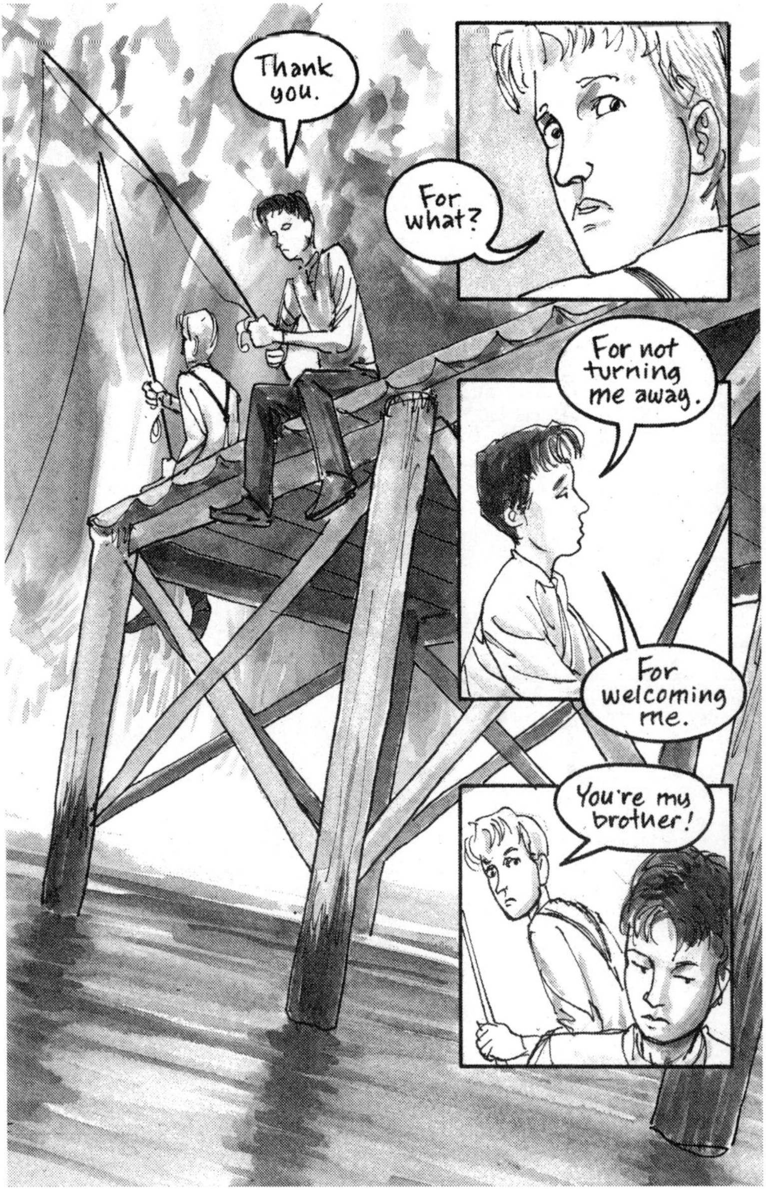

Thank you.
For what?
For not turning me away.
For welcoming me.
You're my brother!

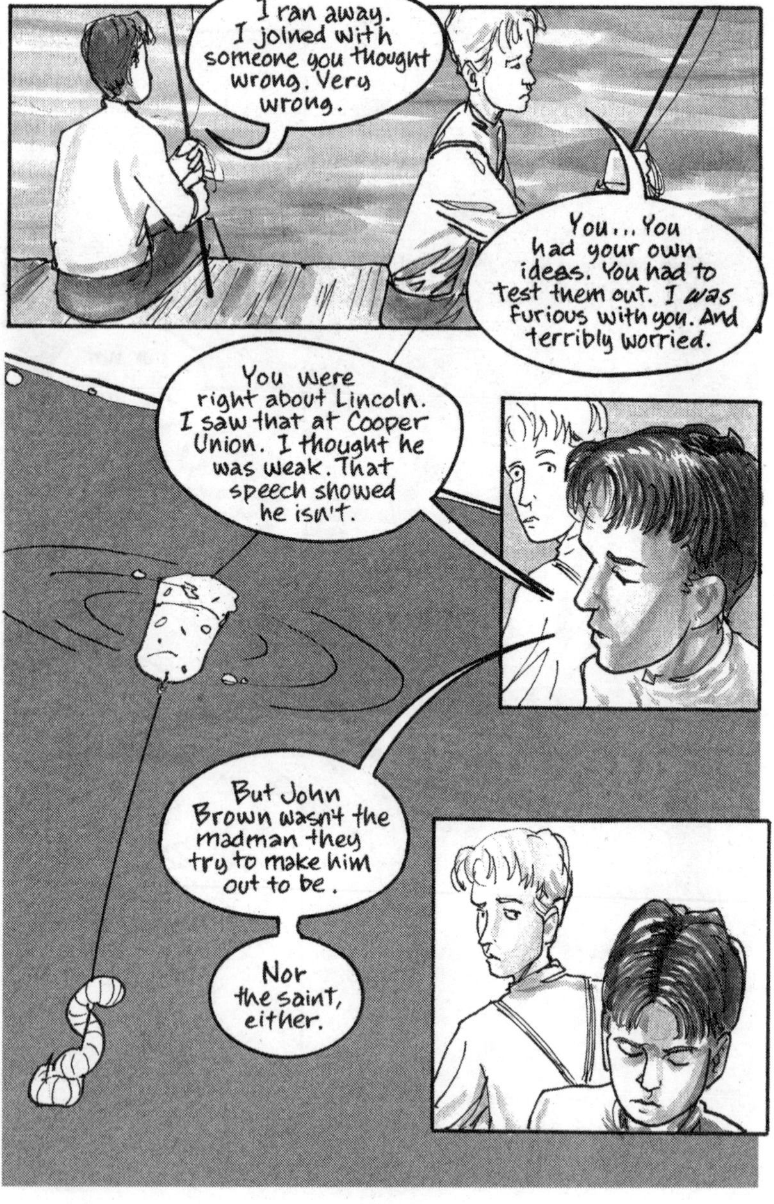
I ran away. I joined with someone you thought wrong. Very wrong.
You... You had your own ideas. You had to test them out. I was furious with you. And terribly worried.
You were right about Lincoln. I saw that at Cooper Union. I thought he was weak. That speech showed he isn't.
But John Brown wasn't the madman they try to make him out to be.
Nor the saint, either.

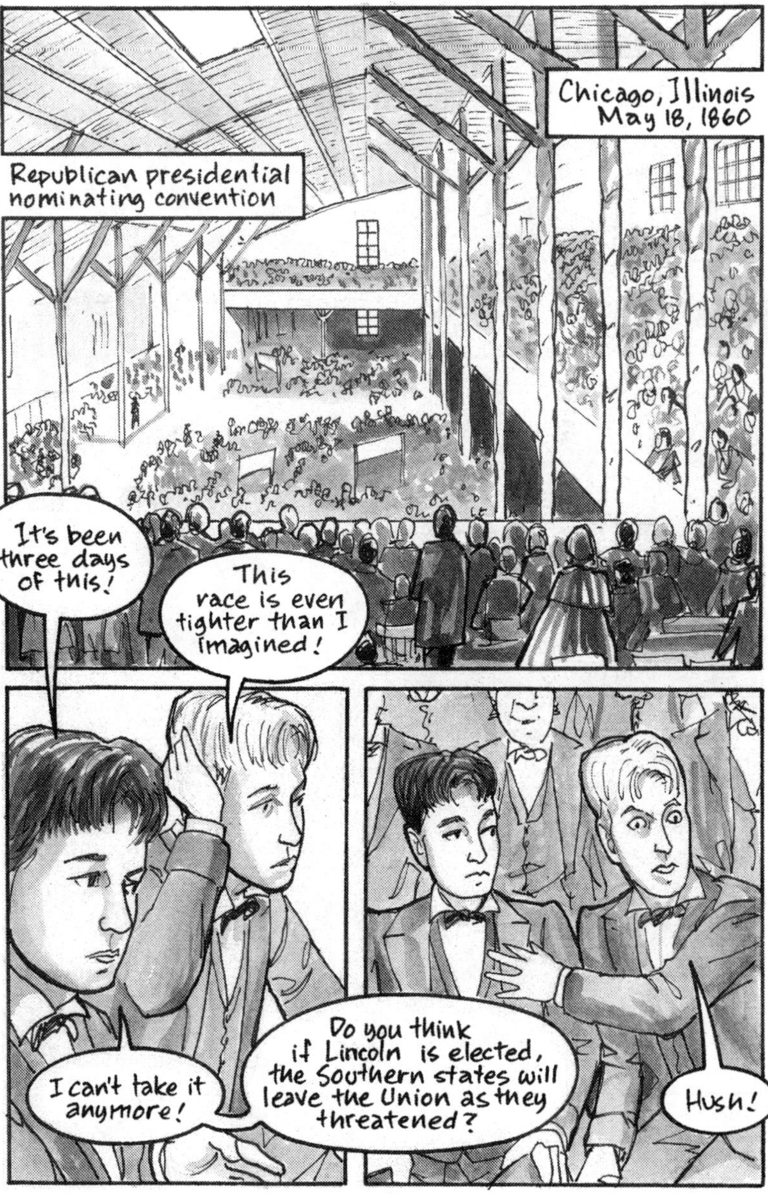
Chicago, Illinois
May 18, 1860
Republican presidential nominating convention
It's been three days of this!
This race is even tighter than I imagined!
I can't take it anymore!
Do you think if Lincoln is elected, the Southern states will leave the Union as they threatened?
Hush!

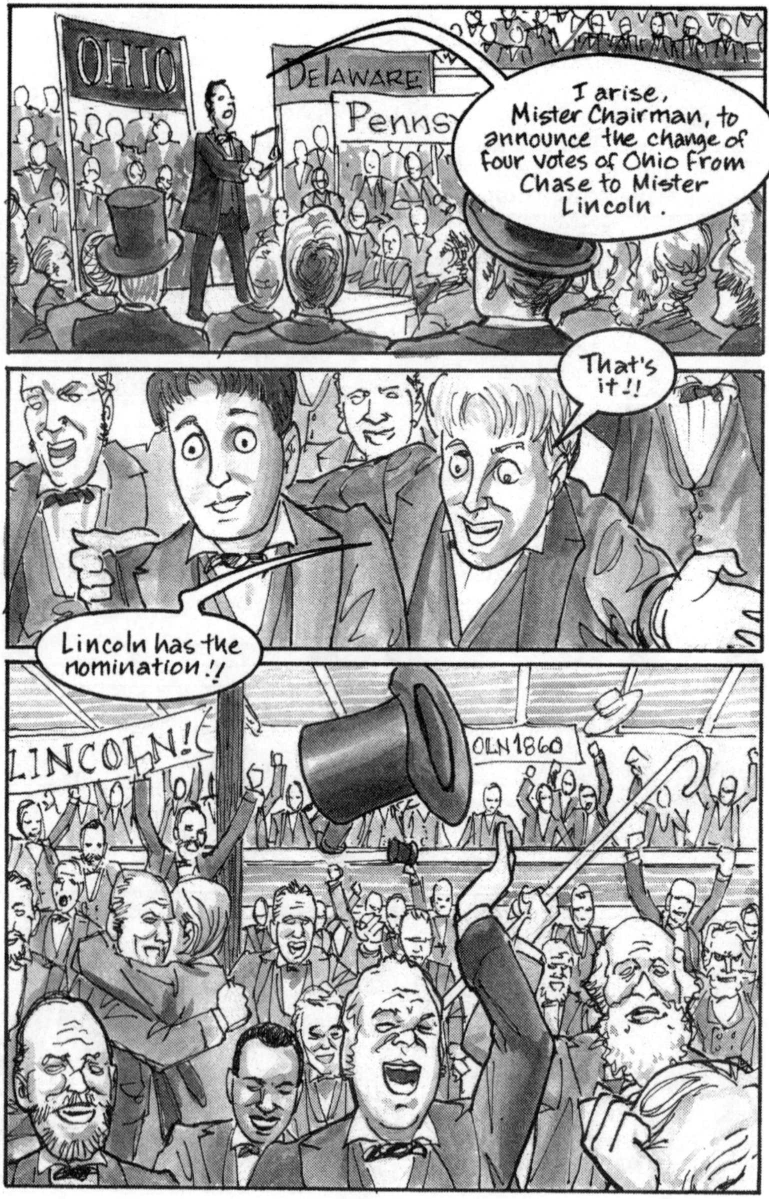
OHIO
DELAWARE
Pennsy
I arise, Mister Chairman, to announce the change of four votes of Ohio from Chase to Mister Lincoln.
That's it!!
Lincoln has the nomination!!
LINCOLN!
OLN 1860

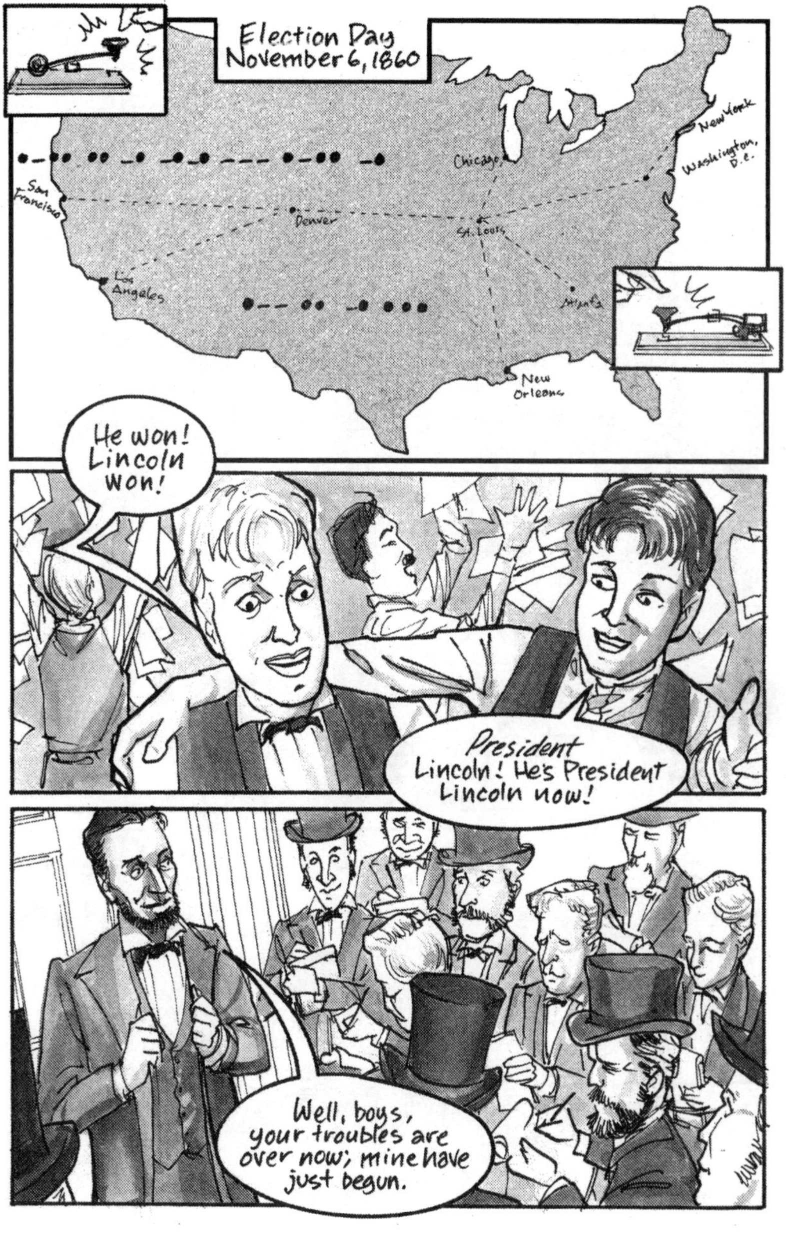
Election Day
November 6, 1860
New York
Washington, D.C.
Chicago
San Francisco
Denver
St. Louis
Los Angeles
Atlanta
New Orleans
He won! Lincoln won!
President Lincoln! He's President Lincoln now!
Well, boys, your troubles are over now; mine have just begun.

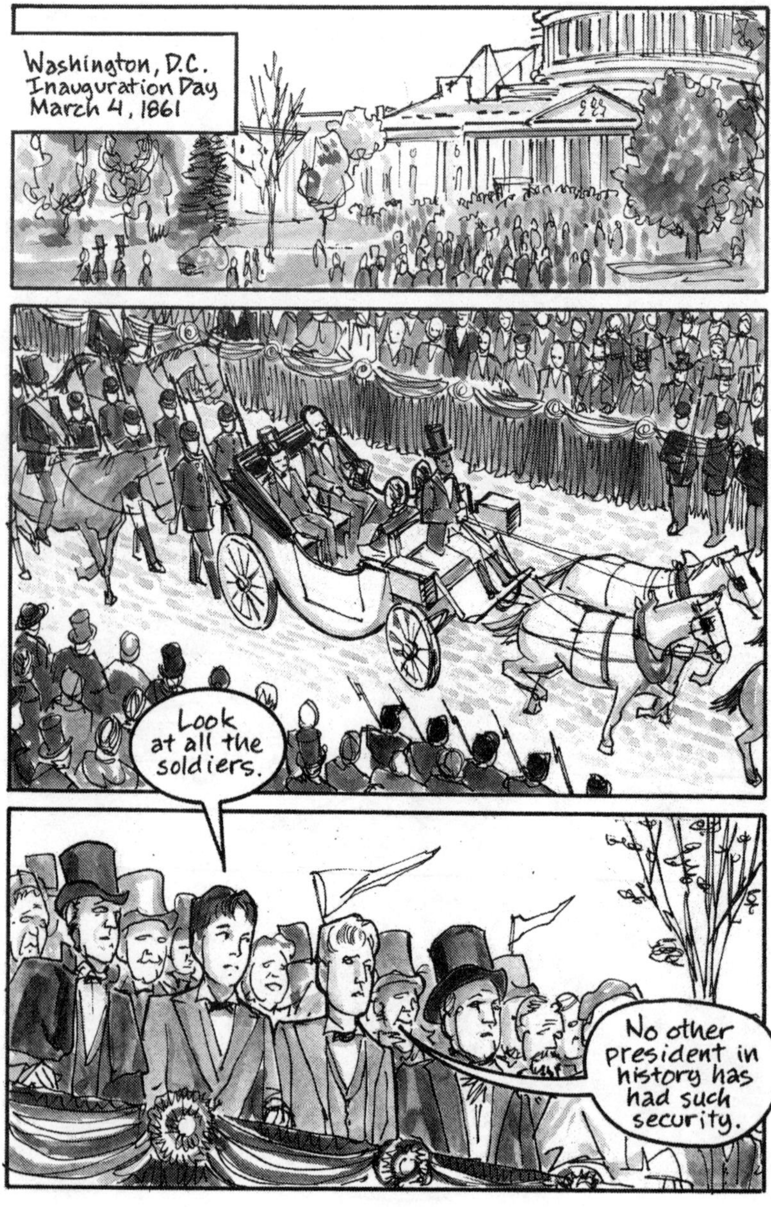
Washington, D.C. Inauguration Day March 4, 1861
Look at all the soldiers.
No other president in history has had such security.

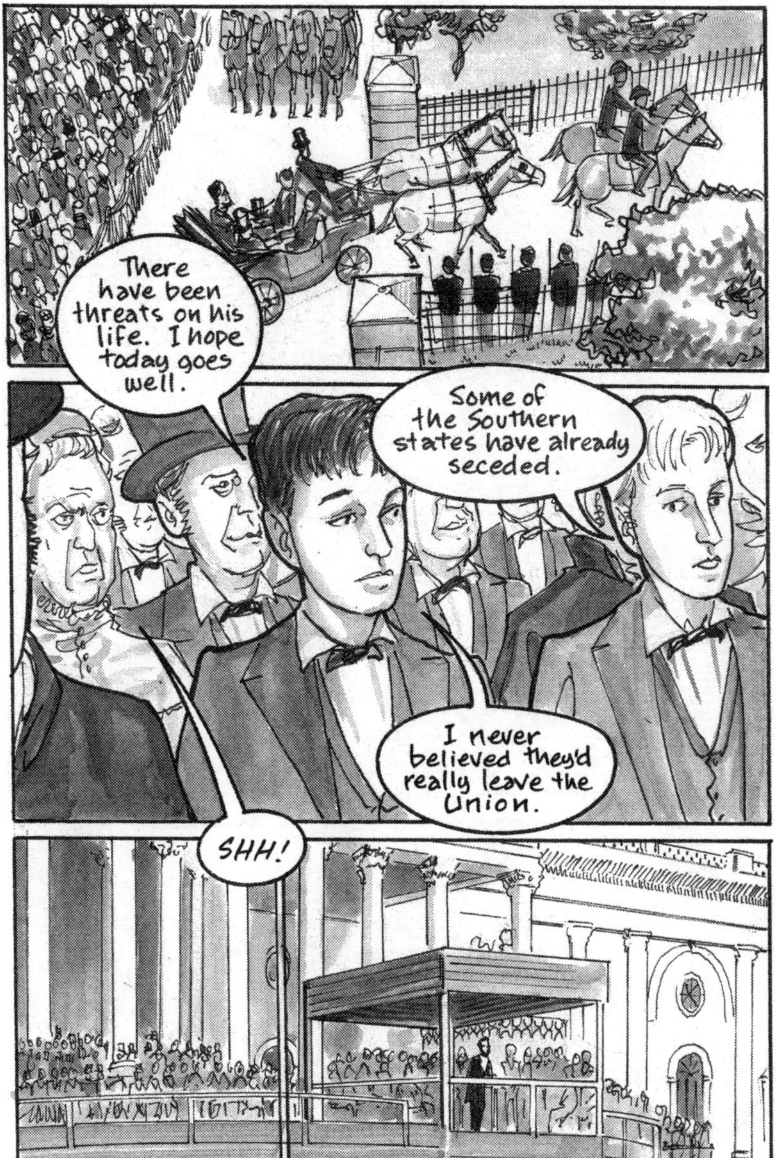
There have been threats on his life. I hope today goes well.
Some of the Southern states have already seceded.
I never believed they'd really leave the Union.
SHH!

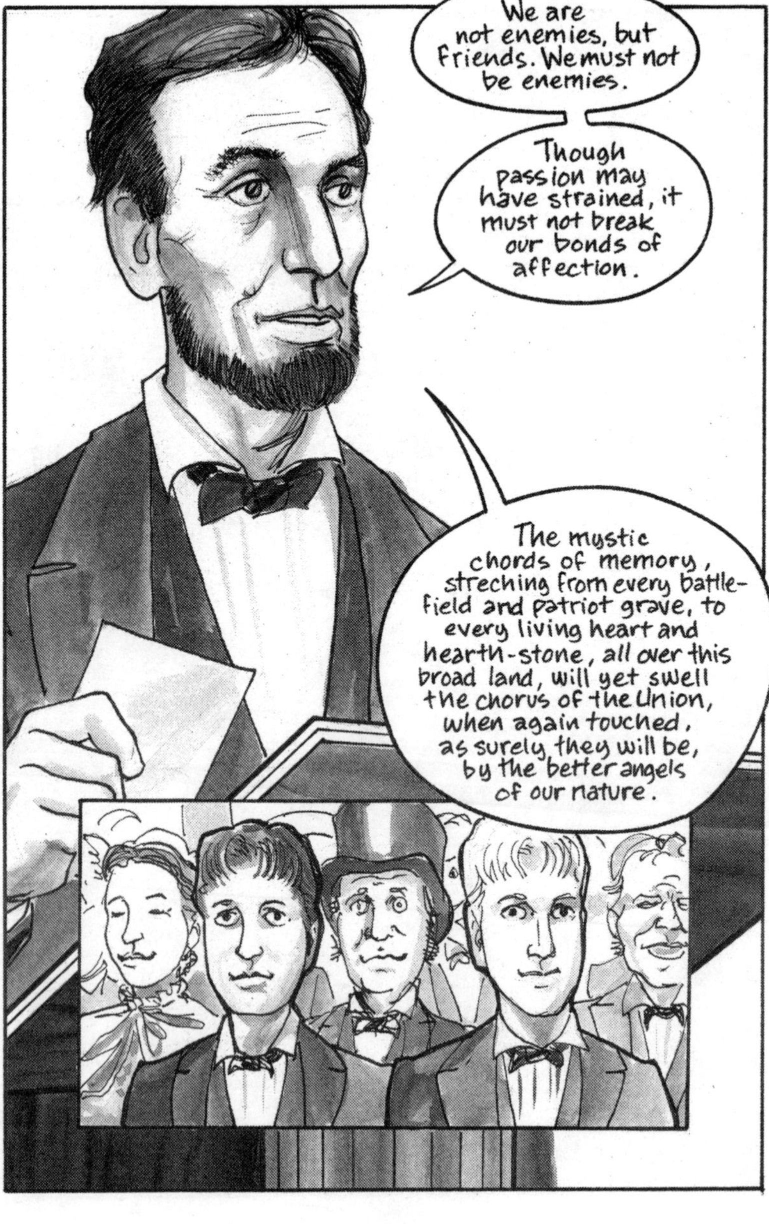
We are not enemies, but friends. We must not be enemies.
Though passion may have strained, it must not break our bonds of affection.
The mystic chords of memory, streching from every battle-field and patriot grave, to every living heart and hearth-stone, all over this broad land, will yet swell the chorus of the Union, when again touched, as surely they will be, by the better angels of our nature.

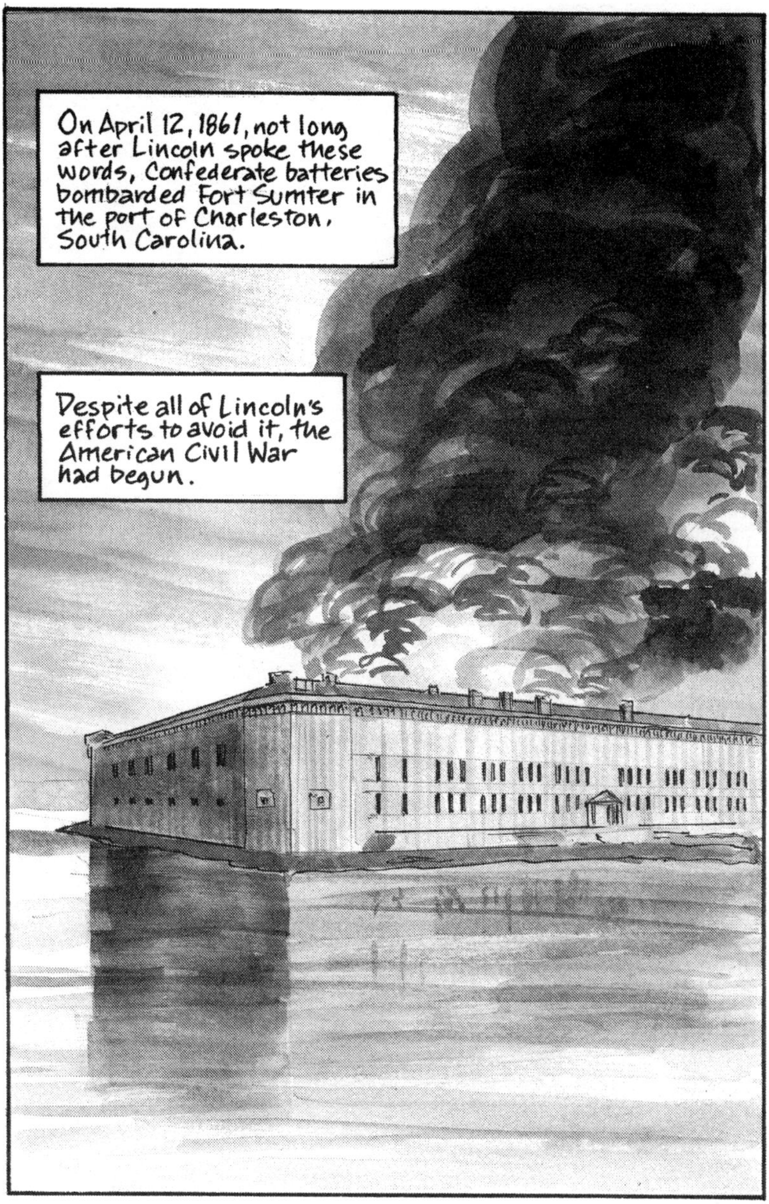
On April 12, 1861, not long after Lincoln spoke these words, Confederate batteries bombarded Fort Sumter in the port of Charleston, South Carolina.
Despite all of Lincoln's efforts to avoid it, the American Civil War had begun.

MARSHALL POE

is an American historian and the author of many nonfiction works. He is currently a writer and analyst at the *Atlantic*. Marshall lives in Iowa City, Iowa.

LELAND PURVIS

is a Xeric Grant award-winning comics illustrator whose work has been published by companies such as Dark Horse Comics. He lives in Brooklyn, New York.

ALADDIN GOES GRAPHIC . . .

. . . don't miss any of Aladdin's exciting graphic novels!

TurningPoints
LITTLE ROCK
NINE
MARSHALL POE
Vote against Integration!
SEPARATE BUT EQUAL

TurningPoints
SONS OF LIBERTY
BY MARSHALL POE
ILLUSTRATED BY LELAND PURVIS

BOOK ONE: THE MERCHANT OF DEATH
PENDRAGON
GRAPHIC NOVEL
Relive the #1 New York Times bestselling adventure!
Adapted and illustrated by Carla Speed McNeil
D.J. MACHALE

BEFORE THEY WERE FAMOUS
Babe Ruth

chiggers
hope larson

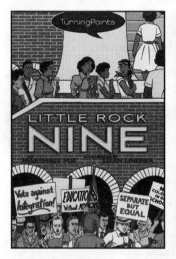

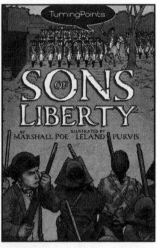

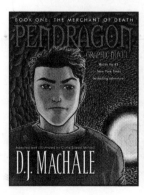

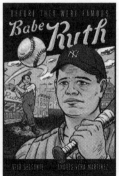

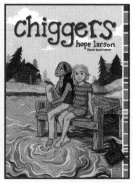